THE
HOSTAGE

THE HOSTAGE

JOHN RYDER

bookouture

Published by Bookouture in 2021

An imprint of Storyfire Ltd.
Carmelite House
50 Victoria Embankment
London EC4Y 0DZ

www.bookouture.com

ISBN: 978-1-80019-292-8
eBook ISBN: 978-1-80019-291-1

To my son, a young man with the world at his feet and a damn fine head on his shoulders.

Jerome Prentice opened his eyes to find himself staring down the barrel of a gun. Not the narrow barrel of a pistol or small handgun, but a shotgun. Its bore an abyss filled with menace and the threat of instant death.

The figure holding the gun was huge, a veritable bear of a man, large enough to make the weapon seem like an insignificant trinket in his hands. A ski mask covered his face and his clothes were black or, at the very least, dark colors.

To his left Jerome felt his wife stir. Always the heavier sleeper, Alicia never woke up easily and he had soon learned that until she had a coffee, she could be grouchy and uncommunicative. Rather than prize open her eyes, Alicia wriggled against him, her breaths warm on his bare shoulder and her mass of crimped hair tickling his cheek.

Jerome envied his wife's oblivious state and was glad of it. She couldn't feel the terror he was experiencing. No serpents of dread could writhe in her stomach. No fears could assault her mind.

"We haven't got anything of value, but please, take what you want and leave us be."

The gunman raised a finger to his lips to silence Jerome.

It was an effort, but Jerome managed to drag his eyes away

from the shotgun and look around the room. It was a room he knew well. He and Alicia decorated it together when they moved in. They'd laughed and cried and made love in this room. It was their private sanctuary, their safe space. Or at least it had been. Until that moment.

In the gloom of the night, Jerome's eyes picked out two more black-clad figures. Both were of an average height and build, but that wasn't what he focused on. It was the pistols in their hands that got his full attention. His first thought was that their barrels were unnaturally long until he realized they had silencers fitted.

The silencers changed things. Jerome was by no means an expert on guns, but he knew shotguns were loud weapons that boom when fired. They weren't used for stealth. Silenced pistols, on the other hand, were designed for stealth. Designed to deal out death with the minimum of sound.

One of the men had his pistol aimed at Alicia, the other was directed at Jerome.

"Jerome." The speaker was the man whose pistol was aimed at Jerome. His accent pure Brooklyn. "We know exactly who you are. Where you and Alicia both work. I can recite your birth dates, your wedding anniversary and your parents' names. In short, this isn't a mistake. This isn't some random home invasion. This is targeted and deliberate. Wake Alicia. Make sure she doesn't make a noise or do anything stupid. We have no desire to harm either of you, but be under no illusion, we won't hesitate to shoot if you force our hands."

The flat tone of the man's voice carried more threat than any yell or shout could. Nowhere in his words was there a chink that may have offered some hope to Jerome. There was just absolute confidence that Jerome would do as he was told.

Jerome wanted to resist. Wanted to fight back, but how could he with two guns aimed at him and a third at his wife?

Alicia gave sleepy grumbles when he shook her shoulder, so he put more force into his shakes. "Alicia, darling, wake up. You need to wake up."

"Wassamatter?" Her lips moved but her eyes remained pressed shut.

"Alicia. Wake up. *Now.*" The forceful tone he used was one that tore at Jerome as he knew the effect it would have.

He was ready. As Alicia's eyes snapped open, he pressed a hand to her mouth. She'd be worried about a fire or some other such disaster, and if she wasn't, she'd be drawing breath ready to rail on him for waking her.

"You need to be quiet, and stay that way. We have a situation."

A situation. What kind of understatement was that? This wasn't a situation, it was a full-on nightmare.

Alicia's eyes widened as she took in the guns pointed their way. Her hands instinctively pulled the bedding up to her chin, as if it would protect her from gunfire. Jerome gripped her shoulder in a supportive squeeze then released his hand from her mouth.

A finger at the lips of the man with the shotgun kept Alicia from uttering a sound, although Jerome could see the fear in her eyes.

"Mrs. Prentice, Alicia." The speaker's tone had softened to the point of patronizing. "You're going to be coming with us for a few days. There's a very specific task we need your husband for. The task is one of redress, of balancing yin against yang, but it's a task he's going to need a total focus to fulfil, so we're inviting you to be our guest for a few days so you're not a distraction to him."

Jerome felt Alicia stiffen beside him. No wonder. She was more than smart enough to work out the subtext. She wouldn't be a guest of the masked gunmen: she'd be their prisoner. And he'd be their pawn. Directed to do their bidding with threats against her to ensure his compliance.

"And if I refuse your 'invitation'?"

The tip of the silencer bounced, indicating Alicia should leave the bed. "Surely you can see that refusing isn't an option? That we have all the cards and you have no options? I don't want to have to threaten you, but..." The speaker let the unspoken threat hang. To Jerome it dangled like a hangman's noose.

"What task could you possibly have for me?" Jerome spread his arm over his wife, making sure it was above the covers where it could be seen. "I'm a corporate accountant, not some drug runner or anything like that."

"We're well aware of who you are. As I said previously, you've been selected for a reason. Now, do I have to do the whole clichéd countdown? Or are you going to just do as I ask?"

"We'll do as you say." Alicia extended a finger out and pointed it at the speaker as she shoved Jerome's arm aside. "But hear me speak. I may be respectable, but I know people who aren't. People who would take down the likes of you for fun. So if anything happens to me or Jerome, you'll pay with your lives."

Jerome would have put Alicia's words down to the stress of the rude awakening had he not become accustomed to her feisty nature years ago. Rather than ensuring their well-being, she was giving these gunmen a reason to kill them both once whatever task they had in mind for him was completed.

"Duly noted." The speaker watched as his accomplices led Alicia from the bedroom.

"Please, you have to understand, I'm a nobody and she doesn't have those connections. She's just talking big."

"Shut your bazoo, Jerome. We both know your wife has more balls than you, so stop with any pleas you're thinking of making. You will be contacted tomorrow. The contact will come via a Twitter message and you will need to be at work. I know that going to work is the last thing you'll want to do, but that's where we want you to be, so that's where you *will* be. Do I need to explain the consequences of you trying to follow us or calling the cops?"

"No." The single word was an admission of defeat, as well as an acknowledgment, as well as compliance. That he had to say it made Jerome hate himself for being unable to prevent his wife's abduction.

Without another word, the gunman slunk out of the bedroom.

Jerome dashed to the window, and saw Alicia being ushered toward a nondescript sedan whose license plate couldn't be seen. A part of him wanted to give chase, but that wouldn't achieve anything. With the implied threats against Alicia, he didn't dare try and follow them. Even waking up a neighbor and using their phone to put in a call to the police—in case his own was bugged—was fraught with dangers. If the police got involved and found the sedan, it would probably result in a direct hostage rescue, where one of the abductors used Alicia as a shield as they held a gun to her head. There was no way he was going to put Alicia's life at that level of risk until he knew what her abductors wanted him to do.

2

Alicia fought to keep herself from succumbing to the panic that threatened to overwhelm her. It reared within her like a beast possessing her normal self, fighting for domination, for supremacy. Nothing about her predicament was good. No matter any threats she may make about retribution, common sense and logic dictated that once Jerome did whatever task the gunmen wanted him to do, their use was over. At that point there was no further reason to keep her alive.

That was her long-term future, and as much as she worried about it, the short-term was of greater concern. The thin silk pajamas she wore might be great for keeping cool at night, but she wasn't comfortable having male eyes other than her husband's looking at her in them.

The task they wanted Jerome to perform was uppermost in Alicia's mind. She was a hostage against that task, a helpless victim to be used as leverage. The very fact she'd been taken suggested the task would be one Jerome wouldn't do of his free will. "Balancing yin against yang" had been the man's words, to provide redress, but if they weren't doing it themselves, it must be either dangerous or illegal. More illegal than kidnapping and extortion.

Alicia knew her husband well and Jerome had a strong moral code. *What if he had to take a life? Many lives? Could he bring himself to do such a thing? He loved her, she was sure of that, but at what point would his limit be reached? At what point would he sacrifice her for the greater good?* She'd like to think it would be never, but at the same time she shared Jerome's view that two lives were always more precious than one. *How many strangers' lives would he deem to be of equal worth to her life? Two? Three? A dozen?*

Alicia tried to steel herself against what might be coming. A few punches, a black eye, a tooth knocked out. All would hurt, but all would be more than acceptable if she survived the experience. If it came to it, she could live with losing a finger or two.

So far the gunmen had treated her with something approaching respect, though. Her eyes were covered and her hands bound, but any physical contact from the men was limited to her arms, shoulders and back as they guided her where they wanted her to go.

The car they were traveling in moved with consideration. Turns were navigated with care, and both braking and acceleration was done with the gentle touch of a professional chauffeur. The interior smelled of Cool Water from the man to her left, and washes of a dashboard air freshener that drifted pine scents her way. A seatbelt held her against the seat and, coupled with a gunman pressed either side of her, she was prevented from making any desperate attempt to jump out when the car was stationary at a stoplight.

Alicia had at first tried to track their direction, counting the turns left and right, ticking off the seconds in her head as she calculated the distances between turns. If she knew her ultimate destination, she figured, then she'd have some small piece of knowledge that may be useful.

The longer the journey went on, the more difficult it became to keep a mental map of where they were going. When the car began to circle constantly Alicia gave up on her attempts to keep a count.

No longer did she have even the faintest clue as to whether the car was traveling north, south, east or west.

Alicia didn't expect pleas to work, but she wasn't too proud to try. "Please. You have this all wrong. Jerome won't be able to help you with whatever task you want done. Like he said, he's a corporate accountant. He won't be of any use to you."

"You underestimate us, Alicia. You also sell your husband short. He's not one hundred percent the man you think he is. You may think he's lily-white, but his hands are far dirtier than you think. Than perhaps even he realizes. You and he have been deliberately selected."

The speaker was the same person who spoke in the house. His voice level, unremarkable. There was no stress, no excitement, and no hesitation to it.

"Please, I beg you. Let me go. Don't make Jerome do whatever it is you want him to do. We're innocents. We're good people. We abide the law and pay our taxes. We give to charity every month. We babysit our nieces and nephews and play games with them whenever they ask. We recycle and think about our carbon footprint."

"That is all terribly commendable of you. But of no importance to us. Your husband is going to help us right a heinous wrong. To extract a retribution for past deeds. There was a selection process and he was the number one candidate. Now if you'll be so kind as to stop talking, I'll be kind enough to not gag you."

Alicia fell silent and waited as the car continued its journey. She saw no point in further attempts to make her case. She guessed the smooth driving style went on for at least an hour, before the car drew to a permanent halt.

The seatbelt went slack around her body and she felt a gentle push on her shoulder. "Ease your way out."

As Alicia slid her way across the seat and rotated her feet out of the door, a hand placed itself atop her head as another took her elbow. "Mind your head."

The level of care was welcome, but at odds with her expectations. *Was it a subterfuge to make her compliant? Or a genuine desire for her not to suffer any hurt?* Alicia's instinct was distrust. Men who kidnapped people at gunpoint to use as leverage didn't care about their victim's welfare. They cared only for their goals.

She couldn't help but wonder if this was a crucial part of their plan. If she was being taken somewhere to be executed. If all of a sudden she'd feel something thudding into her body, or the immediate nothingness of a bullet to the brain.

A strong hand gripped each of her elbows and propelled her forward. Warnings about steps or trip hazards were delivered in a bored monotone.

Wherever she was, it wasn't somewhere plush. There was a mustiness in the air and light debris underfoot.

"This is a staircase. They go up."

Up had to be good, right? Down was basements and holes in the ground.

Alicia trudged up stair after stair. It was clear they were in a stairwell as she was routinely rotated and set toward a new flight of steps. The farther up she went, the more intense the smell of mustiness got.

"The stairs end here. Walk forward, I'll give you directions."

The thought of making a mad dash forward never seemed so good to Alicia. Her hands were bound in front of her so she'd soon be able to reach up and remove the blindfold. However there was no knowing what was in front of her. She could get three steps and trip over something before she'd gotten the blindfold removed. She could hear the footsteps of the men behind her, and there was no knowing if their guns were trained on her back. Just because she couldn't feel one pressing against her spine, didn't mean it wasn't there. Another thing making her compliant was the breeze she felt on her face. If she was on a rooftop she could tumble over the edge long before she'd gotten her bearings.

Most of all, though, she stayed obedient as she knew her captors would be prepared for any escape attempt.

Partway up the stairs she got her next instruction.

"Stop here. Turn to your left."

Alicia stopped. Made the turn.

Strong hands gripped her shoulders and spun her round. At first she thought it was the kidnappers playing rough until she heard the gruff voice again. "I said left, not right."

Alicia had never managed to get left and right set in her mind and frequently got them wrong, especially when she was under pressure. Jerome often joked with her about it. The memory of his good-natured teasing made her whimper out loud.

The hands gripped her again, raising her arms up, and she felt the zip ties binding her being snipped free. There was a gentle push on her back and she let it walk her forward.

"Put your hands out and keep going until you reach a wall. Stay there until you hear the door shut. You can take your blindfold off then."

Alicia did as she was told. Every fiber of her being was locked in a prayer that this wasn't going to be the end of her life. Against her cheek the blindfold was sodden from tears she had no memory of shedding.

The door slammed shut, and using tentative movements Alicia lifted her hands to her face believing she'd being tricked. No further instructions came. No orders, requests or commands.

Her fingers prized their way under the blindfold and lifted it over her hair.

Alicia blinked at the introduction of stark light to her previously dark world. Fraction by fraction her vision landscaped from dancing white spots to clarity.

Alicia examined the room with a dispassionate and forlorn eye. It was maybe fourteen feet by twelve. There was a mattress on the floor, a porta-potty from a Winnebago and what looked to be a small fridge. Atop the fridge there was a stack of battered paperback books.

Inside the fridge were bottles of water, fruit and store-bought sandwiches in clear plastic triangles. There was more than enough food and water in the fridge for her to believe she was going to spend days in the room. But worst of all, for Alicia, were the room's other occupants.

Every corner of the room bore the same signs of occupation, although where the corners of the walls met the ceiling, the spider-webs were at their largest and most ominous.

3

The sun may well have been high in the sky, the subway less crowded than usual and there may have been birdsong audible as he walked from the subway station but none of these things meant anything to Jerome.

Since Alicia had been abducted in the middle of the night, Jerome had spent every waking minute battling indecision and trying to answer a whole range of "what if" questions. Every instinct he possessed had told him that he ought to fight back in some way, but neither he nor Alicia had a gun, and even if they did, a three-on-one gunfight would only ever end one way when they had Alicia as a hostage. Calling the cops was an option, but what could he tell them? The cops would want to set trackers on his Twitter feed. They'd want to monitor his every movement. From what the speaker said, he'd been chosen for a specific reason. He was to go into work. The gunmen had worn masks and as two were silent, it was possible they could be someone he knew from work. In turn this meant they could be watching him. The way the gunmen had gotten into the house and up to their bedroom before he'd woken spoke of their skills when it came to breaking and entering.

After the lengths they'd gone to last night to take Alicia, he'd convinced himself that he was being watched, and that his phones were tapped. Even with the thought he was being monitored, Jerome still pulled out his cell and checked his Twitter messages for perhaps the thousandth time since Alicia had been taken. It was a pointless act as one of the first things he'd done after Alicia had been taken was to change the settings on his cell and social media feeds so the only notifications he got were of new DMs on Twitter.

There were no new messages. Just the same four that had been there the last time he'd looked. For Jerome Twitter was a tool to follow a few sports stars and to keep in touch with friends who didn't use Facebook, his preferred social media feed. He browsed Twitter a couple times a week whereas he spent some time every day on Facebook.

Every few seconds a new thought bulldozed its way into Jerome's brain and created nightmarish scenarios. Each one of Alicia being hurt in some way to coerce him into doing the gunmen's bidding. In his mind's eye he'd pictured her being murdered, mutilated and raped.

No matter how often, or how hard he tried, Jerome couldn't shake the worrisome imagery from his brain. Every part of him was desperate to get Alicia back before any harm came to her, but however he tried to work out how he could save his wife, he always came to the same conclusion: To get Alicia back he must do as her abductors instructed. He must perform whatever task they wanted regardless of how it might compromise his morals or principles. Saving Alicia was all that mattered.

For hours now, he'd been repeating the same seven words as a mantra. "One. Four. Three. Alicia. One. Four. Three." "One. Four. Three" was their way of saying "I love you," made by taking the number of letters in each word.

He walked into the office on autopilot. The usual good morning nods and greetings happened without thought or any input beyond the automatic. If anyone thought he was off they could go hang. He had more important things to deal with. Things that could be the difference between life and death for his wife. His world.

In general his walk through the lobby of the Beck Building filled him with pride as he took in its marble walls and an atmosphere that exuded quiet power. Beck Holdings occupied all thirty-seven floors of the glass monolith. Each floor was dedicated to a different division as Beck Holdings employed upwards of fifteen thousand people in nineteen countries. As a truly international conglomerate, Beck Holdings had interests in leisure, hospitality, construction and myriad other industries. The Beck Building was the company's brain and heart combined and, until today, he'd always been proud to work here.

In the witching hours, as dawn clambered over the horizon, a part of Jerome had puzzled at the reason Alicia's captors instructed him to come to work. His first thought was that he'd be framed for her murder and that she'd never be seen again. As terrifying as that line of thought was, it didn't make any sense. Alicia was drop-dead gorgeous in his eyes, but he knew that to others she was no more than very attractive. Neither of them were from wealthy families so a high-value ransom wasn't available for her. Nor had they any hidden secrets that might stir someone to a revenge attack on them. They hadn't led blameless lives, but beyond a shoplifted Tootsie Roll and a few shared joints during their college days, neither of them had done anything that warranted such an extreme situation. As much as Alicia might be an HR lawyer representing Beck Holdings, she prided herself on mediating disputes and finding settlements that were agreeable to both parties. Even those who'd gone up against her and lost, begrudgingly admitted she'd played fair at all times. The intricacies of employment law energized rather than confused Alicia, although her brain wasn't perfect. He smiled for a moment as he remembered the countless times she was given directions involving left and right, and she'd invariably gotten lost.

The more he pondered the issue, the more Jerome began to think that it was the company who'd be extorted rather than either of them. After all, he dealt with the kind of numbers on a daily basis that would make most people's eyes water.

Jerome took his seat and booted up his computer. The screensaver of them on an Acapulco beach sending an arrow into his chest. The arrowhead's twin barbs of love and fear enough to make his jaw wobble until resolve kicked in and firmed it.

A check of his Twitter account returned the four old messages.

The first thing on his itinerary for the day was a meeting. Not a client meet, just an internal one to update the division's director. Where once he'd been dazzled by the myriad of bosses, separate companies and divisions that were a part of a multinational company like Beck Holdings, he now saw them for what they were. A construct designed to impress while delivering a magician's sleight of hand as power shifted between departments. Some would be strong one week and then disbanded the next as they were consumed by another wing or division in the latest corporate restructuring. It was his job to manage a team of five accountants who paid the bills for each individual division, his job to keep the columns of numbers correct and report to the various CEOs of each division plus the CEO of Beck Accounting, for whom he worked. His was a job of finite detail, and it was a job he recognized he was good at. His feet were on the corporate ladder and if he kept his nose clean, he'd be able to climb high enough to set up the family he and Alicia planned to have for the rest of their lives.

Another check of the Twitter account as he rose to attend the meeting revealed the same lack of fresh contact.

As hard as it was, and against all his instincts, he knew that if he was to get through the forthcoming meeting, he had to banish his worries about Alicia to the back of his mind. As a parent company, Beck Holdings had a rigid policy about the well-being of their staff. If someone showed any hint of illness or inability to focus, they were sent home for an unpaid rest day. It was something Alicia herself had championed in favor of increased productivity, and while it kept people from spreading illness to their colleagues, today it could see him sent home when he needed to be at his desk to comply with the instructions issued forth by Alicia's abductors.

The meeting was scheduled to take place in the Ash suite. An interior designer had been paid to make it feel like an accountant's utopia. If brightly colored prints of computerized columns of numbers, spreadsheets and the NYSE interspersed with quotes on the economy from dead presidents were your dream, they achieved their aim. Jerome hated it and much preferred the Oak suite on the floor where Alicia worked. Its décor was tranquil and suggested calmness in the face of adversity.

Jerome filed into the Ash suite and took his usual seat, one down from the director's right hand. It was a seat he was usually thrilled to occupy as it signified importance, but today it was uncomfortable and restrictive.

In Jerome's pocket there was a vibration. He'd muted all other apps, all signifiers of any attempt to contact him other than via Twitter.

"Excuse me, guys." Jerome was on his feet before the cell had stopped vibrating. "Mr. Carthew isn't here yet, so I'm going to shoot to the men's room."

"If you gotta go shoot, you gotta go shoot. Now go do your shooting." The comment from Pete was typically ribald and drew a couple of laughs, although Jerome made a point of waving a dismissive hand lest any of them think he might be unwell.

Even as he left the Ash suite, his fingers were extracting the cell from his pocket.

Jerome was three steps out of the Ash suite and his finger was hovering over the Twitter app on his cell when he heard the guttural tones of Mr. Carthew.

"Ah, Prentice. Not leaving us, are you?"

Carthew was a tall thin man who used his height as a weapon. He made a point of standing closer than was welcome so he towered over those to whom he was speaking. A stickler for protocol he used surnames to address people, and it was joked that not even his wife was permitted to use his Christian name.

"Just a quick dash to the men's room, sir."

"Can't you wait? Dammit, Prentice, I wanted you to open. The numbers aren't as high as forecasted and I want to know why." The glower that accompanied Carthew's words was enough to shrink a blue whale to a size that would require a microscope.

"Sorry, sir. Needs must. I swear I'll be as quick as I can."

Carthew looked at his watch. His top lip curling into a wave any surfer would be delighted to ride. "You have five minutes. Then I expect your complete and utter focus. Do I make myself clear?"

"Yes, sir. Thank you, sir."

Jerome hated the subservience in his voice as he moved off

toward the men's room, the way he had to kowtow to people like Carthew when his wife's life may well be on the line, but his overriding thought was that after being ordered to be at work today, he must do whatever it took to make sure he stayed in the building. And if that meant eating some of Carthew's crap, then so be it.

As always in a corporate environment, the men's room smelled of cologne and cleaning chemicals. Today Cool Water and Sauvage competed with a lemon-scented cleanser for superiority.

Jerome's finger jabbed the white bird in its blue box and he watched as the Twitter feed loaded. His eyes were transfixed on the envelope on the bottom right of his screen and the blue dot above it. The dot had a white "1" inside it that confirmed both his worst fears and greatest hope.

The tip of Jerome's finger shook as he gently pressed the blue dot to bring up the Direct Message.

The sender's name was Jerome Prentice. The Twitter handle @jboyprento.

@jboyprento: TO GET YOUR WIFE BACK UNHARMED YOU MUST REDIRECT $50,000,000 FROM BECK HOLDINGS. THIS MONEY IS TO GO TO 21 DIFFERENT ACCOUNTS. DETAILS OF THE ACCOUNTS WILL FOLLOW, BUT IF IT EASES YOUR CONSCIENCE, WE'RE GETTING PROPER REPARATION FOR STAFF MEMBERS WHO WERE SEXUALLY ASSAULTED IN THE WORKPLACE. FOR NOW, START WORKING OUT HOW YOU CAN REDIRECT THE MONEY. WE DON'T CARE IF YOU END UP IN JAIL FOR REDIRECTING THE MONEY, BUT WE ARE SURE YOU DO. YOU NOT GOING TO JAIL FOR GRAND THEFT IS YOUR PROBLEM, NOT OURS.

Jerome's fingers went slack and his cell clattered onto the tiled floor of the men's room. He pounced on it and made sure it was intact as he fed it back into his pocket.

A glance at his watch informed him he had less than a minute to return to the Ash suite before Carthew's deadline expired.

One way or another he had to find a way to get the $50 million. So far as Jerome was concerned, if it worked out that he went to prison that was a small price to pay for Alicia's life. As he walked back to the Ash suite, his brain was working on several things. The reply he wanted to send saying that stealing $50 million was impossible. How he would actually get the money, and way at the bottom of the list, the presentation Carthew was waiting for.

Now he knew what the abductors wanted from him, he *had* to make sure he remained an employee of Beck Holdings at least long enough to acquire the ransom.

"So in conclusion, expenditure may have decreased in line with the change in interest rates, but there was also a downward spike, which affected the value of invested resources, and the leveraging we did to protect those resources is sadly reflected in the bottom line. It's my fervent belief those measures weren't only necessary in the short-term, but vital to the continued existence of Beck Accounting as an integral division of Beck Holdings."

With his presentation over, Jerome took a sip of water and eyed Carthew over the top of his glass. Carthew may be hatable in many ways, but he possessed a sharp mind and an intuitive under-standing of the vagaries involved in high finance.

"So, cutting through the crap, Prentice, what you're saying is that the measures you proposed two months ago have worked and will provide future stability for Beck Accounting?"

"Yes, sir." All Jerome wanted was to get out of the meeting and work on his plans to rescue Alicia, but there was no way that could happen until Carthew was convinced. "That's exactly what I'm saying."

Carthew's hand squeezed his chin hard enough to make the loose skin form a butt crack. "So, the man who proposed the idea lauds its success. Why am I not surprised by a word you've said, a graphic you've shown or a number you've quoted?"

Something inside Jerome broke. Not an explosion or a full-on snap, just a little break, a fracture that threatened to widen into a fissure, then a geyser. "With respect, Mr. Carthew, you approved this course of action in this very room. As I recall it, I had the initial idea and then, as you always do, you poked and prodded at my idea to make sure every angle of it was examined and break-tested for fallibility. Then and only then did you give it your seal of approval. I think it's unfair of you to cast this aspersion on my integrity and the integrity of the figures I've just given you.

"If I thought you were a vindictive person, which for the record I don't, I would think you set me up for a fall and today is when you give me that final push. If any of you recall"—Jerome swept an arm round the table at the others present—"my original idea had flaws, which thanks to the probing questions from Mr. Carthew were identified and eradicated."

Around the table nods rippled in a silent Mexican wave, although two people avoided Jerome's eye. "Sir, and again I say this with respect, you know me and the quality of my work. You yourself have promoted me on three occasions, including to the position I now hold. I thought you trusted me. I certainly trust you. You've been a kind of mentor to me. Admittedly not in an arm-round-the-shoulder kind of way, but more by the way you've pushed me. You're the director of Beck Accounting. What I've shown in my presentation is how bold moves have saved the company both in the short- and long-term. As director, the credit for that will go to you. And frankly, it should. My original plan without your refinements wouldn't have worked so well. So please, don't ride me on this one. If you think I've manipulated the figures to make myself look good, you're wrong. Feel free to have someone else run the numbers. You'll see I'm right in every possible way. Yes, the numbers do make me look good. But they make you look better."

"Are you finished, Prentice?" Carthew's face and tone were

unreadable as he rose to his feet and planted the fingertips of both hands onto the table.

"Sir." Jerome jerked a sharp nod and tried not to think about what would happen to Alicia if Carthew fired him.

"I want you all to take note of what Prentice has just said. Yes, unlike Mr. Adamson and his gentle manner, I might ride you all hard at times, but in Prentice's own words, it's to identify and eradicate flaws. To make you all better. To make you all strive to heights you don't know you can attain. To get the very best out of you for the company." Carthew held up a hand to still the muttering that accompanied the astonished looks from around the table. "Yes, it benefits Beck Holdings, but don't think me riding you the way I do doesn't also improve your individual capabilities. In short everyone is a winner and Prentice ought to be applauded for having the confidence to speak his mind to me. For having the conviction to defend himself so passionately." Carthew matched his words with actions and began to applaud. Every person in the room joined in and it was enough to bring a flush to Jerome's face, although he knew it was mostly fueled by relief at Carthew accepting his strong stance with grace and understanding, instead of being offended and ending his career with Beck Accounting.

Jerome had to give Carthew credit for admitting his style was different to that of Adamson. The Chief Financial Officer for Beck Holdings was a genial man, unfailingly polite and always considerate of the feelings of others. His man-management style was encouragement and support: he was the carrot to Carthew's stick.

As the meeting moved on, Jerome's brain was only part focused on the other presentations as he chewed at the few details that could be gleaned from the Direct Message on Twitter.

Twenty-one didn't go into fifty in any neat way. A simple spot of arithmetic told him that if it was divided equally it came out at just shy of $2.4 million apiece; yet he didn't think the abductors were taking such risks to deliver compensation that would result in inexact payouts. Surely $21 million for twenty-one people would make more sense. On the other hand, maybe the abductors were weighting their payments according to the severity of the individual cases. That made more sense to Jerome, but his overriding thought was skepticism. He didn't believe so many people had been sexually assaulted in the workplace without it coming to light.

Apart from anything, Alicia was an HR lawyer for Beck Holdings—the parent company for all the different Beck divisions and subsidiaries. Any claims of sexual impropriety at Beck Holdings, any of its subsidiaries or divisions, were sure to pass through her office, if not across her desk, and while she kept details of individual cases from him, she gave him broad strokes about her day and she'd have been sure to mention allegations of sexual impropriety, even if she withheld the names of those involved.

But never once had Alicia spoken of anything like that, and he trusted she would tell him as sexual misconduct was a hot topic for her, and as part of her role Alicia delivered workshops on what was and wasn't acceptable behavior in the workplace.

Back in their college days, Alicia had walked out of a job she'd had tending bar within a minute of her boss grabbing a handful of her ass. Before leaving the premises she'd left a glowing handprint on the boss's cheek and had made sure every female colleague knew why she was quitting. Upon hearing what had happened, Jerome had for the first time in his life the desire to pick a fight. To go into the bar and beat the crap out of the boss. Alicia had stopped him. Talked him round and made him promise not to do anything he might later regret.

Because of all this, Jerome struggled to believe the claims the money was going anywhere other than to the abductors. The line about reparation was nothing more than a salve for his conscience, an extra motivator for him to do their bidding. The only way the sexual assault story could be true was if it had been covered up before the HR department got wind of it.

Whether the claims were true or not, however, Jerome's biggest issue was finding a way to get the money without landing himself in prison.

It was just as he was beginning to have the first inklings of a possible way to redirect the money that he felt the cell in his pocket vibrate to indicate there was a second message.

Jerome made for the door, intent on getting to his office, when he heard his name being called. Had it been anyone other than Carthew's voice he would have ignored it and kept going.

"Sir?"

Carthew afforded him a rare smile and for the first time ever there was a hint of a twinkle in his eyes.

"That speech you gave. It was very impressive. I want to personally thank you for the passion with which you approach your work. Just because I push you to your limits at times, do not think you are unappreciated."

"I don't, sir. And please understand that I wasn't taking a swing at you with what I said." Jerome didn't want this conversation. He wanted to be back in his office learning how the money was to be paid; planning how he would not just redirect the company's money but redirect it in a way that didn't lead a trail right to his desk. *Why couldn't Carthew leave him alone?*

"I know that, Prentice. Know it fine well." A crease appeared on Carthew's brow. "Are you okay, Prentice? You look a little off to me. Do you need a sick day?"

Jerome had to think on his feet to prevent Carthew from

sending him home. "No, sir. I'm fine to be here. I guess I'm just having a little blowback from what I said. As you know, I put a lot into that project and I felt that my career may well be linked to its success or failure." Jerome gave a self-deprecating shrug. "I guess that's why I spoke out the way I did. And again, sir. Please do not think I was trying to offend you personally with what I said."

"Not once did I think that and I still don't. And to be frank, if my being offended is the best thing for Beck Accounting, then that's what needs to happen. It's about the company as a whole, Prentice, not the individual."

"Sir." Jerome aimed a hand in the direction of the door. "If you'll excuse me, I have plenty to be catching up on now this project has been proven to work."

"Good stuff, Prentice, good stuff."

Jerome's cell was in his hand long before the closer shut his office door behind him.

The first DM had vanished and he was Twitter-savvy enough to work out the account had been deleted. There was though a new DM, and before he even read it, he took screenshots of every line in case things went wrong and he had to explain his actions in court.

This time the sender's name was Alicia Prentice; the Twitter handle @alialiprents.

@alialiprents: THE $50 MILLION IS TO BE CONVERTED TO CRYPTOCURRENCY AND PUT INTO 21 DIFFERENT WALLETS. 20X $1 MILLION AND 1X $30 MILLION. YOU ARE TO CREATE THESE WALLETS UNDER ANONYMOUS CREDENTIALS AND THEN PROVIDE US WITH THE REQUISITE DETAILS TO ACCESS THE WALLETS. EACH NAME BELOW REPRESENTS A VICTIM OF SEXUAL ASSAULT AT

THE HANDS OF A SENIOR BECK HOLDINGS COLLEAGUE. FURTHER INSTRUCTIONS WILL FOLLOW.

Jerome caught the subtext of the message on the first read, but that didn't stop him reading it twice more before he looked at the list of names.

The twenty names meant nothing and everything to him. There was no need to give him these names; getting Alicia back was all that mattered to him. Sure, it'd be noble to help deliver some financial compensation to the assaulted women, but he didn't need the extra motivation of doing something philanthropic. His wife was a prisoner and only he could save her.

Seventeen of the women's names were unknown to him, but three he recognized. One of the three was someone he'd worked with; someone who'd left the company in a hurry.

Lucy Sampson had been one of the secretaries for Beck Accounting. Tall and athletic, she was bubbly and outgoing with an eager-to-please personality. As he thought of her, Jerome realized that while chatty, Lucy kept her private life private. He knew nothing about her family life and he couldn't remember her saying a single word about her folks or a romantic interest.

Of the other two names he recognized, Jerome knew them via reputation and internal dealings but had never met either.

Deneece Tsango was a marketing guru and had headed a sizable team at Beck Marketing. He'd never met Deneece, but had exchanged emails and the odd call with her. She'd been professional and friendly, but always focused their interactions on work, and he'd always gotten the impression he was being kept at arm's length.

Angelique Rossi was someone he knew of but had neither met nor interacted with. She'd been involved in PR for Beck Holdings, and due to her Italian heritage and stunning looks had become something of a poster girl for Beck Holdings. She was another one

who'd left the company without explanation. He'd heard she'd
started up her own company but had failed to attract any clients of
a significant size, despite her ability to put a positive spin on almost
any situation.

All of the information he'd gotten in this message backed up
the claim in the first message that the redirected money was being
used to deliver a latent compensation to victims of sexual assault.

The $30 million was obviously the abductors' cut. That was
their compensation for taking the risk.

To back up his screenshots, Jerome used Messenger to send the
images to himself. That way, as well as on his phone, they'd be
stored on his private feed rather than the office's PC or its cloud.

Next he got a pen and notepad to write down the list of names.
The names were listed in alphabetical order, which robbed them of
any individual significance.

Next, he scrolled through the list of contacts on his cell in the
hope Lucy Sampson's name was there. It wasn't, but he knew he
was connected to her somewhere so he searched Facebook. She
was there!

Jerome's fingers rattled out a message, asking her to contact
him ASAP regarding a job opening he'd heard of and thought she'd
be great for. The lie was to engage her, as he felt the truth of his
asking would be certain to scare her away.

His next move was to search the internet for Twitter tracking
apps. He didn't know if such things existed, but if they did, he was
damned if he wasn't going to try and trace the abductors, to locate
and identify them and save Alicia.

While Jerome was prepared to steal the money from Beck
Holdings, he knew that the odds of him being successful in not
leaving a trail back to himself were so small as to be a fool's bet.

He didn't want to gamble a single dime against Alicia's life, and
his biggest fear was that once he'd gotten the abductors their
money, they'd keep Alicia and demand he get more for them, or
worse, kill her so she couldn't identify them.

His thumbs battered a reply into the cell, but he hesitated before pressing send. A demand for proof Alicia was still alive was a bold move, but he had to know she was alive and well before he did anything else. Even Jerome's breath wobbled as he depressed his thumb and sent the message.

Alicia eased her way through a series of stretches and tried to generate some warmth in her body. The thin pajamas weren't close to keeping her body temperature up to a comfortable level. The mattress in the room was adorned with a worn sheet and, when she wasn't trying to build up some natural warmth, Alicia used it as a shawl to cover her bare shoulders.

Everything about the room suggested it was in an abandoned building. From the decaying plaster to the twin stenches of mold and decay, to the graffiti on the same wall as the door. The floor was uncarpeted and, save the few basic comforts provided by the kidnappers, there was nothing that even hinted at newness or care.

Once she'd gotten over her initial terror at being imprisoned in the room, a sense of desperate outrage had kicked in. She'd examined every inch of every wall, the floor and the ceiling looking for a way to escape the room's confines. There was only one possible way to exit the room and that was the door.

With the door the only feasible exit, Alicia focused her rage upon it. The wooden door was all that stood between her and freedom. One block of ancient lumber over six feet high, three wide and maybe a couple of inches thick.

Alicia retreated until she was pressed against the far wall from the door. Her mind was blank to thoughts of defeat, to the idea that spiders may be scuttling across the wall above her.

Every time Alicia thought about spiders she was carried back twenty plus years to the day when she and her cousins had been playing hide-and-go-seek at Gramps's house. Along with her favorite cousin, Benny, she'd hidden under a tarpaulin in the basement. As they'd cowered and suppressed childish giggles she'd felt a tickling against her bare shoulder. She wouldn't have been too bothered had she not seen Benny's eyes widening in the faint light as he backed away. Alicia had brushed her shoulder with tentative fingers, and when she turned she saw a spider the same size as her hand. Her shrieks had betrayed their hiding place, but that had been the least of her worries as she scampered up the stairs desperate to put as much distance between herself and the huge arachnid.

Alicia leaned forward, planted the sole of one foot against the wall and drew in three deep breaths, before she pushed off and sprinted for the door. At the last second she twisted and led with her shoulder.

Instead of crashing through the door, as happens in the movies, Alicia bounced off, waves of pain radiating through her shoulder. The whole experience had jarred her entire body, but she wasn't going to let pain prevent her trying again and returned to the other side of the room and planted her foot for a second attempt to either break the door itself, or smash it free from its casing.

Five more times she sprinted at the door and launched her shoulder at it. Five times the door repelled her.

Alicia's shoulders ached as if they'd been struck by baseball bats, yet she gritted her teeth as she stood in front of the door and assessed her tactics. Shoulder charges weren't working. She was taking on more damage than the door.

She paused and thought and listened. There were no sounds of her kidnappers coming to see what the commotion was. That made sense to her. She was imprisoned in a place where no one would be likely to find her, where unwitting rescuers wouldn't travel. There was no need for there to be guards outside.

With the door having failed to yield under her previous assaults, Alicia positioned herself three steps from the door. In her mind she was measuring the distance, marking out the positions where she could maximize the impact of her next move. She licked her finger and smeared a damp line on the floor just in front of her toes.

Alicia strode forward and lifted a foot to the door, her sole crashing flat against the timber at handle height. She hadn't given the door her best shot, this was merely a sighter, a test attempt to get her distances right.

On her next attempt, Alicia left a four-inch space between her toes and the wet smear. This time when she moved forward, she put everything she had into her stride and the thrust of her foot toward the door.

Alicia's timing was off. Instead of her foot colliding with the door when it was reaching full extension, it landed as she was still thrusting forward with everything she had. With the door resolute in the face of her attempt to kick her way through it, the force of Alicia's thrust had nowhere to go except backwards.

The power Alicia aimed at the door propelled her backwards and she found herself taking rapid steps as she fought to stay upright. She couldn't do it, couldn't move her feet backwards quick enough, couldn't maintain her balance, couldn't stop herself from falling. She twisted her body, arms extended to break her fall.

Alicia's left hand missed the edge of the mini-fridge as she sprawled to the ground, but even though she twisted her head, the sharp corner of the mini-fridge slammed into her forehead and turned her world black.

8

Jerome walked right past his usual lunchtime haunts. Breakfast had been skipped and he didn't trust the squirming knot that was his stomach to not instantly reject any food he asked it to process.

Food wasn't close to being Jerome's priority; getting Alicia back safe and sound was the only thing he cared about. He'd come up with an idea that would get him the money. The trick was finding a way to make sure he didn't end up doing hard prison time for the theft. If he stole fifty bucks he'd get a fine and maybe a few days' community service; for stealing fifty million, he'd be sure to be looking at a lot of prison time. The company would make sure of that. He knew from Alicia that when anyone was caught defrauding any part of Beck Holdings, the company went after them with everything they had, and for stealing as much as he was going to, it was odds on that Thomas Beck Senior would use his not-inconsiderable influence on the DA and whichever judge he ended up in front of.

The $50 million could be obtained by the creation and payment of false invoices. That though would leave a paper trail as easy to follow as the Yellow Brick Road. To have any chance of getting away with the theft he'd have to be smarter than that, a whole lot smarter. This was why he'd left the office. He needed to make a call and there was no way he dared make the call from either his cell phone or the one on his desk in case they were bugged.

Jerome walked two blocks before he found a payphone that was working. People gawped at him as they passed by, cell phones glued to their palms or ears. They could go hang. Considering what he was having to do, strange looks from strangers were the least of his problems.

Ed Dunsfold was an old college buddy. They'd roomed together and had been on the same wrestling team. Marriage and differing career trajectories meant they didn't see each other more than a few times a year, but their friendship had never suffered for the lack of regular meet-ups.

Where Jerome had trained as an accountant, Ed had gone into computer programming and had spent his years since leaving college working for a company that made online games.

The phone burred twice and then he heard Ed's familiar Boston Irish twang. "Ed Dunsfold, cattle wrangler, legendary lothario and all-round good guy." The greeting was typical of Ed. The only thing he ever took seriously was his work.

"Don't say my name, Ed. I know you'll know my voice." Jerome was gambling on Ed's instant comprehension. "Something's going down that I can't discuss over the phone. Can you meet me at the bar where I first introduced you to my wife? I'll be there from ten after six."

It was a risk involving Ed. A moral man, Ed wasn't the kind of guy to do wrong, to even contemplate doing something illegal, but that's what Jerome was going to ask of his friend.

Before he met Ed, though, there were still other tasks that had to be completed. The primary one of these was to open a bank account to host the money he stole from Beck Holdings. Of course Jerome had his own bank account, but the way he was planning to get the money would leave a trail, and the last thing he wanted was for that trail to lead direct to his door. To isolate himself from his crime he needed access to an account that wasn't his, and the easiest way he could see to get access to such an account was to create one in a false name.

Jerome knew all about bank accounts, about the hoops the banks required customers to jump through when opening a new account. He could change his name and lie about his address, but that wouldn't help him. The bank would want proof of identity and residence. To circumvent all of the bank's precautionary measures he'd have to have these details for someone who wasn't him. He was sure there were hundreds of people in New York who could supply him with a complete new identity and any documentation he required, but as a law-abiding citizen, he had no idea who these people were, how to contact them, or where to find them. Even if he did have all the necessary ID, he couldn't just walk into a bank and present it to a teller and open an account. Banks were laden with CCTV, and any insulation from guilt provided by the false details would be lost by having his face recorded as the person who'd opened the account.

This might not apply for online accounts, but to open one of those he'd still have to have a false identity, or at the very least someone else's. The idea of setting someone else up for his crimes was abhorrent to Jerome, but when set against Alicia's life it was just something he'd have to learn to live with.

Not knowing what he needed was a hindrance he could have done without, so Jerome ducked into a store and bought two cell phones. One to be a cheap burner should he need one, and the other, a more modern cell, to be the one he'd use to research and create an online account.

Jerome expected there to be federal regulations on the opening of an online account. His own accounts were the ones he'd set up years ago and while he might be a corporate accountant, his role wasn't one that saw him opening new accounts for Beck Holdings.

Another problem he faced were the CTRs—Currency Transaction Reports—that banks had to file to the FinCEN—Financial Crimes Enforcement Network—for every transaction over

$10,000. A sudden deposit of $50 million into a new account that was then filtered out to numerous other accounts would surely trigger a rapid investigation by the FinCEN. If he managed to get the money, he'd need to find a way of getting it past the CTRs in a way that didn't bring the FinCEN straight to his door.

Jerome found a bench and took a seat. Around him New York was busy being New York. People hustled and dawdled, they gawped and ignored as they went about their day. Tourists and business people mingled as they passed by Jerome. A homeless guy held up two signs in front of a drug store. One asking for spare change, the other announcing the end of the world.

A drip of rain landed on Jerome's nose but he ignored it, his complete focus on the screen in his hand. He'd opened a private browsing window and was studying the screen. This was about research, about knowing what he'd need rather than stumbling on blindly and crashing into a digital roadblock.

Jerome was careful about the banks he'd chosen as possibilities to lodge the money. The big names such as J.P. Morgan, Bank of America and Citigroup had all been rejected in favor of a smaller bank. At the same time, he didn't want to go so far down the ladder the sudden insertion and then extraction of $50 million would ring alarm bells. He also needed the bank to have the online facility for him to buy cryptocurrency, so he worked his way through what he thought of as middle rankers.

The banks were aligned with what they required to open an online account. To Jerome that made sense, and after seeing the same set of requirements three times over he worked out these must be the federal regulations he'd expected to encounter.

The most troubling aspects he found was most of the banks required an opening deposit, and some required that online account holders already had an account with them. Add to those requirements the requests for a ZIP code and a Taxpayer Identification Number, plus a photo ID, and the task of creating a new bank account in someone else's name became extra hard. Jerome understood the measures were there for good reason, but the more he encountered them, the more he despaired at their existence.

Jerome examined his options from every possible angle and found them far more limited than he was comfortable with. No way could he find the necessary underworld figure to get him the false documentation he needed in time to save Alicia. And there was every chance he'd end up being blackmailed by the forger too.

His next option was to obtain the details from a real person. Another human being. This too was fraught with dangers, and that was before he considered the moral implications of stealing another person's identity. It would be wrong on every level to involve another person, an innocent, just so he could steal the money. Wrong to drag their lives into the gaping abyss that was his current ordeal. Wrong to have them implicated in the theft of the money required to save Alicia.

But, and it's a but Jerome had no problem understanding, if he didn't act, Alicia would be the one to pay the price. She would be the one who suffered.

The cell got switched off and put back into his pocket as he weighed the consequences for his hapless victim. As soon as the theft was discovered, the police would be called and digital forensic experts would trace where the money went when it left the Beck Holdings account. That would lead them to Mr. Victim's door. Mr. Victim would be innocent. Very innocent. Mr. Victim would explain he had nothing to do with the theft. The digital forensics guys would dig deeper. They'd look at when the account was opened. They may even trace the account's origins back to the device that opened it. From there they'd look at triangulation and then trace back to the location in the hope of finding some CCTV footage. This meant that if Jerome did have to create an account online, he'd need to get somewhere private so he couldn't be linked to the account in any way.

As for Mr. Victim they'd be grilled by the police. They'd be able to claim, with complete honesty, they had nothing to do with the theft, and would in all probability have a cast-iron alibi. There would be witnesses as to their whereabouts, and if the police did trace the location where the account was created, they should be able to prove they were elsewhere.

In short, as best as Jerome could calculate, Mr. Victim would suffer a few days of discomfort and worry. They'd be questioned relentlessly by the cops but would ultimately be released without charge.

Compared to the danger Alicia was in, it was a no-brainer for Jerome. Sure, he'd feel bad for the hapless soul, but he knew he'd feel a lot worse if he didn't do everything in his power to make sure Alicia came home safe.

With the decision made, Jerome turned his mind on to the how. No way could he outright mug someone. That wasn't him, he couldn't stick someone up. Couldn't look into their eyes and force them to hand over their wallet. Even if he could, that person would be alert to things happening. They'd stop their bank accounts and take extra precautions over their security, both in real life and online. All this would make using their details to open an account so much harder, if not impossible.

Jerome realized he'd have to steal the details in such a way as to leave Mr. Victim unaware of the theft, or at least under the assumption that they'd lost their identifying documents. To achieve this he'd have to pick a pocket or burglarize a house. Neither of these options appealed to Jerome, but of the two he'd much sooner pick someone's pocket than try to break into their house. Maybe he'd get lucky and see an unattended jacket or purse he could help himself to, but with the way his luck had been going, he doubted he'd get that kind of break. He'd kept his eyes open for such an opportunity in the office, but hadn't been presented with a decent chance. It was also far too close to him for comfort. With a stranger there was far less chance of the theft being traced to him. With a colleague who'd be able to trace the theft of their wallet to the office, there would be an immediate link to his workplace.

As Jerome rose to go back to the office he saw a man stumbling his way along the path. The man's head was down as if looking for dropped money, and the others on the sidewalk dodged out of his way, their disapproving expressions telling an entire story.

Jerome tracked the man with both his eyes and his feet. Other than his drunken state, the man looked to be a professional. He was well-dressed, sported a hundred-buck haircut and shoes that were a long way from needing a cobbler's attention.

Why such a man was so drunk so early in the day was his own issue. He could be an alcoholic, or just some poor soul whose world had collapsed through a discovered infidelity or sudden bereavement.

The man lurched forward, and Jerome fell in behind him. The man was suffering his own private hell, but so was Jerome, and in Jerome's mind it was very much a case of survival of the fittest. Jerome also recognized how his luck changed when Mr. Victim stumbled across his view, so he planned to follow Mr. Victim until he had a chance to steal his wallet.

Jerome kept himself ten paces behind Mr. Victim as the man stumbled his way along the sidewalk. He was close enough to hear the tuneless singing emanating from Mr. Victim's lips. It was a cheery tune about freedom and new beginnings.

Other pedestrians tossed amused glances at Mr. Victim, but none of them engaged with the lunchtime drunk.

Mr. Victim finished his song and with a leaned-back bellow launched into a spirited if not tuneful rendition of the Beatles' "Here Comes the Sun." Despite everything he was going through, Jerome couldn't help smiling at Mr. Victim's lusty singing. He'd been wrong in his assumptions about the man being down, but that didn't mean he was prepared to ignore him as a source of ID.

Mr. Victim lurched in the direction of a bar on a street corner. Jerome followed, hoping none of the staff would decide Mr. Victim had already had enough and refuse to serve him.

Jerome hung back as Mr. Victim levered himself onto a bar stool. The bar was a typical New York bar. Neither a dive nor an uber-trendy place, it was a regular bar with menus on the tables and a sense of genial bustle about it. There was laughter, food smells and one-sided telephone conversations in the air.

"Scotch rocks." Mr. Victim's voice carried across the room as he beamed a misshapen grin. His hand slapped down on the bar then was raised in a victory salute. "And a picture, oops, a pitcher of beer for every table."

Jerome sidled across to the bar and took a stool four along from Mr. Victim. He had his old cell in his hand and was both checking for a new Direct Message on Twitter and making a concerted attempt to not look as if he was paying Mr. Victim any attention.

Mr. Victim's voice cut across Jerome's act. "Hey, buddy, c'n I getcha drink?"

"I'm good, thanks. Just in for a soda before I get back to work." Jerome slid his cell back into his pocket and focused on Mr. Victim. There had been no Twitter message. No instructions and no proof Alicia was still alive. If he stole Mr. Victim's wallet to get his ID, he'd be doing so in the faith Alicia was still alive.

Jerome had to believe. Had to keep that faith, and he knew that until he had irrefutable proof Alicia couldn't be saved, he'd have to keep progressing his plans forward, to keep continuing with his schemes regardless of the risks to himself.

"Come on, buddy, join me for a drink." Mr. Victim raised his left hand and used a stirrer to point at his naked ring finger. "I've finally gotten myself free." He patted a pocket of his jacket. "My divorce was finalized today and I plan to celebrate being shot of that woman. No more will she control me. No more will I return home to be attacked by the most vicious mouth on the planet. I'm free, and she's had to settle for a fraction of the alimony she wanted. Life is good. Damn good."

Jerome lifted his hand in a mock toast. "Happy days."

"Happy days indeed, my friend." A hand was waved to the bartender. "Grab this dude a drink. Whatever he wants."

Jerome ordered a soda and watched as Mr. Victim reached into his jacket for his wallet. "Thanks." Jerome paid special attention to where Mr. Victim's hands went as he put the wallet back into his jacket's inside left pocket.

Now he knew where the wallet was kept, he was in a better position to steal it. At least that was his plan until Mr. Victim stood, shrugged off the jacket and folded it before planting it onto the stool beside him.

Jerome copied the act as he stepped forward to join Mr. Victim, with his left hand he laid his jacket atop Mr. Victim's as he extended his right and introduced himself with a false name. "I'm Frank."

"Beau." Beau cast his eyes round the room. "Man, it feels good to be free. Good to know that I can sink a few cold ones and some whiskey today, and then begin to start over tomorrow. How 'bout you? You married? You with someone?"

Jerome pulled a face at the question. "Married, and very happy with her, before you ask."

"Good for you, Frankie. I'm happy for you. Just because my Norma screwed me over, that don't mean I can't be happy for others. I picked a bad one, but man, man oh man oh man, I still believe in love. Still believe there's someone for everyone."

The goofy way Beau spoke played into Jerome's hands while kicking his morals in the groin. Beau had gotten his name wrong, which made for a great indicator of how little he was absorbing of what was going on around him. His comments about being happy for Jerome were a kicker, though. They showed Beau to be a decent guy. His sharing his good fortune by sending a pitcher of beer to each table was another plus point in his column.

Jerome had to push down the feelings of self-loathing at what he was planning to do to Beau. Had to quell the uprising as his gut knotted and twisted itself to send bile up his throat.

Jerome watched as Beau aimed his eyes around the room until they locked on the signs for the bathrooms. As he levered himself upright he leaned into Jerome, cascading beer and whiskey fumes over him. "You look after your girl. Look after her real good."

The words cut at Jerome. Slashed at his psyche. He'd already failed to look after his girl. Alicia had been taken. Stolen from their bed and taken to an unknown location. Again he had to swallow down the toxic bile of his conscience's revolt.

As soon as Beau disappeared in the direction of the men's

room, Jerome rose to his feet and scooped up the two jackets on his way to the door. He was doing everything he could to shield Beau's jacket with his own, but he was three steps from the door when he heard a raised voice.

"Hey, dude. I think you've got that drunk guy's jacket as well as your own."

Jerome froze. He had two options. Return the jacket and pass it off as an innocent mistake, or run.

He ran.

The thump at the door made Alicia's head spin. The noise couldn't be described as a knock, more the banging of a fist's heel against the door.

An egg-sized lump had formed above her eye from where she collided with the mini-fridge, and she had a pounding headache that hadn't eased since she picked up the injury.

"Jerome?"

Please, God, let it be Jerome. The man of her dreams, the love of her life and the person whose arms she wanted to die in.

Alicia missed Jerome like never before. If he'd been in here with her he probably wouldn't have been able to escape either, but he'd at least have kept her spirits up. His good cheer was infectious, and even when life took a swipe at him, he never let himself get beaten down. Sure, his pedantry and general OCD about untidiness could be as irritating as hell, but right then all she wanted was to see his smile, feel his arms around her and hear his voice. Knowing Jerome, he'd calmly explain why everything was going to be all right, then make some stupid joke to allay her fears.

"Step away from the door and go to the other side of the room." It wasn't Jerome's voice, but one belonging to a captor. Its tone brooked no argument so Alicia did the only thing she could do, and obeyed the instruction.

Whatever the men were coming into the room for, things would always go better for her if she did as they said. Her first thought was that Jerome had failed to complete whatever task they'd set him and they were here to kill her. Her second was that she was about to be raped. Both of these thoughts had her pressing herself against the far wall.

She'd already searched the entire room looking for anything that might be used as a weapon. The best she found was a plastic water bottle and she rated that as useful as a handful of feathers in terms of deadliness.

Alicia heard the sound of locks being turned and bolts being slid open. The door squeaked open and two figures stepped into the room. One was the size of an NFL linebacker and the other wasn't. Both wore ski masks and the big one held a pistol he aimed her way. The smaller one held a generic brown bag that he laid on top of the small fridge.

He opened the bag and removed a newspaper. When he turned her way and held the newspaper out to her Alicia shrank farther away, the coarse wall scraping furrows into her back.

"I take it you injured yourself while trying to break through the door?"

Alicia nodded. The act instinctive, but enough to double her headache.

The small guy gave no acknowledgment of her nod as he unfolded the newspaper enough so Alicia could see it was the *New York Times*, and waggled the paper at her. She reached out a hand and took it as understanding swept over her. A rapid glance at the newspaper's date confirmed her theory.

Alicia took the newspaper and held it in front of her as Small Guy took out a cell phone.

"I get that you're providing Jerome with proof I'm alive, but I have some questions." Neither of the men answered so Alicia took a half step forward. Now she knew they were in communication with Jerome and he had the good sense to insist on proof of her well-being, she was less afraid of the men and what they might do to her. "How long do you plan on keeping me here? What are you getting Jerome to do? How can Jerome and I trust you to let me go when he's done whatever you want him to do?"

Neither man spoke. They didn't even look at each other for a reaction. For all they didn't respond to her questions, there was still a defined difference between the two men. The smaller guy held her eye, his gaze hard and uncompromising. It was as if he was daring her to speak again.

The big guy wasn't so subtle. Instead of staring her out or looking elsewhere, he let his eyes caress her chest with a suitor's intensity. The thin pajamas Alicia wore kept few secrets about her physique, and Big Guy was absorbing every detail. A part of Alicia wanted to stand still and let Big Guy's examination of her be met with the contempt it deserved. She couldn't do it, though. Maybe if it had happened in a different time and place, she could have endured the humiliation of being so blatantly ogled. But here, in this room, when held captive at gunpoint his gaze creeped her out, made her skin crawl like a million spiders were scuttling over her body.

She folded her arms across her chest and glared at Big Guy. "Get a good look, did you?"

His eyes dropped. Not to the floor in shame, but down her body, down to her waist and below. That was bad enough, but when his Adam's apple bobbed in response to a swallow, it was all she could do not to turn away and offer him her back. The only reason she didn't do so was that she wanted to keep him in her sight.

Small Guy retreated to the door and waited for Big Guy to do the same. Big Guy backed out of the room, his gaze offering every bit as much a threat as the gun in his hand.

Alicia wanted to sink onto the mattress. To weep out the stress of the encounter and the humiliation of Big Guy's lechery. She didn't. To cry now would be to crumble. She couldn't crumble. She inherently knew she must remain strong, stronger than she'd ever been. Whatever way this went, good or bad, she had to be ready to face it. If she survived she could cry after it was all over, and if she wasn't fated to survive the whole thing, then she planned to go down fighting. No matter how powerful and strong Big Guy might be. No matter how much of a height and weight advantage he may have over her, if he tried coming back alone with rape on his mind, she'd claw at his eyes, send knees, elbows, feet and fists toward his groin and his Adam's apple. She'd bite, tear and scratch regardless of what he did, or threatened to do to her.

As much as she was mentally steeling herself for the worst, Alicia wasn't so stupid as to be unafraid. She wanted to live. Wanted to see Jerome and her folks again. Wanted to raise a family with the man she loved.

Alicia knew it would be a waste of time, but she checked the room once again, looking for any area where she may be able to effect an escape.

Jerome hurtled along the sidewalk at his best pace. Sprints were never his strongest suit. He was always better at distance running. He was giving it everything he'd got, though. His one free arm pumping like an Olympian's, the other tucked tight against his body, clamping the two jackets to his side. Beau's for the precious ID it would contain, and his own because it carried his own ID, and the last thing he needed with Alicia taken was for the cops to be after him.

Jerome rounded a corner and risked a look back. Bad idea. Two young guys who'd been in the bar were coming his way. To his frantic eyes they looked much fitter than he was, and he set off again, desperate to rid himself of the tails he'd picked up.

As Jerome powered along he heard a yell. "Stop that man. He's a thief."

Ahead of Jerome a guy in his fifties set himself like a blocker. Jerome's high school football days came back to him. It might be a lot of years since he last ran down the line, but the principles and moves were as much a part of him as his blood type.

Jerome adjusted his course until he was aimed to the guy's left, near the asphalt of the roadway. A hard-planted right foot sent him into a wide sidestep that should have seen him pass to the older guy's right.

The older guy was wise to the move and shifted his body enough to intercept Jerome. This should have been a problem, but wasn't. Jerome had pulled this move a hundred times on the football field. His next sidestep aimed him back to the guy's left again, but even as Jerome's right foot was making contact with the sidewalk, he was shifting his bodyweight and sidestepping back to the guy's right.

The guy's fingers grasped at thin air, but the whole encounter had slowed Jerome down and up ahead there was a pair of guys who looked like they planned to make an attempt to intercept him.

Off to Jerome's right a crosswalk was beginning to flash the Don't Walk sign, but Jerome paid it no heed as he sprinted across the four lanes of asphalt. Tires screeched and horns blared, but he could care less, he was getting away.

A rushed look back saw his pursuers interrupted by the traffic, so he shucked on his own jacket and set off running again. He took the first corner at great pace then slowed to a walk, his hands fumbling for the contents of Beau's pockets. He got the wallet, the divorce papers and a couple of letters. These all got stuffed into his pockets, and he was about to lay Beau's jacket over a newspaper stand when he got thumped sideways, sending him tumbling to the ground.

A man stood over him. He wasn't one of the young guys who'd chased him from the bar, nor the guy he sidestepped, or the pair who were preparing to stop him. It was someone else. A stranger. A Good Samaritan.

"I saw you. You were going through the pockets of that jacket. The way you scudded round that corner it's gotta be stolen, so I'm making a citizen's arrest."

"Screw you, you jerk. You've got it all wrong." Jerome tried to rise but the guy gave a stomp on his chest that sent Jerome back to the sidewalk.

"Yeah, well, you can explain that to the cops."
The guy pulled a cell from his jacket and started to dial.

Jerome's mind raced as he tried to think of a plausible lie that he could deliver in time to be free of the Good Samaritan before his pursuers caught up with them. His first idea was to say the jacket belonged to a guy he'd caught with his wife, but it wasn't the most credible excuse.

He used a similar lie instead. "The jacket belongs to a guy my sister has just started dating. She's only been seeing him a month and already he's asking her to loan him money. He asked her for twenty grand, and I wanted to know more about him. I tried asking. Of course I did, but all he gave me was a load of bull."

"A month? Twenty grand?" Jerome captured a look at the Good Samaritan as the man stood over him. He seemed a regular guy.

"Yeah. That's right."

Jerome levered himself to a sitting position and, seeing no further signs of aggression from the Good Samaritan, began to roll onto his front so he could stand. As he straightened the Good Samaritan leaned forward and entwined his hand in the front of Jerome's jacket.

"If what you're saying is true, then it sucks, but so I'm not being fooled by you spinning me a line, I'm still going to call the cops. You can explain your story to them."

With his free hand, the Good Samaritan went back to dialing on his cell.

Jerome couldn't allow the police to be involved. Couldn't let the call be connected long enough for the Good Samaritan to tell his story and a cop to be dispatched.

The hand grasping the front of his jacket had bulbous knuckles that were white with the strength of the Good Samaritan's grip.

The hand holding the cell was loose, relaxed as the Good Samaritan tried to use the device one-handed.

Jerome swung a straight arm upwards, his hand arrowing toward the Good Samaritan's elbow. The top of his balled fist thumped into its intended target, the sudden impact tossing the cell from the Good Samaritan's hand and up into the air.

To prevent the cell being caught, Jerome took three steps backwards, rotating his body so the Good Samaritan careered into a signpost.

"You asshole. I knew you were feeding me a load of bull." The Good Samaritan's eyes flicked to the cell on the ground. Its screen now black and spiderwebbed with cracks. His other hand came forward, misshapen knuckles clenched tight as they arrowed toward Jerome's face.

Jerome couldn't avoid the blow, but the attempt he made was enough to diminish the punch's power so that he wasn't knocked cold. Rather than let the Good Samaritan wind up another blow, Jerome powered his right foot forward. He wasn't trying to deliver a clever move, just to kick the Good Samaritan good and hard in the shins.

His kick achieved its aim and drew a yelp from the Good Samaritan. Jerome recognized the grip on his jacket had loosened, so he repeated the kick and added a little more venom.

His second kick landed and pulled a curse from the Good Samaritan, but the punch that had been coming his way connected and because he'd been focused on his own attack, the blow exploded pain into Jerome's cheek.

From the corners of his eyes, Jerome saw people were starting to take notice of the scuffle, so he grabbed the wrist of the hand holding him and took three rapid sidesteps to whip the Good Samaritan across his body and backwards into the trash can. Then he used the movement to throw a sneaky elbow in the Good Samaritan's ribs. It worked; the Good Samaritan's grip loosened enough for Jerome to rip himself free.

He lifted a hand and aimed a finger at the Good Samaritan. "I told you, it's over. Now please stop harassing me. We're done. Through. Forever."

Chuckles broke out around them, but Jerome paid no heed to the onlookers as he snatched up the jacket and set off at a steady trot. He was late back for work and sure as night follows day, Carthew would notice and comment.

It wasn't until Jerome was in the visitor bathroom on the ground floor of the Beck Building that he got enough privacy to examine the items he'd stolen from Beau. The wallet held some credit and debit cards. All were for the same bank, which limited his options but there was little else of value. He'd been hoping for a driving license, as they included the date of birth, which was a key detail that he needed as well as a photo that could be used as ID.

Jerome considered using Beau's account to receive the money, but it was too much of a risk as Beau would be sure to stop all his accounts when he realized his wallet was gone. It was also a racing certainty that the bank would be watching the account for any activity and that would just lead cops to Jerome's door.

The envelope containing Beau's treasured divorce papers was just as useless. Worse than useless, it sent inflammatory pangs of guilt throughout Jerome to have deprived Beau of it.

At least the envelope gave him an address for Beau, but nowhere on any of the documents was the necessary Tax Information Number. The address would at least allow him to return Beau's stuff when he'd gotten Alicia back.

Two pieces of key information were missing. The guilt he felt for stealing was nothing more than an unnecessary burden. The bruises he'd collected from scuffling with the Good Samaritan, the risks he'd taken to steal Beau's jacket and the headlong dash that had left him late for work and thereby drawing further attention to himself. All were for nothing. All were a waste of time and energy.

Jerome knew he was in over his head. Knew he wasn't the right man to have the task he had. Knew he'd have to get smarter about his methods and do so rapidly. Alicia's freedom and possibly her life depended on him delivering the $50 million. No way could he let her down. No way could he have any further failures. Not when Alicia's life was at stake.

Alicia was the girl whose dazzling smile entranced every male who fell victim to its wattage. Assured, graceful and smarter than anyone else he'd ever met, she breezed through NYU as if the classes were designed for kindergarteners. When not studying she'd helped out at a homeless shelter and worked in a busy bar to pay her way. Alicia's moral compass was on a heading for compassion, and she never failed to offer help when she encountered someone who needed it.

He'd had to put his foot down when she'd wanted him to visit a pet rescue center. He knew her too well. If she saw all those animals awaiting a new home she'd want to take them all. It took him two hours of patient explaining. They both worked long hours commuting into New York, and while maybe a cat could work, there was no way it would be fair to rescue a dog and then leave it alone eleven hours a day, five days a week. As he always did, he sought compromise. Rather than leave her hopes dashed, he promised that when they were ready to start a family, they'd rescue a dog or two and maybe a cat. Alicia had cried at that vision of their future. Kids and pets. Individuals for her to look after, who would rely on her. Those were the things she wanted more than anything in life. She was looking forward to living her dream life staying at home to care for with one boy, one girl, two dogs and three cats. When the kids were in school she'd return to work on a part-time basis. Even her career as an HR lawyer had been chosen because she felt she could do good work for people, could help the downtrodden, and even though she worked for a multinational company, she made sure that the workers got fair contracts. At a work function, Alicia's boss had once confided in him that Alicia saved the company a fortune each year because the meticulously comprehensive employment contracts she drew up were so agreeable to the workers, they were rarely challenged in the courts and when any issues arose, she could always mediate the situation to leave all parties content, if not happy.

Jerome exited the bathrooms and made his way back to his own floor. When the elevator doors opened, he put his head down and set off for his office. He made it ten paces before he heard his name being spoken. By Carthew.

"Good Lord, Prentice. What on earth happened to you? You look like you've been in a fight. You need to explain yourself. And to get some ice on that eye." Carthew snapped his fingers at a hovering intern. "Go get an ice pack; failing that, bring some ice wrapped in a towel."

Jerome started at the accusation. Did Carthew know more than he was saying? How could he tell? He looked down at himself. His trousers bore dirt from his time on the sidewalk. And his eye, what was wrong with that? He raised a hand to his face and winced when his fingertips alighted on the swelling below his right eye, where the Good Samaritan's best punch had landed. With his full focus on rescuing Alicia, the injuries had hardly registered, but now he thought about it his palms were grazed and the muscles of his legs were protesting at the sudden dash without the benefit of a warm up, or even the slightest stretch to prepare them.

Carthew looked at him waiting for an answer. Jerome couldn't tell him the truth. Not here, not where so many ears could overhear. Pernicious as the man might be, Jerome trusted Carthew and a part of him wanted to get his boss somewhere private and tell him everything. Explain how he was being forced to steal from the company to secure Alicia's release.

Two things stopped him. Carthew was a company man through and through. His first thoughts were always about what was best first for Beck Holdings and then for Beck Accounting. The second reason was more practical, more rational. The people who'd taken Alicia seemed to know a lot about Beck Holdings and all its subdivisions. To have this knowledge they'd need people on the inside, and for all Jerome might be sure of Carthew's integrity to the firm, he knew he didn't dare trust any employee of Beck Holdings.

"Are you going to say what happened?"

There was more concern and less demand in Carthew's voice, but Jerome needed to deliver an answer.

"It's not what it looks like. I was getting some lunch and I heard a shout. Some punk had stolen a woman's purse. He was running my way so I tackled him. There was a bit of a scuffle, he got away from me, but at least I got the woman her purse back."

"Jeez, Prentice. You're full of surprises today. First you call me out, and then during your lunchbreak you turn into a crime fighter. Are you okay? Do you need to take some personal time this afternoon?"

"I'm good, sir. It wasn't that big a deal." Jerome gestured to his office. "If you'll excuse me, I have a lot to do."

"Of course, of course. I will naturally be keeping an eye on you, Prentice. To make sure you're okay, of course."

That was all Jerome needed. Carthew's way of keeping an eye on him would involve impromptu visits to his office, which meant he'd have to be very careful not to get caught researching anything online. Carthew's concern seemed genuine, but a cynical element of Jerome's character suspected Carthew wanted to make sure he was capable of doing his job and wouldn't be making any mistakes. After all, with the figures he dealt with, something as simple as a misplaced decimal point could be disastrous.

Jerome pushed open the doors of Melvilles and drank in the atmosphere the way he always did when entering the bar. Named for the New York author Herman Melville, there was a prominent theme to the bar that reflected his most famous book, *Moby Dick*. Each of the four walls was decorated with prints depicting the struggles the old whalers faced when hunting the mammoth beasts. A traditional harpoon was fixed above the bar, and an old whaling skiff hung from the ceiling. Copies of the novel could be bought from Melvilles and, according to legend, they'd sold as many copies as any dedicated New York bookstore. Melvilles had a character of its own, and as such it had become a regular haunt for Jerome back in the day. He'd always been a reader and his way of dealing with the daily commute was to escape into a world of mystery and action thrillers. A bar with a literary theme was always going to be a haven for him, and Melvilles was a well-run establishment that looked after its customers with aplomb.

As Jerome expected, Alicia had never shared his affinity with Melvilles. Her love of all animals prevented her from ever feeling comfortable in the bar, even if the novel was nothing more than a fictional account of a true story.

Ed was seated in a booth against the back wall. The booth was big enough for six, but Ed had positioned himself at the entrance to the booth, and as Jerome walked over, he saw Ed shake his head at a trio who gestured at the empty seats.

"Hey, dude. What's so important you have to interrupt my life as an international playboy and all-round achiever of the impossible?"

The greeting was typical of Ed. For all his jocular nature, he didn't ever fail to get straight to the point. If something bothered him, he spoke out there and then. He wouldn't wait to think things over, wouldn't give any slight time to fester. He'd just open his mouth and let the conversation flow wherever the tides directed it.

How to start? How to give voice to the nightmare that was his life? How do you tell someone your wife has been abducted? That you have to steal $50 million from work to get her back alive? Jerome didn't have the answer to any of those questions, so he adopted Ed's tactic of getting straight to the point. "Alicia was abducted last night and I have to steal fifty mil from work to get her back."

"You're having me on." Ed shook his head. "Come on then, let's have the punchline."

"There's no punchline, Ed. I'm deadly serious."

Ed's face blanched. Not an easy feat considering he covered his natural pastiness with a sunbed tan.

They fell silent when a server appeared. "Good evening. I'll be your server tonight. Is it drinks and dinner or just drinks?"

"Two boilermakers, please. Budweiser and Jim Beam." It was Ed who ordered. Jerome couldn't make his mouth work. Now he had spoken out about Alicia's kidnapping, his resolve threatened to fail him. He felt as if he was going to either hurl or cry. The release of sharing his problem had floored him. "Can we also get two plain burgers with fries, please?"

"Sure thing." The server wheeled away, her ponytail swishing as she went to fill their order.

"That's big, dude. Real big. What did the police say when you called them?"

Jerome didn't have to answer the question. Ed could read his face as easy as a kids' comic.

"Scratch that. Stupid question, there would be enough threats to make sure you didn't dare. So, you've obviously asked me to meet you because you need my help. Consider it given. But before I can help you, you're going to have to tell me everything, and I mean everything."

Jerome waited until the server deposited their drinks before launching into his tale. How typical of Ed to specify the brands of beer and whiskey.

As Jerome spoke Ed sat still. No fidgeting, no taking notes and no looking around the room. His focus was on Jerome and the words he was speaking. Jerome could hear his own voice cracking at times, and he saw the reflected concern on Ed's face as he ran through the day. The one semi-positive spot in his tale was the Twitter message that had arrived in the middle of the afternoon. No words, another Twitter account and a picture of Alicia holding up a copy of the *New York Times*. There was a bruise on Alicia's forehead that looked painful, but Jerome had expected to see her in a far worse state, so while he loathed seeing evidence of her being mistreated, he could accept a minor injury to her as he'd imagined her suffering far greater harm.

It was at this point Ed asked his first question. "The picture, I take it you zoomed in and checked the date on the paper?"

"Yes." Jerome nodded as he tried a first tentative sip of his beer to moisten his mouth after speaking for so long. "I also checked their online site and the headlines were the same."

"Good. That gives us something of a timeline and tells us quite a lot. You asked for the picture late morning; they delivered it mid-afternoon. Let's say there was a three-hour time span between you making the request and them sending the picture. First off, although they are deactivating the accounts they're using to contact you, they're monitoring them whenever they are active. Now let's count this back. Within a second or two of you sending the message asking for proof of life, it would be out there. What's uncertain is how much time passed before they saw it. Now, we have the question of who is monitoring their accounts. You said three people abducted her last night. That tells us there's a minimum of three people involved in this, although I think there are probably more. My guess is that it'd be someone mid-ranked within their organization, or team, if that sounds less scary to you."

"It all sounds scary. We gotta get Alicia back." Jerome lifted his beer and took a slug from the bottle. The first sip hadn't felt bad and if he'd ever needed a beer, it was right at that moment. "We've gotta save her."

"We will. Now, back to what I was saying, if the person who read the message wasn't the top dog, he'd have to pass it up the chain of command. Then the decision maker would have to think for however long and then issue the command. If they didn't have a copy of a newspaper with them, they'd have to get one. Depending on where they are holding Alicia it might take two minutes, or it might take them an hour. Then they have to get Alicia to hold the paper, create another Twitter account, if they haven't already set up several, take the picture and send it to you. A lot of that is unknowns in terms of timings, and if as you suspect some of their organization are employees of Beck Holdings, they may not be able to respond immediately to messages or calls."

"And what if it was the top man who read my message and he could get a newspaper in a few minutes. Why did they delay for so long before sending me the picture?" This is the part Jerome couldn't understand. Why the abductors would torture him by delaying when they would surely want him to get the money as soon as possible.

"That's obvious, dude. You're strung out. You're damned near at your breaking point and they want to keep you there. The more time you spend worrying about Alicia, the more you're likely to do their bidding. They're just screwing with you." Ed lifted a silencing finger as Jerome opened his mouth to speak. "Think about your rep, you're known as a good guy. Someone whose honesty is unimpeachable. You have integrity, you are very good at what you do and you're known for being a stand-up guy. That makes what they're asking of you a morally tough ask. Alicia is their leverage, and so long as they have that leverage, they're going to maximize its use."

Jerome couldn't help but scowl at Ed's irrefutable logic. Ed always saw the big picture, and everything Ed had just said he should have worked out for himself, but he knew he was too close to be objective. Alicia looked scared in the picture. There was some defiance in her features but there was no mistaking the fear in her eyes. Most telling of all about the picture was the slight lack of focus on the newspaper itself. It suggested it wasn't being held still. That spoke of shaking hands. Of a body filled with trepidation and terror.

The picture was a double-edged sword. It showed Alicia was alive and relatively unharmed. That was brilliant. It was the best news. Alicia might look terrified, but she was alive and that knowledge quelled Jerome's worst fear, although the way Alicia looked broke his heart. He just wanted to reach into the picture and hug her fears away. To sweep her up in his arms and bring her to a place of safety. To smooth her hair and tell her that she was safe. He wanted to fix things for her. Not when he could get the money. Now. This instant.

He couldn't do that. He had to play the game the abductors wanted him to play. He had to leave his honest life behind and commit grand theft.

"What do we do? I reckon I can find a way to get the money from the company, but it's fifty-fifty as to whether I get caught and sent to jail. To be honest, I'm more worried about them not releasing Alicia."

"Let's come back to the points we were discussing earlier."

Jerome paused while their burgers were served. The offer of ketchup and sauces was declined, but Jerome's first action was to push the plate away from him. Ed used a small handful of fries as a pointer. "Eat. I know your stomach is probably roiling, but you need to eat. You need to refuel your body. You're no use to Alicia if you're exhausted and either unfit or too damn tired to think straight. Eat. If not for yourself, for Alicia."

Jerome picked up a lone fry and bit an inch off the end. Against his wishes and expectations, his saliva glands stormed into action and he realized he was ravenous. Ed was right. He needed to keep his strength up for Alicia, even if the idea of eating made him feel sick.

"Now, about the Twitter accounts. It's possible for multiple users to access the same account, but you say that the first message you got came from an account that got deleted. This tells me that they're taking precautions to make sure they can't be traced. It also tells me they don't know much about technology."

"What do you mean don't know much about technology?"

"Instead of deleting their account they could simply use a VPN to shield their IP address and location."

"Maybe they're doing both?"

"Perhaps, but my guess is they'd trust the VPN if they knew about it." Ed rotated his beer through ninety degrees. 'It's practically impossible to trace a user who has VPN installed." Ed lifted his burger. "You haven't mentioned a deadline. Did they give you one?"

"No." Jerome felt a new sense of dread. There was no deadline. Therefore there may be no end to this nightmare. No point at which he could believe it would be over. "But I want to get it done as soon as possible. I have to save her, Ed. Have to get her back before they hurt her."

"Of course you do. That's a given. But the lack of a deadline is telling. It suggests they have no idea how long it will take you to steal the money for them. If everything they've told you is true, it suggests they're not professionals at this type of thing. That they're more or less regular people who've decided to take a drastic course of action. Them not giving you a deadline tells me they've no real experience and they don't dare set one that's too tight, as it'd mean they'd either have to progress from kidnapping to homicide, or fold and release Alicia unharmed when their deadline expired."

Thank God for Ed and his irrefutable logic. Jerome loved that his friend could see the big picture, but even this common-sense overview was layered with bad news. If Alicia had been taken by professionals, they'd know what they were doing. They'd follow the best practices of their felonious industry and would be calm. There were none of these reassurances to fall back on when dealing with amateurs. Amateurs made mistakes. They panicked and made those mistakes worse. As horrendous as the idea of Alicia being in the clutches of hardened criminals might be, Jerome believed she would be safer than she would if amateurs had her.

As much as it pained Jerome to do so, he parked his worries about Alicia and looked Ed in the eye. "You said you'd help. I have a plan, it's not the greatest, but I have an idea of how to get the money. The problem with my idea is that I have no way of covering my tracks. Ten minutes after the theft is discovered, whomever discovers it will know I am the person who stole $50 million from Beck Holdings. I know you're an IT wizard and that you develop computer games for a living. I want to know if you can, and will, because this is a big ask, use some of your contacts to find out if there's a way to access our system and erase all the files that pertain to the money being taken. This will need to include any emails from me as I plan to create dummy invoices and have them paid from Beck Holdings."

Ed drummed his fingers on the table and stared at the ceiling. "I might know someone who I could ask, but wouldn't it be simpler for you to just pay the invoices yourself and then we find a way to erase all traces of your involvement?"

"I don't have that level of access. My job is to verify the figures are correct and then sign them off. Carthew double-checks them, or at least makes random checks in case I'm making errors, and from him they're sent to a central paymaster who either issues checks or makes bank transfers for the appropriate accounts."

Ed's lips pursed as he considered the details. "Seems complicated, but I suppose there will be reasons for all the checks. The big one being the amounts of money involved."

An idea came to Jerome but it was a big thing to ask of Ed. Far bigger than he'd ever intended making. With Alicia's life at stake, he couldn't not ask. "My idea will get us the money, that part I'm sure of. What it doesn't do is insulate me from the crime. How about we do something different? If someone could hack into Carthew or someone else's email and then forward on stuff from him to the paymaster. Then when the money is transferred the hacker goes back in and deletes all traces. They'd also need to file the CTR reports that banks have to send for transactions of over $10,000 and make sure the money moved on before the bank or the FinCEN had time to ring-fence it."

Ed's head shook. "That seems more practical than your first idea, but it's fraught with risk and it all hinges on us getting the timings right. Quite frankly there are too many things that can go wrong and, as much as I have your back, if we get caught I'll be telling the cops the whole truth. Plus, it's a big ask of the hacker, and while I might know one or two, I really don't know if they'll be happy taking the kinds of risks we're talking about. I also wouldn't be surprised if they asked for a sizable fee for helping us. Another thing: if you go ahead with this plan, you'd essentially be selling out Carthew or whomever else's email we chose in the process. How do you feel about that?"

16

"Alicia's life is at stake. I don't care what happens to Carthew or anyone else at Beck Holdings. I only care about getting her back." The words came easy to Jerome, but the truth of the matter was that he hated the idea of someone else paying for his crimes. A significant part of him wanted to take all responsibility for the theft so that any potential prison term would be handed to him as the guilty party, rather than an innocent patsy. If prison—and so being separated from Alicia for years—didn't terrify him as much as it did, he'd take the chance and face the consequences of his actions.

Ed raised a silencing finger. "Hush up a minute, will you? I may have a better idea."

The last few fries were fed into Ed's mouth and he chewed on them distractedly. For Jerome the wait was interminable, but he used it to take a bite of his burger. It was cooler than he'd prefer, but he knew that was his own fault for not eating it sooner.

"Okay, how about this? You create enough invoices to cover the fifty mil plus any fee a hacker requires. Then, we skip Carthew and send them straight to the paymaster. Not from you or Carthew, from someone further up the paygrade. I'm thinking one of the Becks themselves or, at the very least, a board member. With the invoices there will be an instruction to pay them at once. What we'll get the hacker to do is insert a few lines of code into the email attachments that will allow them hidden access into the back of the paymaster's screen. Essentially they'll be able to see what he's doing without him knowing we're watching. Once the money is paid the hacker could trigger a virus bomb on the paymaster's computer that will wipe his emails and trash his access to the bank accounts. They could also set one off in the online account he pays the invoices from. This will help to hide where the money went, but we can't be certain we'll have time to do this as there's a good chance every bank will be different, and until we know which bank he's using, the hacker would only have the time the paymaster takes making the transfers to make the necessary tweaks to his coding. If we do it this way, when the money is noticed as missing, there'll be no trace of where it's gone unless the paymaster prints or saves the emails to his computer. Even if he does that, there's no trail back to us. For your part, you'll need to get a secure account to put the money in, just in case the hacker doesn't have enough time to create a proper code. We'll also need the email of the paymaster and the email of whichever member of the Beck family you want to use."

"Wow, Ed, you're really thinking of everything here. Do you honestly think we can pull this off?"

Ed dropped a nonchalant shrug. "If the guy I'm thinking of asking is willing to play ball, I'm sure we stand a better-than-even chance."

"I'll get the account and the email addresses, no sweat. Thank you, Ed. Thank you for your help." Jerome knew the words of gratitude were inadequate. Ed was risking everything to help him.

"You'd do the same for me." Ed dismissed the thanks with a shrug and a wave and reached for his whiskey.

A notion struck Jerome and it was one he wasn't proud of. One he wasn't even sure how to say. He put a voice to it all the same. "You know, if we could steal the ransom and get away with it, we could take more."

"We could. But that's not who we are. I can just about live with myself for stealing if it's to save Alicia, but I got to tell you, Jerome, if you plan on suggesting we take some for ourselves, even a cent, I'm saying that not only will I not help you, I'll go to the cops myself because you'll no longer be someone I can think of as my best buddy."

Jerome's hand shot out to prevent Ed from continuing. "I agree, I don't care about getting rich off this, I only care about getting Alicia back as soon as possible. It's just that it's not as simple as you might think. What do you know about Bitcoin and cryptocurrency?"

"I know they exist, but I've never had any dealings with them. Why do you ask?"

"I've looked into them. They come with costs, handling fees, that kind of thing."

Ed shrugged. "That stands to reason, the people facilitating them will need to get something for their work." His eyes narrowed. "Are you suggesting we take more to cover the fees?"

"Exactly." Jerome washed a hand over his face. "I have specific amounts to go into each of the crypto accounts I've gotta create. If we don't take more, there will be a shortfall and I daren't contemplate what that will mean for Alicia."

"What are you proposing will be a suitable amount to cover any fees? And what happens to any money that's left?"

"Two million, plus any extra we need to entice your hacker friend, and any that's left should go to charity. You can choose the charity if you like."

"Okay. I'm in. As for the charity, there's a center for abused women back in Boston. Charlestown to be precise. They looked after my mom and me when she finally left my scumbag of a father."

"Deal. That's a worthy charity and one I know is very important to you." Jerome didn't like to manipulate Ed this way, especially when it came to events he knew traumatized Ed's childhood, but he was taking every advantage he could find.

17

Jerome eased back in his seat and took a long pull at his beer. Now he had Ed's full support, he also had a sounding board for his ideas, some wise counsel to help him navigate the uncertain waters he must traverse.

"The account you have the stolen money sent to, it needs to be totally untraceable back to you. And another thing, the invoices, how are you going to fabricate several invoices that have to be paid to the same account? Even the most lax paymaster will see a red flag with that."

"I've thought about that. I'm going to borrow someone else's identity to open the account. In an ideal world, I'd have had the paymaster convert the money straight to Bitcoin, but there's no way they'd do that. Don't ask me how I'm going to borrow someone else's identity; the less you know about that side of things, the better. For the invoices, Beck Holdings has interests in a construction company that's heavily involved in a new runway at Charles de Gaulle Airport. All of us in Beck Accounting have been alerted to the fact that some hefty invoices are expected to cross our desks in the next week or two. I plan to create several invoices, no more than ten, and they'll be for various amounts but will add up to a shade over the $52 million we need because these things never come in perfect round numbers."

Ed nodded his approval. "Okay. Until one of us is on a deathbed, I never want to hear how you get another identity." He rubbed at his chin. "What do you know about your company's internal program, and the email software? I want brand names, password protocols and everything you know about firewalls, electronic cut-outs and anything else that's installed for security reasons. My hacker friend will need to know all that stuff."

"Finance First is the accounting software we use. Email was Outlook for everything, but they swapped that out for an internal system called TriMail. Apparently there are three levels of encryption protocols built into it."

"What about emails coming in from other sources? Like me, or one of your satellite offices raising a query?"

"They all come through on TriMail."

Ed's fingers drummed a military beat on the table. Jerome knew his friend well enough to recognize when he was deep in thought chewing over a problem. Ed was a creature of habit and would show differing mannerisms whenever stressed, thinking or preparing to tell a joke. What his fingers or arms were up to was a sure indicator of where his mind was.

The server cleared their plates with efficiency and a wider smile than necessary. "Can I get you guys some more drinks?"

"Two beers, please. No whiskey." Jerome slid his Jim Beam across the table until it was in danger of becoming a casualty of Ed's rattling fingers.

As bad an idea as a lot of alcohol was, Jerome was wise enough to recognize that a second beer wouldn't be enough to do any harm, and the one he'd already had had relaxed him enough that he could think straight.

The shot of bourbon disappeared into Ed's mouth in one swooped glug. The action reminding Jerome of their time at NYU when after long days of studying, they'd hit the student bars and try to pick up girls. Those days had been among the most enjoyable

of Jerome's life, especially when one of the girls he'd met introduced herself as Alicia. She hadn't been an easy girl to date. She'd
made him work for the affections she'd given away as if rationed.
Once he'd broken down her defensive walls and proven himself,
she gave herself to him completely and made his life better than
he'd ever dared hoped or imagined it could be. Until she was taken
last night, his life had been damn near perfect.

"Finance First is something I've heard of. It's used by quite a
few companies like yours and is geared toward multinational
conglomerates rather than small businesses. I'd guess it can be
breached, but TriMail will be a different story. It's specifically
designed to prevent people doing what we've suggested. Of all the
emails systems out there, TriMail is reputedly the most secure."

"Damn." Jerome regretted giving his whiskey to Ed. Right
about now the fiery tang a shot of Jim Beam delivered was exactly
what he needed. "Does that mean we can't do it?"

"No, it means my hacker friend is probably going to have to
work harder than we originally thought. Remember a few years ago
I worked for Rhodes Inc. doing the embedded software testing?
Well, one of the pieces of software we had to test was TriMail."

Jerome had a vague memory about the embedded software
testing Ed used to do. The process was about creating programs
that ape a human user pressing random button configurations, to
see how the software being tested coped with the unpredictability
of human beings.

"Does that help at all?"

"Sort of. Once we'd done our tests and identified the weak
spots, they challenged us to breach TriMail's security. There was a
bonus of ten big ones on the table for the first person who got in,
provided they showed the TriMail guys how they'd done it."

Jerome cast his mind back but recalled nothing about Ed
earning any such bonus and he was sure he'd have been told. "Did
you go for it?"

"Sure did. I got a little way in, but hacking isn't my thing so I wasn't able to breach it. The guy who did is who I'll be asking to help us."

"If he did that, he sounds like our guy."

"He's our best hope. How soon can you get the account set up and the invoices created?" How typical of Ed to gloss over the minor stuff and focus on the next thing.

"I can create the invoices tonight. I've already grabbed a copy of a template and I plan to have them all set ready for tomorrow." Jerome spread his hands wide. "I don't know about the account. I've a few things I need before I can open one of them, and I don't know how quick I can get them."

"Yeah, well, that comes firmly under the Too Much Information act."

Jerome's cell phone let out a beep before he could reply. He snatched it from a pocket and aimed a nervous finger at the Twitter icon.

When he saw the message his first thought was to launch the cell across the room. He didn't, though. Instead he turned the cell to show Ed the message.

"'Why are you drinking beer with a buddy instead of getting us the money to buy your wife's freedom?'"

As he read the message aloud, Ed's tone was harder than Jerome had ever imagined it could be.

The instruction to step away from the door wasn't what Alicia had wanted to hear. A gentle tapping followed by Jerome's voice was the only sound she wanted to assault her ears. There was no way for her to mark time in this room, but she was convinced it must only be a few hours since the men came in to take a picture of her with the newspaper.

Alicia's every thought was a fearful one. There was no question in her mind Jerome would do everything in his power to save her, that there would be nothing short of mass murder that he wouldn't do to get her home safe again, but there was always a chance the demands were so outrageous that he'd refuse to do what the kidnappers wanted him to do.

A different thought struck her. The picture that was taken earlier could have had only one purpose, proof she was alive and unharmed, therefore Jerome had insisted on it. She knew her husband and everything about him. He wasn't a gambler, he wouldn't take risks by stalling, by making demands of the kidnappers. Therefore his request for proof of life was a genuine request, because he didn't want to commit to what would surely be a criminal course of action without knowing she was unharmed. As much as Alicia wanted to believe otherwise, it wasn't credible Jerome had already performed the required task.

That left only one reason for the kidnappers to be coming back so soon. Big Guy wanted some alone time with her.

Alicia felt her skin crawl as she subconsciously pressed her knees together. She glanced at her nails. Due to the amount of computer work she did, they weren't as long as she'd like them to be, but they were long enough to scratch a face, to gouge an eye.

Small Guy entered first with Big Guy on his heels. As expected, Big Guy's eyes slithered over her body again. If only she'd thought to grab the thin sheet and drape it over her shoulders, it would have hidden the contours of her body and denied his hungry eyes their feast.

Alicia couldn't work out if Small Guy was here to help pin her down, or if there was another reason for his presence.

"Relax." Small Guy's voice was calm. "We're not here to hurt you, but we do have some questions we'd like answers to, and we'd much prefer that you give us the answers without us having to make, or carry out, any threats to your well-being."

"What do you want to know?" Alicia wanted to kick herself for allowing her fear to show. Whatever the men had in store for her, she wanted to face it with her head up. With defiance shining from her eyes instead of fear.

"Your husband is currently sitting in a bar drinking beer. He's deep in conversation with someone we assume is a buddy. We want to know who this buddy is and why your husband is talking to him instead of doing our bidding."

Alicia knew it was decision time for her. That she'd have to make a choice between resisting and suffering the consequences of that resistance, and giving them the information. In the end it was a simple choice. She knew that for all she could be feisty and tough when necessary, she wasn't strong enough to withstand torture.

"You're going to have to describe the buddy for me." Alicia had already guessed who the buddy was. It had to be Ed. It was always Ed that Jerome turned to when he needed help. Whether he needed a strong pair of arms to move a cabinet, or a sounding board for something that was on his mind, Ed would be Jerome's first choice after her.

From the kidnappers' perspective Ed could be anyone. A cop buddy. A private eye. She got why they were nervous.

"He's a shade over six foot, maybe two-fifty pounds, with neat brown hair and a squashed nose."

"That's Ed, he's Jerome's BFF. Whatever it is you want Jerome to do, chances are he's asking for Ed's help."

"I see."

Two words. Each a single lonely syllable, but the loaded tone Small Guy used made them say much more than the two words themselves said. To Alicia's ears there was disappointment at Jerome sharing, acceptance that perhaps Jerome needed help and finally an ominous undertone that spoke of a potential retribution.

Alicia kept her chin up as she looked at Small Guy and willed her voice to not betray her terror. "Ed's not a cop or anything like that. You have no worries on that front. Jerome will do whatever you ask him to do so I can be released."

"If this Ed guy isn't a cop, what is he?"

"He works with computers. To be honest a lot of what he does bores me, or goes way over my head so I kinda tune out when he talks about his work, but I do know he works for a company that makes online games. He's a good guy, a stand-up guy."

Small Guy turned his head to look at Big Guy. They nodded to each other. This was crunch time for Alicia; either they were happy with what they'd heard, or they were agreeing to something that wouldn't bode well for her.

When they turned back to her, Small Guy held her eye while Big Guy slid his over her chest.

"What else can you tell us about him? Is he married with kids? Where does he live? Just how good are his IT skills. Is he honest?"

"He's married. His wife is a lovely woman. No kids yet, but I understand they're trying. He lives near Central Park." A defensive thought came to Alicia so she played down Ed's IT skills.

"From what I understand, he's good at what he does, but no more than that. He's told me a bit about his job and from what I can gather he designs the backgrounds. He's always had an artistic side. As for his honesty, he's scrupulous in that regard. If he finds a dime on the street, he'll put it into a collection tin or give it to a panhandler instead of his own pocket. I'd happily trust him with my bank card and PIN, and I know Jerome has."

"I see."

Those two words again. Not spoken with quite the same inflection the second time, but still enough to make Alicia shiver inside.

"Have you been truthful with us?"

"Yes, of course I have. I don't have anything to gain by lying to you, do I?"

"Nothing I can see, however"—Small Guy gestured at Big Guy —"if we find out that you've not been truthful with us, we will come back and my colleague here will make sure we get the real truth from you. Please believe me when I say he's got some excruciating ways of obtaining honest answers."

Rather than labor his point, Small Guy then strode for the door with Big Guy falling into step behind him.

Jerome's primary instinct was to look round, to try and spot the person who was following him. To search the crowd, to have his eyes looking for a familiar face, as he was sure Alicia's abductors were people connected to Beck Holdings.

He didn't turn his head. Didn't make any obvious effort to scan every face in Melvilles. His eyes swirled over the faces he could see. Ed's face was a picture of confused consternation, but something inside Jerome clicked into gear. That one damning Twitter message made him raise his game, elevated his consciousness to a new level.

For the first time since Alicia was taken he felt a growing anger replacing the numbness. Whether it was like the stages of grief, and he'd gone through disbelief and denial, a cold murderous fury was growing in his gut. The writhing eels of fear replaced with a pit of coiled vipers. He was ready to strike out, ready to take proper control of the whole mess.

"How dare they say that of you? If only they knew what we were talking about."

Ed's affront was a comfort but also a distraction.

"They're needling me. Trying to goad me into doing what they want. If they were pros they'd already be looking into you. When they found out you are an IT whizz they'd either take fright in case you traced them via Twitter, or they'd realize that you're helping me. The abductors may have already worked this out and are just trying to get me to get the money sooner. The fact they've tailed me is informative. It means they'll have seen my attempts to steal someone's ID, therefore they'll know that I'm doing their bidding. That message is their equivalent of a deadline."

"Are you sure? You're not worried they think you don't care about Alicia, are you?"

"Nope. Not for a second. They took her out of our bed. If they've targeted me because of where I work and their story is straight up, there's every chance I'll know one or more of them. Therefore they'll know me and it's no secret that I'm happily married. You know how Alicia and I are, that we make no secret of the fact we're crazy about each other. Both of us have been hit on at work and both of us turned the offers down. I was specifically chosen for this and Alicia is their leverage. Trust me on this, they might be amateurs but they'll have made damn sure they picked the right person."

"Okay, dude. I'm just trying to look at all angles."

"I know, but that message has left me pissed at them. I want to punch their faces in. Alicia has got to be terrified. I'm terrified for her, and I'm not having it."

Jerome plucked his cell from Ed's hand, accessed the TwitterSpy app and typed in the handle the latest message had come from. If it picked out a location in Melvilles, that more than anything would identify the person spying on him and Ed.

As much as he wanted to wait for the app to do its thing, Jerome knew he needed to keep advancing his plan forward. The hardest part of the whole operation would always be getting someone's ID.

Jerome leaned over the table and whispered the number of his new cell into Ed's ear then pulled back. "I've got to go. I'll let you know as soon as I have the new account set up."

"Cool." Ed nodded. "I'll get in touch with my hacker friend."

The street outside Melvilles was busy, but evening busy rather than daytime busy. Jerome would have preferred it to be quiet so he could potentially spot his tail, but as soon as he had the thought he cursed himself out. He was an accountant, not a spy. His name was Jerome Prentice, not James Bond. He didn't know the first thing about spotting a tail beyond what he'd seen in the movies or read in a thriller. When Vin Diesel or Dwayne Johnson spotted a tail, they'd hop between subway trains, change taxis, double back and somehow end up tailing the guys who'd started off tailing them. Life wasn't like the movies. Those things might look good in the cinema, but when you're alone on a busy street those moves aren't quite so simple.

Jerome hailed a taxi because other than what he'd seen in the movies, he didn't know what else to do.

A taxi pulled over and the cabbie leaned back in his seat, head twisting to speak over his shoulder. "Where you goin', buddy?"

The cabbie's accent had the sharp tones belonging to a native of Queens. His hair was bubble-permed and there was a bobble-headed Jesus stuck to the dash.

"Just drive, I'll direct you."

The cabbie shrugged and set off. The movement causing Jesus to give a series of vigorous nods.

For the next half hour, Jerome kept giving directions that saw the cab zigzagging across Manhattan. At times he doubled back on himself and at others he went five blocks without instigating a change.

When he made it to his destination on Lexington Avenue, he waited until he saw the sign for City Hall Station before delivering his final instruction and reaching for his wallet. "Can you drop me here, please?"

"Sure."

Jerome paid the cabbie and descended into the subway, where he proceeded to ride the subway back and forward until he was convinced he'd done everything he could to lose his tail. Maybe the movie moves had worked, and maybe they hadn't. Either way, he'd easily be picked up again, either at home or work the next morning.

He considered booking into a hotel, but he couldn't face that idea. Alicia had been stolen from their home and he was damned if he was going to let her abductors drive him out. Besides, the one thing he'd been looking forward to all day, the one crumb of comfort he had left to cling to was the fact that Alicia's scent hung like an early morning mist around the house. The essence of her filled every part of their home and because she was currently absent from his life, he wanted to do everything in his power to feel close to her. He wanted to fall asleep with his head on her pillow and her aroma in his nostrils, but before he could do that, he had work to do. A plan to put into action.

20

Jerome cast his eyes around the subway carriage. Half the seats were taken and, as always with the subway, there was an eclectic mix of people. An old couple sat side by side looking at each other with rheumy eyes, their gnarled hands touching. Two guys dressed for business were deep in animated conversation, while a construction worker made faces to amuse a Hispanic kid who was emitting giggles of pure innocence. Further along the carriage a teenager chatted with a woman old enough to be her grandmother. The girl all in black with multiple facial piercings and the edges of tattoos peeking from the hems of her clothing. The older immaculately dressed in couture fashion. Both were happily engaged in the conversation and Jerome caught the respectful looks between them.

It was normal and usual and typical and New York. A vast melting pot of nationalities and ideals and personalities that managed to rub along together despite their many differences.

None of the people in the carriage had faces Jerome recognized from Melvilles. None were people he knew from work. So far as he could tell, he'd lost his tail. This wasn't something he was confident about, but the more he rationalized it the more he came to realize it didn't matter if he was being tailed. He was going to do whatever he needed to do to save Alicia, and there was no reason for a tail to stop him doing that. In fact, in a situation like the one with the Good Samaritan, there would be a chance the tail might step in to help him out.

After spending so long trying to lose a tail, this realization left Jerome feeling dumb and furious with himself for wasting time.

He was checking his cell at every station where the Wi-Fi kicked in. The TwitterSpy app had been his app of choice. He'd fed in the details of all the Twitter accounts used to message him and gotten their results. The first three were a bust due to them being deactivated before he set the app on them. The most recent message, the one mocking him for meeting Ed, had returned better results, although they weren't brilliant. He did though have an email address, so at the next station he prized himself off the seat and rushed up the stairs. The sooner he could get Ed or his hacker friend to dig into the email address the better. Though Jerome didn't hold out much hope the email would yield much as it was a generic Gmail account.

21

Ed answered on the third ring. "Dunsfold Investigations. Lost cats our specialty. Here, puss, puss, puss."

Jerome got what Ed was trying to do with the daft way he'd answered the call. How his buddy was trying to take the edge off his worry with his usual silliness. Many were the times Ed and he had provided ever weirder greetings to each other and they'd usually keep the joke rolling for at least two minutes. Ed was being normal. Keeping things level. He recognized that as much as Ed was trying to help him with actual support, he was also providing emotional assistance by not changing his demeanor. But this time Jerome ignored Ed's joke greeting and plowed ahead with his point. "Ed, I've got an email address attached to the Twitter handle that sent me the last message."

"Good stuff, I expect you want me to get my guy to run it down. I'm no hacker but that ought to be something I can do myself. Message it to me and I'll dig into it as quick as I can. With luck I'll be able to track where it's been used. If not a specific location, then certainly a general area. Give me a half hour and I'll get back to you as soon as possible. In related news, I've spoken to my hacker friend and he's on board. When I told him about the sexual assault aspect he said he was happy to help as his sister had been raped by a boss."

"Thank God. Please, Ed, make sure he knows how grateful I am for his help. When this is all over, I'll get him something, something real good to show that gratitude."

"I've already told him all that. He gets it. He's just married so he understands what you're going through."

Ed's words about being able to find a location had Jerome looking over his shoulder again. If he got a specific location for where the email address had been sent, then he'd be able to go and scout the place out. Then he'd maybe be able to find where Alicia was being kept. Once he'd done that he'd be able to call the police. They'd swoop in and save Alicia.

Before Jerome could go on any scouting missions, he'd need to be one hundred percent certain that he'd lost his tail. As soon as he started wandering around anywhere near where Alicia was being held, or where one of the gang was based, the abductors would either move Alicia or harm her.

A look around presented him with a sea of unfamiliar faces. As best as he could, he memorized them and set off for a bar a half block ahead. Breezy was one of the uber-trendy bars Alicia loved and they'd often go there for a Friday night dinner before heading home together.

Breezy was a target of his for a specific reason. It sat on a corner and had three entrances. One at the corner itself and one on each of the streets. He swung open a street door and walked into Breezy, where he was immediately assaulted with the aroma of their specialty, a clam chowder whose recipe was reputed to be two hundred years old and a famously guarded secret. He passed by several people as he made his way to the opposite door. At one point he had to lean back as a server passed by carrying a tray that had to be three feet in diameter.

Twenty seconds after entering Breezy, Jerome was at the far door, but rather than exit immediately, he stood at the door and watched both the door he'd entered via and the corner one. He was watching the faces of those who entered either door for anyone scanning the room.

A couple in their twenties were the first to enter. She blonde and aloof, he wide and dapper. They took a table and didn't look beyond the menu. Next through a door was a guy who'd fit everyone's clichéd ideal of a private detective. Rumpled suit, check. World-weary expression, check. Eyes that never rested, check. His eyes alighted on a couple in their forties and they raised a hand in greeting. He joined them, making sure to attract the attention of a server with a "drink" gesture of his right hand.

In the minute Jerome waited, three more people entered. None were making obvious signs of looking for him and all took menus from the server who pounced to greet them.

Jerome slipped out of the street door and turned his head toward the corner door. Logic told him that if he still had a tail and that tail hadn't followed him into Breezy, they'd station themselves by the corner door so they could track his exit whichever way he left Breezy.

As he skimmed his eyes across those on the sidewalk he saw none of the faces he'd earlier committed to memory. He cast his gaze wider, across to the other side of the street and into those using the crosswalks at the intersection. Again, none of them fired a synapse of recognition.

He turned and set off at a brisk walk. His pace hard enough to make his calves burn. Anyone trying to keep up would either have to punish themselves in the same way, or break into an identifying trot. After a block and a half of this, Jerome wheeled to look through the window of an electronics store, his eyes casting back along the sidewalk looking for anyone who may be following him. Nobody was slowing a trot to a walk. Nobody was running who wasn't dressed for it, and the one person who was running was setting a pace far greater than Jerome's speed walk.

Despite these precautions giving him peace of mind, Jerome carried out the same moves a second time using a different bar and a longer speed walk before he dared believe he wasn't being followed.

Jerome's cell rang and he listened as Ed outlined his findings. He had three locations where the email address had been used.

"How specific are the locations? Can you pinpoint a specific place or does it only give you a block?"

"Somewhere in between. I've run the co-ordinates against a street map and, in order of use, they are on the corner of West Fifty-Seventh and Ninth, the general vicinity of the Beck Building and the third is in Hoboken, halfway between Sixth and Seventh on Willow Avenue."

"Beck Building means there's definitely an inside man. Have you had a look at what's at the other two places?"

A pause long enough for Jerome to hear two breaths come through the phone. "I hadn't until I started dialing as I figured you'd want me to call you as soon as possible. I've had a quick look using Google Maps and both seem to be apartment blocks. Do you know where West Fifty-Seventh and Ninth is?"

"Southwest of Central Park is where I'm thinking. Hell's Kitchen is that way, isn't it?"

"Correct on both counts."

Being right gave Jerome no satisfaction. None of this was about being right, it was all about getting Alicia back. About holding his wife in his arms again.

He was as confident as he could be that he didn't have a tail, so he set off for the nearest subway station. He wanted a close look at the two locations. It seemed unlikely to him that Alicia was being kept in an apartment where neighbors might hear her screaming for help, but he and Ed had already worked out the abductors weren't professionals, so he figured nothing was off the table in terms of possibilities.

22

Hell's Kitchen was closer than Hoboken so Jerome set off toward it. Darkness was beginning to fall as he arrived at the corner of West Fifty-Seventh and Ninth. That didn't matter to Jerome, he was on a scouting mission and as such was doing little more than a drive-by, albeit on foot.

Jerome stopped in at a thrift store that sold various oddments of clothing and picked up a second-hand Yankees jacket and a backpack. He'd also gotten a baseball cap he pulled down until his face was shielded. As disguises went it was up there with the plastic moustache, false nose and glasses used for larking around in a photobooth, but it was better than nothing and Jerome's biggest fear was Alicia having to pay the price of him being spotted by one of the abductors.

To this end he kept his distance from the doors and his head down at all times. What he did do was memorize the building names, addresses and every other detail he could. Some of the apartment blocks had a list of names beside buzzers.

Jerome was tempted to step forward and scan the names looking for one he recognized. Or take a quick photo he could use to capture the names so they'd be at his disposal when he could check them against the Beck Holdings database. The database only held names, direct dial numbers and professional email addresses, but that would be enough. He already had someone's physical address. The problem with stepping forward was that by doing so he'd be making himself conspicuous. He'd be too close to discovery. If one of the abductors caught him doing that level of investigation, the possible consequences for Alicia were unimaginable. That didn't stop him from imagining them, though, and with every new thought he felt less confident the payoff would be worth the risk.

In addition to the guy with the falafel stall on the corner, there were people walking back and forth and moving in and out of the various apartments he was passing. In the end he gave up on the idea of photographing the names against the apartments and carried on with discreet research. Somehow or other, he'd have to find a way to get addresses for all the employees of Beck Holdings and its subsidiaries.

With the memorized details keyed into his new cell, Jerome set off for the subway station. His destination Hoboken.

———

Hoboken was quieter than Hell's Kitchen, but there was still the odd person on the sidewalk. The last of the daylight had long dipped below the horizon, so Jerome had to conduct this reconnaissance by streetlights alone. Thankfully it was a good area and he was able to see the street addresses well enough to commit them to memory.

Jerome was halfway along Willow Avenue between Sixth and Seventh when he heard someone calling out. He ignored the voice until he heard the next sentence.

"Hey, Yankees Guy. You lookin' for someplace special?"

He *must* be Yankees Guy. No one else in sight wore any Yankees–branded clothing. Jerome half turned, making sure to use the cap's visor to keep his face in shadow.

An elderly man was walking his way, his cane giving him the

same slow pace Jerome had employed. Gray hairs sprouted from his nose and ears, but his head was egg-bald.

"Not someplace. Someone. A guy I went to college with lived round here and I was looking to catch up with him. I was in the area for work and thought I'd take the opportunity."

"This time of night?" The elderly man nodded at Jerome's left hand. "You got a ring on your finger. Folks don't call round for a catch-up so late. I'm guessing you got your ass kicked onto the street because you been putting it where you shouldn't. Either that or you'd gotten home and caught her acceptin' what she oughtn't."

"You got me. I need to find my buddy or I'm booking into a hotel." Jerome hated how well he could lie. Yesterday he'd been an honest man. Sometimes to the point where his honesty had gotten him into trouble. While he hadn't confirmed which of the old man's accusations was correct, Jerome felt his gut knot that he could lie about him or Alicia being unfaithful. That was something he'd never worried about. He was damned lucky to have her, and she'd never once given him even the slightest reason to feel afraid she'd be attracted to another man. She'd never even teased him that she found some other guy attractive.

"What's your buddy's name? Lived here a long time and 'cause I had me a small store, I've gotten to know most of the folks who been here a number of years."

Jerome cast his brains for a plausible but unmemorable name. Eventually he recalled a temporary alias used in the movie *Die Hard*. "Bill Clay."

"He 'bout your age?" Jerome nodded as the old man creased the bushy gray caterpillars that were his eyebrows. "That name don't ring no bells, son. There was a Claymont family a few years back but as I 'member it, they only had girls."

"Bill didn't have any sisters." Jerome gave the old man a thumbs up. "Thanks for trying to help. I guess I'll just have to find a hotel somewhere."

Fifteen minutes later Jerome was halfway back to the station. He'd completed his reconnaissance as best he could under the old man's watchful eyes. The records on his phone were updated and he was beat. Every part of his body felt heavy and sluggish, and as foreign as the idea of sleep might seem to him, he knew he needed to get some rest. That he needed to restore his strength so he was in the best possible shape to deal with whatever the next day threw at him.

23

Jerome looked around him and saw nothing of any great note. The closer the little hand got to twelve, the less packed the subway was. That was just a fact of life. Every commuter who stayed late in the city knew the later trains home had fewer travelers than the ones running at peak times.

There were six people in the carriage. None were together. All had their own interests, a cell phone, a newspaper, or a Kindle; whatever their distraction from the boredom of the commute they were engrossed by it. Rapt eyes staring at screens or reading old-fashioned print.

Except one guy. The guy two seats to Jerome's left. He hadn't brought any source of amusement or entertainment. Like Beau earlier in the day, this guy was drunk. Unlike Beau he wasn't filled with an infectious and generous bonhomie. This guy was passed out. His clothes were good and suggested the man had a decent job. The briefcase trapped between his legs was in good condition and looked expensive. His hair was mussed, no doubt from the time spent drinking, but enough of it fell into a natural position for Jerome to be confident it wasn't a ten-buck special from a barber college.

The train pulled into a station and three of the carriage's occupants left. Two others got on. A mid-thirties couple, but from the way they were going at each other, it was debatable as to whether they'd still be a couple at the next station. He was taller than her, tall enough to rest his chin on the top of her blue hair. Both were dressed in casual clothes, but for all the woman was almost a foot shorter, she wasn't prepared to cede any ground to her partner. Nor did either of them seem bothered about conducting their fight in such a public place.

"I don't care what you say to me now. You told me it was over between the two of you. That you wouldn't go back to her."

"I didn't go back to her, babes. I went to see my kid. To see Little Mike."

"Oh yeah. Little Mike. The hook she has embedded deep into you. I know you love him, and I'd think less of you if you didn't, but jeez, come on. You gotta be stupid not to see how she's using him to try and get you back. That date she was supposed to be on, that was just to make you jealous."

"Well, it didn't work, did it? Honestly, babes, you're being paranoid."

As the argument raged back and forth, Jerome edged along the seat toward the sleeping guy. The man snuffled and snuggled into a different position. His legs now splayed apart and his movements causing his jacket to gape at the front. Jerome could see the guy's wallet poking up from an inside pocket. It was a large wallet. The type which held lots of credit cards and miscellaneous items like receipts or ID-rich cards.

"How dare you call me paranoid? How dare you, you piece of scum. Remember when we got together? How you got yourself so tied up about me and Ferdie? How you didn't believe he was just a friend?" She jabbed his chest with a stout finger. "In the end the only way I could convince you was to out him as being gay. That was a secret he trusted me with."

"Come on, babes, how many more times are you going to throw that in my face? That was two years ago."

"Yeah, right about the time when you and I were running

behind your wife's back. Zebras don't change their stripes. My momma, God rest her soul, was right. Once a cheater, always a cheater."

Jerome had gotten close enough that he could reach over and pluck the sleeper's wallet from his jacket pocket. The arguing couple were providing an ideal distraction. He kept his head down, used the baseball cap to shield his face. Trains had CCTV, but he'd never heard of anyone ever being identified using them. All the same, it would be stupid not to take precautions.

"I ain't never cheated on you, babes. Never have. Never will. But I can't go on like this. Can't have you pulling me one way and Little Mike the other. You know I ain't gettin' to see him often as I'd like. When I got the chance to sit him, I snapped it up. You coulda come joined me. Instead you refused to step into my old house. Said you couldn't breathe the same air as her. We gotta be better people, babes. I want Little Mike brought up proper. I want him to know and love you like I do. But you gotta not ask me to choose between you." Jerome cast his eyes at the carriage's other occupants. They were all watching the drama of the couple's fight, so he extended his hand toward the sleeping guy. "Because if you do, you'll be asking me to do the impossible."

Jerome's fingers caressed the soft leather of the sleeper's wallet. They tugged on it and wrested the wallet free, although it was so bulky it turned the pocket inside out.

"Are you saying you couldn't choose?"

The wallet got secreted into Jerome's pocket.

"I'm saying that I could, but no matter how much I might find it impossible to break up with you, there's no way I could ever give up on my kid. And, babes, do you want me to be that guy? Think how you'd worry when we have *our* kids? I want to have Little Mike in my life because I want to be a daddy. A good daddy." A cheeky expression perked his bony face. "Anyway, think of it like this. I'm learning with Little Mike. I'll make mistakes, but I'll learn from them and then I'll be an even better daddy for *our* kids…"

Whatever he said next was silenced as she enveloped him in a hug so tight even a bear would think it excessive.

The carriage started to slow as they neared another station. This was Jerome's stop. He was desperate for it to arrive, to get off the subway and abscond with his stolen goods. At least he was until he saw every passenger except the sleeping guy preparing to leave. Papers were folded. Cells were tucked into pockets.

Jerome wanted to leave, but the briefcase between the sleeping guy's legs called to him. If the carriage was empty at the next stop, he'd be able to get off then and take the briefcase with him.

Lots could go wrong with that plan. The guy could wake. More passengers might board the carriage.

Nothing went wrong, although Jerome felt he was having a major heart attack when the man started talking in his sleep.

Jerome kept his head down as he exited the station and trudged up the stairs with the briefcase in his hand. Before he even made his way home, he wanted to check the wallet and briefcase to see what he'd managed to obtain. If it was a bust he could take both back to the station and claim to have found them. That way the sleeping guy would have a chance of getting them back.

Jerome slid into the booth of a late night diner and made sure he couldn't easily be observed. The briefcase had a combination lock, but he was confident that in the confines of his garage he'd be able to get into the briefcase. He just wouldn't be able to return it if it proved to be a bust.

A server schlepped his way, her feet scuffing the tiled floor with every sliding step. Her hair was up in a mussy bun and appeared to be secured by three pens.

"What you after, honey?" Her voice was thick with phlegm, and there was an extinguished twinkle desperately trying to reignite in her eyes.

"Can I get a coffee and a Danish, please?" He didn't want the food and drinking coffee this late at night was never his thing, but he knew the combination of caffeine and sugar would give his body the fuel it would need. If the wallet and briefcase came through for him, he'd need to be fully alert to create the new account where the Beck Holdings money would be transferred to, so he could then buy the cryptocurrency. The sooner he could get the account up and running, the sooner he could steal the $52 million and get Alicia back.

As the server scuffed her way back to the counter he pulled out the wallet and prized it open. It was stuffed with credit and debit cards. He found a driving license and a bunch of store loyalty cards.

His victim's name was Oliver Welsh. Knowing this gave Jerome's conscience a metaphorical kick in the groin. It was one thing ripping off a drunk, another altogether ripping off someone whose name he knew. There was a picture of Welsh in the wallet; he was beaming with pride and had two kids sitting on his lap. Seeing the proud father with his kids was enough to add a second, harder kick.

Jerome pushed on, pressing his guilt down into the basement of his subconscious and slamming the door on it. Welsh wouldn't get into too much trouble. Chances were he'd get a good grilling from the cops when the theft was reported, but there would be no other evidence against him, and if he'd previously reported that his wallet and briefcase were stolen then he'd quickly be exonerated.

A look through the flaps of the wallet revealed $179 in various sized bills and a plethora of random receipts. Jerome pulled out the driver's license and checked Welsh's date of birth. It was a long shot, but he fed it into the briefcase's combination locks.

As with the stuff he'd stolen from Beau, Jerome planned to return everything to Welsh once he'd gotten Alicia back home.

When Jerome slid the locks sideways they both popped. He had to check himself so his jaw didn't drop. Welsh was lax about his security. That shouldn't have taken Jerome aback considering how easy it had been to rob the man, but he found it hard to believe anyone would be dumb enough to use their date of birth as a security code.

A disheartening thought hit Jerome like a counterstrike. What if the briefcase had a simple code because it held nothing of value? What if all it contained was the *New York Post*, the remains of a sandwich and some stationery?

Jerome lifted the lid as the server bumped a well-used coffee mug and a plate with the Danish onto his table.

"Honey, you need to take a break. Whatever you got in there can wait till morning. You look more frazzled than me."

The server's comments were well-intentioned, but Jerome just wanted her to vanish.

"Thanks for your concern, but there's something that can't wait." He dropped a rueful nod at the briefcase. "I should be finished in a half hour, though."

"Make sure you are." She flashed him a smile that was more grimace than tooth. "No matter how much money you make, ain't no pockets in a shroud, and if you keep pushing yourself too hard, that's what you'll be wearing."

The server's warning held more resonance than Jerome cared for. If he was getting a health warning from a stranger, all his fears for Alicia must show on his face and in his body language.

He opened the briefcase fully, expecting to find little of value. It held several large manila envelopes. The first bore a pair of handwritten names either side of the shorthand "vs." The second the same. Jerome figured Welsh must be a civil action lawyer. It was the third that saw him strike paydirt. Its inscription was the best thing Jerome had seen since Alicia was taken.

In Welsh's scrawling handwriting were the words "United Bank Application." Jerome tore his way into the envelope not daring to believe his luck was this good.

It was. The envelope held everything that could possibly be needed to create a bank account. The forms were all filled out, all supporting documents were there.

As Jerome checked through the envelope's contents he felt a rush of belief flooding through his body. For the first time since Alicia had been taken, he was starting to believe, truly believe, he'd be able to get the money that would secure her release. Until now it had all been an abstract concept. Almost an out-of-body experience as he went through the motions, acting more in hope than certainty.

Jerome kept going through the briefcase and found a cell phone beneath the envelopes. It powered up with great ease and no password. When Jerome saw there was an app for United Bank already installed he wanted to punch the air in glee. One of the biggest problems he faced when opening an online account was that most banks specified an initial deposit be made.

With his finger shaking Jerome touched the app and waited as it sprang to life. It kicked in asking for a passcode. Jerome's own online banking code was an eight digit one, so he expanded Welsh's date of birth to eight digits and keyed it in.

A whirling circle appeared on the screen as the app buffered and then changed to another screen. He was in. Welsh had $15,983 in his account so there was no issue about him having the necessary funds to facilitate a new account.

Now was the moment of truth. The point he'd been preparing for since he'd realized he'd have to break the law to save Alicia. And here he was. Breaking it. Creating an account to distance himself. To save himself and implicate an innocent. To do such a thing punched every one of Jerome's morals square on the nose and then added vicious kicks when they were down.

The only hesitation Jerome allowed himself was the time it took to examine his surroundings with respect to any future investigation. The diner was a half mile from the subway station. There were no cameras in here and at this time of night the patrons were minimal. The server was the only person he'd interacted with and he doubted she'd provide an accurate description of him should cops eventually make their way here. Even if she did, he wasn't known to the police in any respect and he could always claim innocence and leave the burden of proof upon the police should they ever get to his door.

There were no obstacles Jerome could see so he used his burner cell to create an online account with United Bank and then transferred the necessary funds to it using Welsh's cell and account.

The act of implicating Welsh was tempered by his newfound confidence there was a chance he'd get Alicia back safe and sound. And that was something he'd do anything for.

With the account now set up and the access codes memorized, Jerome left the diner having paid cash for his coffee and Danish.

As he walked the mile to his house, he dropped various parts of the burner cell into drains at random intervals. This wasn't an original idea of his, but he'd read a book where a spy had done the same and it made logical sense to him.

He could update Ed in the morning, and when Alicia's abductors next contacted him, he had a new plan to get them to provide proof she was alive.

The train into the city was its usual rush-hour scrum. Where Jerome normally detested the daily commute and endured it by losing himself in his latest read, he was facing it on autopilot today. His every thought on Alicia and what he must do to get her back.

Ed's response to his message informing him the account was set up and he'd formulated the necessary invoices wasn't the one Jerome wanted, but he didn't show any of that to Ed in his reply.

There was no doubt in Jerome's mind that Ed's friend was doing everything in his power to help. It wasn't the fault of either of them that both Finance First and TriMail had updated their security measures. Ed's friend had promised to find a way into both operating systems, but Ed's message had stated that due to the new security measures, it could be as long as forty-eight hours before he could get the necessary access in a way that couldn't be traced back to him or Jerome.

This news tore at Jerome in the same way a wild animal worried at its prey. Forty-eight hours of further separation from Alicia was unthinkable. It would be worse for her, imprisoned wherever the abductors had her. She'd be petrified every waking second. Only she would know the torment of her thoughts, of her fears, but that didn't mean he wasn't imagining them.

With the ability to be reactive to Alicia's plight now delayed, Jerome was holding far more thoughts of proactivity. It had been his intention to try and identify the employees of Beck Holdings who lived in Hoboken and Hell's Kitchen at some point today, but that had now become a priority.

Also on his to-do list was buying another cell. As wise as it had been to ditch the one he'd used to set up the online account, replacing it was a chore he could do without. He couldn't think of a better way, as he was afraid the IP address of the cell used to create the account may be traced and he didn't want to have the cell anywhere near his home or on his person after it had been used to create an account that would be used for grand theft.

He'd brought his iPad with him so he could run searches on it that were untraceable in case his office computer was being monitored.

The biggest problem he had getting addresses for employees was that he had no access to such information, and could think of no good reason to get that all-important access. Names were available via an intranet, addresses were kept private.

Also on his list of tasks was the creation of a crypto account so he could buy the untraceable Bitcoin. Once opened, the account would need to be separated into subaccounts, or "wallets" to use the correct terminology.

With everything he'd have to do to maintain a semblance of his usual work output, and not fall foul of Carthew's all-seeing eye, Jerome knew he was in for a tough day.

His cell beeped and he withdrew it from his pocket in a swift movement. The Twitter message he found awaiting him was bad enough, but the crude picture attached to it compressed his heart in a vise-like grip.

26

The day had so far passed with an interminable slowness. At every opportunity he could get, Jerome researched the opening of a crypto account. He'd kept any relevant details of Oliver Welsh that he might still need and, as he'd created a new email address to create the online account, it hadn't been too hard for him to get his ducks lined up.

The biggest problem he'd faced was the lack of focus created by the Twitter message he'd received earlier. He'd been clever and had set his phone so the message showed on his screen without him having to actually access the app. This bought him some time, which he used to run the latest Twitter handle through TwitterSpy and then send the email address to Ed via Snapchat.

YOUR RESPONSES HAVE FOCUSED ON YOUR WIFE'S WELL-BEING. YOU HAVE NOT TOLD US YOUR READY TO SEND US WHAT WE REQUIRE. THIS MUST CHANGE SOON, OTHERWISE WE WILL NEED WHAT'S IN THE PICTURE.

The message was to the point, and, as he'd expected nothing less than directness from the abductors, it wasn't too worrying. It was the words after the comma and the accompanying picture that filled it with menace.

No matter how many times Jerome had screwed his eyes shut in dread, the image never left him. It was seared into his mind's eye. Etched into the fabric of his being.

The picture was a woodland scene with a shallow grave dug in between a pair of towering pines. Jerome received the message loud and clear. While they hadn't yet given him a deadline, they were putting pressure on him to get the money.

Jerome's thoughts were the swirling circular motion of a draining sink. Each one disappearing down the plughole of terror that he might lose Alicia forever. He flipped and flopped between returning to his original plan and just stealing the money to get Alicia back and dealing with the consequences, and holding his nerve. There were times when he considered opening a crypto account for himself and stealing more than the $52 million. That way he and Alicia could disappear over the horizon and never have to worry again. The thoughts of stealing extra didn't sit well with him, though, and every time his brain went down that route he retrieved it a second later.

The more he rationalized it, the easier he found he could hold his nerve. As terrible as the thought of Alicia being dumped in a shallow woodland grave was, so long as he kept insisting on proof of life, he knew he had a small amount of leverage over the abductors.

The misspelling of "you're" was telling. Okay, in today's world fewer people seemed to get such things right, social media was proof of that, but for something as important as communication between an abductor and their captive's family, Jerome expected enough know-how to ensure correct spellings.

He opened the Twitter app and picked out a reply. His words brief and to the point.

DOING EVERYTHING POSSIBLE TO GET YOU MONEY ASAP. CREATING ALL THOSE CRYPTO

ACCOUNTS ISN'T A QUICK PROCESS. I WANT TO
SEE A PICTURE OF ALICIA HOLDING A COPY OF
THE LATEST GAME INFORMER MAGAZINE AS
PROOF OF LIFE.

The fact he'd specified what Alicia had to be holding was his
way of verifying the picture was up to date. That the abductors
hadn't taken several snaps yesterday in an attempt to fool him. His
reasoning wasn't so much to catch them out as to keep them
honest. To give them continued reasons to keep Alicia alive.

He hadn't been lying when he'd said it would take time to set
up all the various crypto accounts. From what he'd learned with
his research, his best guess was that it would take him several hours
to set up all the accounts and that was a task he'd earmarked to do
after work, at a location where there were no cameras, and using a
new cell phone.

27

Jerome strode out of the elevator and along the corridor toward the HR department with purpose. A brainwave had brought him here and he needed to stay focused and front things out.

"Hi, I'm Alicia Prentice's husband, I called ahead asking to pick up Alicia's laptop."

The receptionist gave a delicate shrug and pressed her face into a professional smile. "I'm sorry, sir, but company property cannot be given to spouses, much less taken off the premises, even if you are an employee of Beck Accounting."

Jerome returned the smile and set off toward the HR department, leaving the receptionist floundering in uncertainty. He supposed she'd leave the problem he was creating to Alicia's boss, but he heard a pair of heels and polite remonstrations following him.

Rather than get into it with the receptionist, Jerome lengthened his stride and entered the HR department at pace, his eyes scouring the room for Alicia's boss.

At the back of the room a prim man rose to his feet. More dapper than the finest tailor, Hubert, never-Hugh never-Bert-or-Bertie, Jessop was Alicia's immediate superior. Jerome had never worked out whether the British ex-pat was a little in love with

Alicia, or someone who'd just never possessed the confidence or seen the need to come out. His gestures and speech patterns were effeminate, and when Jerome had broached the subject with Alicia she'd said that Hubert often mentioned a partner called Jamie, but had never assigned a gender to the name. Whatever way his tastes lay, Hubert was the epitome of a nice guy and Alicia always spoke highly of the man, and that was good enough for Jerome.

The receptionist said her piece before Jerome could address Jessop.

"Thank you, my dear. Now, Jerome, how is poor Alicia? Really, she shouldn't be thinking about work when she's laid up. Now I've had a chance to think on the subject, I won't hear of you taking her laptop back to her. She must rest, the poor dear."

"She's fine. In pain but fine." Jerome leaned in as if conspiring. "To tell the truth, she's embarrassed more than anything. Like I said when I called you yesterday, she went to kick a soccer ball back to the neighbor's kid and twisted the ankle on her standing leg." Jerome held his hands six inches apart for emphasis. "You should see the size of it. Anyway, she wanted me to pick up her laptop so she can do a few tasks from home."

"I'm pretty sure you know the company policy on sick days, and I'm certain she does. She should rest up and not worry about work."

Jerome gave Hubert a self-deprecating look. "I know, and I *have* told her all that. But if you've ever tried to argue with her, even for her benefit, you'll know what success I had. Or perhaps lack thereof. She says she's not going to do anything current, more that she's devised a way to arrange her files so she can work with more efficiency and wants to do it in her own time so she can be more focused when she returns to work."

"I can only imagine your odds of winning that argument." Fondness washed over Hubert's face. "Very well. But please, tell her to take it easy and not to rush back until she's fully fit. But, most of all, please tell her we're all wishing her the speediest of speedy recoveries."

. . .

As he walked back to the elevator with Alicia's laptop, it was all Jerome could do not to leap into the air and click his heels together. He now had access to a database that listed all employees of Beck Holdings. Next he had to figure out Alicia's passwords and start running some searches.

Alicia's passwords weren't something he knew, but he did know his wife. Her loves and loathes. Her memories and her passions.

With every step back toward his own office, Jerome ran through options, discounting those too outlandish, and storing the possibles in his memory. He had a vague memory of her saying she used their dream future for some password or other, so the first thing he typed in was the future Alicia envisioned for them.

Oneboyonegirltwodogsandthreecats.

The system ran out of possible characters after "dogs" so he tried again cutting the password down to the base elements. Something he knew Alicia frequently did. 1b1g2d3c.

This didn't work either. Jerome thought of the software he used. It needed a capital letter so he tried again with 1B1G2d3c. Despite the fact her job often had her seeking balance between genders, sexual orientation and ethnicity, Alicia wasn't a woke warrior who tried to cancel opposing points of view; instead, she listened to all sides and tried to find common ground rather than the no man's land between warring factions. Jerome knew Alicia also held enough feminist principles that meant there was no way she'd capitalize a male and not a female. Or vice versa.

The pop-up password box disappeared and allowed him in.

He closed it down for the time being. He had another task he wanted to get into. A part of his job was to check all payments due were accurate before anything was paid, but another of his weekly tasks was to check the correct amounts had been sent. To that end he had limited access to the company's bank accounts.

For years the task had irked him as he never found more than a dollar's discrepancy, but there were certain payments that were regular. Including the fact Beck Accounting paid a monthly fee to Beck Holdings for the office space it used in the Beck Building. It was a tax dodge, plain and simple, but it happened and he'd never questioned it. Nor the maintenance contract, nor the payments for utilities. He checked those now. In detail, purely because if there were payoffs being made, they weren't going through the normal company accounts and must therefore be paid from a different account. A slush fund. And that slush fund had to have its own source of income, which logic dictated would be the various accounts attributed to Beck Holdings.

Jerome picked out the payments and dug into where the money went. The utilities and maintenance money went to the central account for Beck Holdings and were distributed on to either the utilities company, or the people who had the maintenance contract. The payments for the office rent went elsewhere. The same amount of money moved each month. Regular as clockwork. When Jerome checked the account number, he saw it was different from any account he'd ever known the company to be associated with. He used his iPad to run a search on the bank's branch code and found it belonged to Grand Valley Bank from a place called Vernal in Utah. This made no sense. Beck Holdings paid for the construction of the Beck Building back in the sixties. They might have leveraged the finances to do this with mortgages and loans, but that didn't explain why the money for "rent" should be paid to a small bank in a small city that was nearer the Pacific than the Atlantic. All Jerome's years of experience told him the same thing. This money was being siphoned off. Snuck out of the company accounts and sent to the middle of nowhere for a reason. A nefarious reason. He figured this account must be the company's slush fund. Money for discreet payments would be taken from this account and washed through two or three like it before being used to pay off disgruntled employees, or encourage reluctant rulemakers. He'd always suspected something like this existed, but he'd never had the need or desire to go looking until now.

The phone on his desk rang. Jerome listened to the speaker and agreed to go and speak with him in his office. He had no idea why Lenny Zeller wanted to speak to him. Zeller was the CEO of Beck Accounting.

Jerome had made what he thought were discreet enquiries about Lucy Sampson yesterday, but he was now doubting himself. If word of his questioning had gotten back to Zeller, he might be fired. That couldn't happen. No way could he allow Zeller to can him. Alicia's life depended on him being able to get the money. As Jerome reached out to knock on Zeller's door another thought hit him. Had he somehow triggered an alert by logging into Alicia's laptop? Was that the reason for this summons? Or had his boss somehow learned of his searches into the destination of the "rent" money?

Six floors up from Beck Accounting, the penultimate floor of the Beck Building held all the department heads. The views were panoramic and the air crackled with power and influence.

Jerome made his way toward Zeller's office and saw the door was standing open. As he approached a well-dressed man strode out, his genial face pleasant and welcoming.

"Jerome, nice to see you. Mr. Carthew told me earlier about your presentation and the good work you've been doing. Well done, well done indeed."

And with his usual drive-by cheeriness, Adamson was gone. He might be the CFO for Beck Holdings, but he never once looked as if his role placed any stresses upon him. Jerome had always thought that if more bosses could be like Adamson, the workplace would be a far happier environment.

Lenny Zeller's office was as spartan as the man himself. Devoid of anything that might give it a touch of humanity, it was a large space—as befitted his status—that had only what was needed—as befitted his character. There were no plants to breathe life into the room, no pictures on the walls depicting colorful scenes or personalities met. Even his desk was about function over style. A plush chair for him, and two less plush chairs for visitors.

Two file cabinets stood against a wall and beyond the PC, his desk held three files, a plain white mug and a cheap pen.

Jerome stood in the open doorway and knocked twice on the door.

"Come."

Where Adamson was polite, Zeller was brusque. Lean and in possession of a simian face, Zeller wasn't an easy man to like and respect. This got harder whenever he opened his mouth and let his guttural tones run free.

As CEO of Beck Accounting, if Zeller wasn't directly involved in Alicia's abduction, he'd surely know about discreet payments being made to former employees. Whichever he was, Jerome viewed him as the enemy. Jerome had no proof other than circumstantial, but his gut told him Zeller had either been guilty of a cover-up, and therefore the reason Alicia was abducted, or was himself one of the abductors.

"You wanted to see me, Mr. Zeller?" Jerome did what he could to keep his tone and expression light and unconcerned, but even to his own ears his words sounded strained.

There was no invitation to take a seat so Jerome stood behind one of the two visitor chairs. His mind pulsing with reasons why Zeller might have identified his guilt.

"Yes. I've recently had conversations with several of your colleagues across varying positions. I have to say I was surprised at how often your name was mentioned. And the context. Phillip Carthew spoke highly of you, as have your direct peers. One of the secretarial staff was less than complimentary, seems you pushed her to perform her duties when she was slacking so I have no issue with that. I do though have an issue with you. Would you care to guess what this issue might be?"

Jerome had several theories as to what the issue might be, but there was no way he'd give voice to any of them. "I honestly can't think, sir. I come to work, give the company and my job one hundred percent. I don't engage in office squabbles, don't waste time. I do what I'm paid to do and then go home. Could you enlighten me, please? Whatever it is I'm sure it can be rectified. Self-improvement is such an important goal, don't you think?"

The last three sentences may have been impudent or cocky, but Jerome wasn't prepared to give any ground. Zeller wasn't a bully per se, but his nature made him come across that way at times, and Jerome had long ago learned the best way to deal with bullies was to stand up to them.

"You can't think, you say. Let me elaborate for you. Carthew told me in great detail of the play you suggested and put into motion. He credited you as the instigator of and the driving force behind that play. For your good work there, the company owes you a debt of gratitude. Carthew also told me how you stood up to him. That shows moral fiber. You ought to be commended for that, also."

As much as Zeller may be complimenting him, Jerome felt the nice words were little more than an executioner drawing back his axe and tensing his muscles ready to decapitate the condemned figure below him.

"Thank you, sir, but as I said earlier, I give one hundred percent to the company. It's my way of showing my gratitude for all the opportunities the company has given me and my wife."

Zeller nodded without speaking. In Jerome's mind the executioner was identifying the spot at the back of his neck where the axe would strike.

The silence dragged on. Jerome knew what Zeller was doing. That his boss was trying to make him uncomfortable in the hope he'd babble just to end the silence.

Jerome started a quick count in his head. When he reached fifty he opened his mouth and turned ready to leave. "If that's everything, sir, I'd better get back to my desk."

"Not so fast." Zeller held up a halting hand as if he could detain Jerome by sheer force of will. "I find it odd you haven't asked again what the issue was. That you haven't pressed me to tell you. You talked of self-improvement, but when I gave you the opportunity to learn of your failings you stayed quiet. Why is that?"

The sinews on the executioner's arms stood out as he prepared to strike.

"I'm sorry, but I did ask, sir. You didn't speak. Therefore I thought it may be a delicate matter and you were unsure of how to approach it. You're my boss's boss. The CEO of Beck Accounting. You hold a position of respect within not just Beck Accounting, but Beck Holdings itself. You have my respect, sir, and I'd rather leave wondering than put a man such as yourself in an awkward position. You may think that sounds a little kiss-ass, if you'll pardon my choice of words, but the truth is if it was serious, I'd have been fired by now. If it was trivial, Mr. Carthew would have raised the issue with me. He hasn't. Instead, you have. That all tells me whatever your issue with me may be, it lies in the middle ground."

Jerome knew he was taking a chance, but he had to get Zeller to speak his mind so he could head off the problem.

"You speak well. No wonder Carthew thinks so highly of you." Zeller's fingers steepled as he planted his elbows on the desk. "I think otherwise. Upon hearing what everyone else had to say about you, I decided to watch you work. You know everything you do on your computer can be tracked. It's told to you on day one of your employment. So, I watched you for less than ten scant minutes and I found something I didn't like. Something very concerning for the company." Zeller's features drew back into a baboon's snarl. "Would you care to tell me why you were examining regular payments the company makes? Why you didn't stop there, but looked at the accounts those payments were made to?"

Now Jerome knew what the issue was, he could deal with it. Zeller's silence had been nothing more than a trick used to get him talking. The CEO had used the time to think, to assess then reassess.

The fact Jerome had been caught almost as soon as he'd misstepped was a worry. It meant that he'd have to be ultra-careful going forward. He needed to keep his job safe in the meantime.

Rather than let things play out and keep a stealthy watch on him, Zeller had reacted at once and summoned him to his office. That could be a sign of guilt, or an honest man doing his job. Except the Utah account had few suggestions of honesty. To Jerome its hallmarks had all the grubby feel of a slush fund.

Jerome had only seconds to think of a decent reason, so he set his sights on one that would appeal to Zeller's instincts as the CEO of the accounting side of a multinational corporation. "That's all a misunderstanding, sir. An easy one to make. You said Mr. Carthew told you how I'd come up with a proposition to help Beck Accounting through a seriously bad quarter." Jerome held his arms wide and painted a smile into his tone. "I was looking for ways to save the company more money. Obviously the rent is a big expenditure that can't be altered. It's money moving back and forth between various parts of Beck Holdings so that the company as a whole pays less tax. That's smart, even if it is a standard move. The IRS will see it for what it is and know what we're doing. Now, when it comes to utilities and maintenance, those are different matters. We've been with the same companies for at least the last five years. My recommendation to you is that you have those services checked out to see that we're still getting the best possible deals."

"That's a matter for Beck Procurement, not you."

"I completely agree, sir. However, as much as I don't want to cast aspersions on any of our colleagues over at Procurement, five years without a change in any utility company or maintenance contractor seems odd to me, and it's made me wonder about the company focus of the individual awarding those contracts, because if anyone who worked for Beck Holdings was likely to be offered an incentive, financial or otherwise, to award a contract to a specific supplier it would the people at Beck Procurement."

"They are thoroughly vetted. Background checks like you wouldn't believe."

"As they ought to be, sir. Yet those contracts have been in place for a minimum of five years, and neither you nor I could guess how many more years they have left to run at their current arrangement. I may be wrong and it could all be on the level, but I may be right." Jerome let his words hang in the air between him and Zeller. The CEO was no fool and now Jerome had shifted the finger of suspicion elsewhere, Zeller would want a moment to process his thoughts.

Zeller's eyes narrowed, but gave nothing away. A finger detached itself from the steeple and rasped at the underside of his chin.

This was the moment of truth for Jerome. He'd either get the executioner's axe, or a last-minute pardon.

"I see now why people speak so highly of you." *A pardon?* "However noble your intentions may have been, I'm still left with an issue." *The axe?* "I'd still like to know why you pulled up the account details for the rent payments. Can you explain that to me, please?"

"Of course. I was curious where the money was going because I haven't found it showing elsewhere in the Beck Holdings' accounts. Can I be fully honest with you, Mr. Zeller?" A nod gave confirmation. "I got a buzz from saving the company all that money. Of devising a plan and then successfully executing it. As much as I enjoy what I do on a day-to-day basis, I got a far bigger sense of achievement from that project. I was actively looking for ways to replicate that, improve on it even. That's why I was looking so closely."

The hardness in Zeller's eyes softened from granite to sandstone. "That's very admirable. A man like you could go far in a company like this. In fact, if I hadn't caught you snooping, because snooping is the only word that accurately describes what you were doing, right around now I'd be offering you the promotion Mr. Carthew recommended you for. However, I did catch you and that's not something I can forgive lightly. Your ambition is commendable, but it's cost you a promotion. There are protocols, Mr. Prentice. Had you possessed the foresight to bring your ideas to Mr. Carthew or myself, then you would have received not just permission but our help to achieve your goal. Instead you chose to snoop. Mr. Adamson himself set up the Utah account. And you know his reputation."

"I do, sir." Jerome did. Adamson was the ultimate company man. He worked hours that would exhaust someone half his age, he sacrificed his personal life for his professional at every turn and regardless of the situation, he always put Beck Holdings first.

Zeller eyed Jerome the way a crocodile observes prey approaching a riverbank. "I wouldn't go so far as to say you've made it hard to fully trust you, but you haven't made it easier. Your future with Beck Accounting, and indeed Beck Holdings, because I can see you on their board one day, is in your hands. You can do things the correct way and soar to great heights, or you can continue to snoop and find yourself unemployed. It's your choice. Needless to say that should you find yourself unemployed, no references would be forthcoming and while it would be entirely inappropriate for me to suggest anyone associated with the company would ever blacken your name, all the senior people in comparable companies are known to at least two or three of us. We talk, we network the same way colleagues of your level and below do. It may seem like a big old world out there, but the truth is it's a lot smaller than you think." A spindly arm left the desk and pointed at the door. "I would advise that you heed my words as you walk back to your office."

"Yes, Mr. Zeller, sir. Thank you for your time."

The choice facing Jerome was simple. Snoop and save Alicia. Or conform and lose her. It was a no-brainer. He'd just have to get better at snooping so he didn't get caught.

Jerome was used to working alone in his office. As a rule he enjoyed the solitude. He could work in peace, free from the distractions that went hand in hand with being in a communal office. After the conversation with Zeller and the threats that were levelled his way, his office seemed empty and utterly devoid of life. If this was a normal time, he'd ping Alicia a message and she'd come back to him with one of her many pearls of wisdom. These weren't normal times, though. They were far from it.

He drew his chair forward and made a point of not looking at Alicia's laptop. It sat on a spare chair teasing him with its untapped knowledge. He wanted to dive fully into its secrets, but after Zeller's threat he didn't dare access it again unless it could reasonably be argued Alicia was the one trawling through the files rather than him. But when both he and the laptop were in the office and Alicia was at home, there was no way he could offer up any credible explanation as to why the laptop was in use.

Time and again Jerome tried to work out if Zeller could be complicit in Alicia's abduction. Thoughts of distrust and loathing gnawed at him like a ravenous jackal, yet he was somehow making a pretense of doing his job. The actions he did so often as part of his job were performed by reflexes, muscle memory and a humanoid version of autopilot.

Jerome pulled out his cell and checked the Snapchat app. It was how he now communicated with Ed. He knew Snapchat was nowhere close to being as infallible as many people believed, but it was as secure a system as he could access until he got another burner cell.

Ed had left him a message giving co-ordinates to the location of the email address at the moment the Twitter message had been sent. He'd also left a tip on which app gave the best results for pinpointing the locations on a normal map.

Jerome sent silent thanks to his friend. As much as he wanted complete results from Ed, he knew Ed was doing everything he could so his hacker friend would be able to concentrate on getting the necessary access so they could steal the money undetected.

Jerome scrawled the numbers down on a piece of paper, the last four digits memorized just before the screen went dark.

He rebooted the device and checked Messenger. Lucy Sampson hadn't yet read his message. Jerome considered using the app to call her, but knew that if he did that either he'd scare her off, or she'd simply not answer. He needed to arrange a face-to-face meet with her so that he could examine her face for signs she might be lying. Naturally if he did call her, he couldn't do it from the Beck Building in case Carthew or Zeller decided to drop into his office.

There were three locations from Ed. The first two used once apiece. The second three times.

Jerome had his iPad in his hand in two seconds. The first set of co-ordinates were typed into Ed's recommended app inside twenty. They brought up a grid that overlaid a map of New York. An inverted red teardrop acted as marker. He recognized the location and felt no satisfaction when he zoomed in and the marker denoted halfway along Willow Avenue, Hoboken. The second took him to the Beck Building. No surprise with that result either.

The third set of results bore the most fruit, but Jerome didn't know if that fruit was rotten or not. Long Island was the location depicted by the third set of co-ordinates. From what Jerome could tell from the size of the shapes delineating buildings on the map, it seemed to be a semi-industrial area, but from what he could judge it was more like small businesses than a full-sized manufacturing plant.

Jerome jotted down street names near the marker and looked them up on Google Maps. As soon as he was confident he had the location right, he dropped the yellow man onto a street and entered StreetView.

Color flooded the screen and deserted Jerome's face. This wasn't the glamourous part of Long Island. It wasn't even a functional part. This area was down-at-heel. Depressed to the point of being suicidal. Windows were boarded up. Graffiti decorated every surface and a burnt-out car sat sullenly before what looked to have once been an apartment block.

The apartment block was where the marker had pinpointed the Gmail account. The building was so far into the stages of abandonment only the homeless would choose to sleep inside it. Any color it had once possessed had decayed and, even looking at it on a screen, Jerome could smell its dankness and the urine of the feral animals that would surely have invaded its sanctity.

As a place to store a kidnapped woman, it'd be ideal. It was everything Jerome had imagined, and worse.

He wanted to leap from his seat and race out there at once, but he knew that was a rash course of action that could cause more problems than it solved.

The beep of his cell made him jump. The hand that went automatically grappling for his chest was redirected to his pocket so he could pluck the cell free. The kidnappers had sent a picture of Alicia holding the latest *Game Informer*. She looked scared, but otherwise unhurt. It was up to him to make sure she came back before any harm came to her.

30

Doubts pummeled Jerome like a storm surge. Every instinct he possessed was telling him to race out to the building on Long Island to find and rescue Alicia. He could take the police with him. He could rustle up a few buddies as backup if the cops didn't believe his story.

He didn't do any of those things. The doubts won his internal battle. Alicia's life was too precious for him to take even the slightest chance.

As per Ed's advice, he forced himself to think with his head rather than his heart. It was possible the abductors were using the building as nothing more than a base of operations. His biggest fear was that he hadn't thrown the tail, and last night's surveillance of the locations in Hell's Kitchen had been observed. There was nothing the abductors could do about historical data regarding their email address usage, but they could make sure future uses were from a location that held no connections to them. Worse, they could pick a deserted location in the hope of setting a trap for him should he be foolish enough to try and enact a rescue.

It was this fear, this set of doubts, that kept Jerome's butt in his seat. The more he thought about it, the more he was convinced that he mustn't show up at the Long Island address until he was one hundred percent certain that's where Alicia was. The risks associated with making an unsuccessful attempt to save Alicia were too terrible for him to consider.

He would be the one who earned the punishment, but it would be Alicia who'd receive it. At the very least she'd be moved to a new location. At the worst... Jerome couldn't allow himself to think what the worst might be. It was hard enough thinking about Alicia being in the hands of the abductors; the idea that harm may be done to her because of him wasn't something he could ever contemplate.

It was possible there was only one person in the building. A lone member of their gang stationed there for the sole purpose of communicating with him from a desolate location nowhere near where Alicia was being held. Jerome wasn't a violent man. He'd only had one fistfight in his life and that was back when he was in grade school. All the same, he could easily envision himself tackling the lone abductor and getting Alicia's location from him. He knew enough submission holds from his college wrestling days to extract information. The problem with that idea was that he didn't know whether the person sending those messages was alone or surrounded by buddies.

The more Jerome tried to persuade himself to act, the more problems he ran into. Even if he did manage to convince the cops that Alicia was being held in the building, it was unlikely they'd dispatch a SWAT team on his word alone. They'd want to run surveillance, maybe the surveillance would be done right, and maybe it'd be a bored cop who didn't bother to take a proper look. On the flip side, the cop given the task of surveillance may see a chance for personal glory and would try to rescue Alicia themselves. That could end any number of ways and few of them good for Alicia. Jerome's biggest fear was that when threatened with exposure and capture, the abductors would see their smartest move to be the disposal of the evidence against them. The most damning of which was their captive. Alicia.

Jerome's jaw tightened until his teeth ground together as he assessed his options and corralled the errant thoughts pinballing around his head.

He needed to do this himself. One man against a whole gang might be terrible odds but he wasn't afraid for himself, only Alicia. Whatever the obstacles, whatever the dangers, he'd face them down and overcome them one by one. He couldn't trust Alicia's safety to anyone else. He *had* to be the one to save her. She was *his* wife and it was his duty to protect her. So far he'd failed, but that was just something he'd have to put right.

Another huge fear of acting was that he'd rush out of the office intent on getting to the building only to find it deserted. Used a couple of times as a decoy and then abandoned. He was at work. Under the close scrutiny of his big boss. His work gave him access to the funds he may need to secure Alicia's release, therefore he couldn't do anything that would jeopardize his job.

Jerome leaned back in his chair and rested his hands on his knees as he diverted the part of his brain dealing with work toward the idea that was beginning to form. Before he could mount any advance, by himself or the cops, on the Long Island building, he needed to be much more certain that was where Alicia was being held. To do that he'd have to find a way to get the abductors to communicate with him two or three times in close succession and have Ed on standby to trace their locations.

The easy way to do that would be to send them a Twitter message asking for further proof of life. That avenue was closed off. Barricaded against entry by the abductor's deletion of each Twitter account once it had served its purpose. That didn't mean Jerome didn't have an idea on how to communicate with the abductors.

A Snapchat message to Ed got him on board with his new plan.

The next part was the area where things may not work out right, but as he had no other choice, Jerome accessed his Twitter account and tapped out a public post.

@JerPrent WHEN YOU NEED YOUR WIFE TO SOLVE A
WORK PROBLEM AND SHE ISN'T PICKING UP. THAT!
@AliciaHR

As a further indicator that he was reaching out to the kidnappers, Jerome added a meme showing a man screaming for help.

It wasn't the most subtle of messages, but that didn't matter to
Jerome. If the abductors were monitoring his account they'd hopefully realize he was saying he needed Alicia's help to get them their
money. Even if they contacted him to tell him to do it himself,
dialogue would have begun and the longer he could keep it going,
the better Ed's chances were of getting a fix on the location.

31

It took a half hour for Jerome's cell to beep. Thirty long minutes of wondering whether his tweet would have the required effect. Eighteen hundred seconds of self-doubt where no attempt to distract himself with work came close to assuaging his worry.

Jerome's fingers trembled as he accessed Twitter. The message could be anything. It could tell him to go it alone. That there was now a deadline. He pushed all the doubts and fears to the back of his mind and opened it.

The message was from a new Twitter account and contained a screenshot of his post and six bare words.

@JboyPrenty WHAT DO YOU NEED TO KNOW?

This part was crucial. Jerome had thought hard about what to ask. It had to be cryptic enough that only Alicia would have the answer, yet not so obscure she couldn't answer it. It also had to relate to work in some way as it was clear the abductors were connected to Beck Holdings.

Jerome tapped out the question. His fingers shaking so much he made typos he had to correct.

@JerPrent OUR FIRST AL FRESCO MEAL. WHERE WAS
IT AT?

The answer was engraved in Jerome's memory. It had been a
fantastic meal on a beautiful summer's night. It was their fourth
date and had cost him a week's salary from his job bussing tables
after college classes, but it had been worth every cent. Alicia's
beauty and infectious laugh had turned heads, and they'd laughed
and chatted all evening. He'd had a sublime vegetable terrine
followed by a pork steak so succulent it melted in his mouth. Alicia
had savored her way through a five-leaf salad and then a pasta dish
whose sauce she'd described as heaven in a bowl. They'd returned
many times since and it was their "occasion" place. Birthdays and
anniversaries and general celebrations were all marked with a meal
at The Rooftop.

It was only after Jerome joined Beck Accounting that he
learned The Rooftop was held within the Beck Dining portfolio
along with many other of New York's finest restaurants. Beck
Dining was, of course, a subsidiary of Beck Holdings, which added
the work connection to the question.

While Jerome waited for the reply, he fired off a Snapchat to
Ed to activate his traces. He didn't have to wait long. Ed's response
of a thumbs up arrived in seconds. The response from the abductors came within three minutes of him sending the question.

@JboyPrenty THE ROOFTOP
    WHAT DOES BECK DINING HAVE TO DO WITH
THIS?

Jerome had anticipated the question. He knew he'd meet some
resistance and this was the least he'd expected. It also played into
his hands. The longer he could keep the dialogue going the better
Ed's chances of getting the location.

@JerPrent I NEED TO SEE MY WIFE IS OKAY. SEND ME A VIDEO OF ALICIA. SHE IS TO WAVE WITH HER RIGHT HAND AND BLOW ME A KISS WITH HER LEFT. THEN I'LL EXPLAIN WHY.

The speed of the first response suggested that the abductors were close to Alicia, or were in contact with someone who was. How quick the video came back would be very informative.

The cell beeped in less than two minutes. The message contained a video. One hundred and twenty seconds was not a lot of time for the abductors to relay messages back and forth. Certainly not enough to kick things up and down a chain of command, record and then send a video. The person he was conducting the conversation with must therefore be where Alicia was.

@JboyPrenty YOU'RE ANSWER?

The video was the one he'd asked for. Alicia stood tall and proud with her head held up, but the fear in her eyes put a heart-sized lump into Jerome's throat.

Her mouth moved and broke Jerome's heart. There was no sound to the video, but Jerome didn't need it to know his wife was asking for help and telling him that she loved him. She'd even used their own way of saying it. "One. Four. Three." Alicia used the wrong hands for the requested actions, but that was either Alicia being Alicia, or the video being reversed due to the way it was filmed. Jerome didn't care, he simply found it endearing. On the second viewing he noticed the bruise above her eye had swapped sides, so the video must be a reverse image.

That didn't matter. Alicia was alive.

That mattered. That was all that mattered.

Jerome wanted to toss the cell across the room to vent the frustration he felt at his helplessness, but he didn't. That would achieve nothing. Instead he made sure to save the video. To keep it for posterity.

He picked up on the spelling mistake, though. That was the second time the person sending the messages had confused "your" and "you're." Perhaps it was a trait that he could use at a later date to identify at least one of the people involved in Alicia's kidnapping.

A ping from his iPad had Jerome reaching across the desk. Ed had come back to him. How he'd gotten the information so fast was beyond Jerome, but he'd be forever grateful to Ed for it.

The location from Ed was a series of numbers. Jerome didn't need to match them against a map. Didn't need to cross-reference them against anything except the co-ordinates already seared into his brain.

The person messaging him was in the building on Long Island. They were with Alicia, ergo Alicia was in that building. He knew where she was, and that meant he could save her.

There was just one final thing he needed to do to confirm Alicia's location. He examined the first picture he'd been sent of Alicia. As hard as it was to do, he didn't look at his wife, at the person he loved more than life itself. Instead he looked beyond her at the place she was being held captive. It was a bare room devoid of any feature. The walls an institutional green with flaking paint. The paint flakes were where he directed his focus, and he sketched the shapes onto a pad on his desk.

The second picture filled his screen and while Jerome couldn't match all the flaking areas of paint to his sketches, he matched enough to be convinced both pictures were taken in the same room.

Next he brought up the video. Alicia's head and her huge head of hair obscured much of the background, but as she blew him the kiss, her head bobbed forward enough to reveal a now-familiar shape in the flaking paint.

This was the confirmation he so badly desired. That he needed before he could begin to think of what to do next. Now he had it.

Magically, wonderfully, both of the pictures and the video had all been taken in the same place. He now knew where that place was.

Jerome's relief at receiving this confirmation was so profound he found himself blinking back tears as he spoke to her. "Don't worry, Alicia, darling. I'm coming to save you. One. Four. Three."

Alicia was smart. Super smart in fact. She did crosswords for fun, the more cryptic the better. Jerome was trusting his wife to decode the messages he'd sent her. Both in the question he'd posed and the specifics of the video he'd requested.

He meant it. He *was* going to go save her. Going to the cops could end up with a showdown with the abductors, where a gun was aimed at Alicia's head. That wasn't going to happen. If he couldn't rescue Alicia, he'd still be able to steal the money and buy her freedom.

32

Alicia didn't pay any attention to the door crunching shut. Every part of her brain was focused on the question Jerome had asked of her. It made no sense at all for him to ask that. Jerome knew the answer. Of course he did. It was Jerome who'd book their usual table at The Rooftop whenever they had something to celebrate, it was he who'd first found the place and it was he who got all excited about their next visit. Jerome knew the answer to his question as well as he knew his own name.

Realization hit Alicia as hard as a runaway freight train. Jerome wasn't asking a question; he was sending a message. Her kidnappers wouldn't know how often they visited The Rooftop, therefore Jerome had hidden his message inside the question. The fact The Rooftop was owned by Beck Dining could be his way of informing her that someone within Beck Holdings was behind her kidnapping.

The request for the video was so typical of Jerome. He'd wanted to see her. Not a day went past without her catching him staring her way with unconditional love. She adored that about him. Jerome wasn't some macho dude who hid his feelings behind gruffness and a seeming lack of care; he wore them loud and proud for all to see. That he'd asked her to wave and blow him a kiss, something they never did to each other, was strange but she guessed it was his way of making sure the video was new rather than one taken when she was first captured.

"One. Four. Three. Jerome."

The words fell from her mouth unbidden as she started to put the pieces of Jerome's puzzle together. Shivers of comprehension danced up and down her spine as she began to make sense of his question and the video request.

The blowing of a kiss was the strangest part as it was so out of character for him to request affection in that way. He'd also been specific about the hands she was to use despite him often teasing her about how she always got her lefts and rights mixed up. She'd had to perform an action with her left hand; that was unusual for them. Left not right. A wrong gesture with the left, not right hand. The wrong hand.

The more she thought, the more she understood his unspoken message. Jerome was planning to do something she wouldn't expect him to do. Something outside his normal behavior, outside his skills. Something that may be wrong.

The question was, what was this thing he planned?

Jerome wasn't a man of action. He was no hero. Sure, he'd stand up for what he believed in, and he certainly wasn't a coward, but he wasn't one to engage in angry confrontation.

The best Alicia could figure was Jerome planned to do her kidnappers' bidding. It was wrong but he was going to do it to save her. His hidden messages were his way of telling her not to worry, that he was complying with the kidnappers. That he was working to have her released.

It all made perfect sense apart from the reference to The Rooftop. It didn't fit with anything else he'd suggested. It had no place in his reassurances. Memories of better times were fine, but even the worst memories she had paled when compared to her current predicament.

Alicia thought about every aspect of their trips to The Rooftop. How Jerome always booked the same table. How the maître d' and sommelier both remembered them as semi-regular customers. Her mind went forward to the terrace where they'd savor a couple of after-dinner drinks before heading home. She even replayed some of the conversations they'd enjoyed there in case there was relevance in them.

None of these things had any connotation that she could assign. Nothing about them made sense until she cast her mind to the start of their experiences of dining at The Rooftop. Not the chronological dates they'd went there, more what happened in the run up to them leaving home to head to the restaurant.

Whenever they visited The Rooftop, Jerome wanted to get there as soon as possible so the experience could begin as soon as possible. They'd get ready to go at their usual pace, but as The Rooftop was such a special place for them both, she always made that extra bit of effort. Invariably, she'd be running late while Jerome sprang around like an overexcited puppy as he tried to rush her. He'd jokingly threatened to put her over his shoulder on a few occasions, and once because she was feeling playful, she'd time wasted until he did just that, his free hand patting her butt as he gave her a fake telling-off. They'd left the house in fits of giggles that night.

That's what Jerome was telling her. He was coming for her. Coming to take her away from this. To rescue her. Some of what he was doing, or prepared to do, might be wrong, but he was coming to get her and that was the best news possible.

Alicia's elation at Jerome's intention brought unstoppable tears to her eyes as she both marveled at her husband's resolve and worried for his safety.

33

The afternoon passed with the kind of slowness Jerome would normally associate with a Friday afternoon. It had been four hours since he received confirmation of Alicia's location. Two hundred and forty minutes spent quelling down the urge to race out to Long Island with practicality and common sense. He'd been watched yesterday and while he'd lost that tail, he knew he'd be picked up again upon leaving the office. He could go through the rigmarole of losing the tail again, but to do so during working hours would be sure to instigate a reaction and would take far too long. He reasoned that it was best to do it once in case the reaction might be to move Alicia to a different location, so he'd sat tight and tried to dispel negativity from his thoughts while researching all he could about the building on Long Island. It hadn't been a surprise to him to learn the building was owned by Beck Construction—the property development wing of Beck Holdings. Everything about this mess circled back to Beck Holdings. But why would they want to defraud themselves, or perhaps a better question was why were they going to such lengths while risking so much? Not just for themselves, but for the company that paid their salaries.

Now he was free of the office, he could start in on his plan. His first move was to lose the tail, so he spent an hour switching between subway trains, taxis and ducking into and out of various places that had multiple exits. Only when he was convinced he'd done everything he could to lose the tail did he start procuring the items he'd decided he would need.

The whole idea of storming a building to rescue Alicia was foreign to him. He was an accountant, not a cop or a soldier, but that didn't deter him. Alicia was at risk and that trumped any fears he possessed for his own safety. His one and only fear was failure. Failure to save his wife. Failure to rescue her from the nightmarish scenario she was in. Failure to protect the woman he'd sworn to cherish, to forsake all others for.

He'd thought about enlisting Ed to come with him and discounted the idea. He was prepared to take his own chances when doing this, but to ask Ed would be to put his friend in an untenable position. Despite his height, Ed was even less of a fighter than he was and would be more likely to be a hindrance than a help. Anyway, he needed Ed working on his algorithm, which was the fallback plan if he couldn't find a way to rescue Alicia.

Jerome found a thrift store where he bought himself a backpack, a black hooded sweat top and a pair of black jeans. His suit was swapped for the new clothes and the backpack slung over his shoulder as he went looking for a hardware store.

The hardware store was filled with useful items, but he was mindful of his lack of carrying capacity. He had the backpack and that was it. He loaded a number of items into a basket and approached the counter.

The clerk paid him no heed as she rang up his purchases. When Jerome left the store his backpack now contained a flashlight, a screwdriver with interchangeable heads for different screws, a twenty-five yard hank of rope, a two-foot prybar, a hammer and a Leatherman utility knife. There were also two rolls of duct tape and spare batteries for the flashlight. His feet now sported a pair of workboots. He hadn't intended buying them, but when he saw the box proclaiming they had steel toecaps he'd added them to his basket. They'd protect his toes from stamps and, more importantly, add an extra layer of injury to any kick he delivered.

Jerome stepped in front of an ATM and maxed out every card in his wallet. His final purchases wouldn't be cheap, but he wanted to continue paying cash for things on the off chance the abductors were monitoring his spending. The last thing he wanted them to do was deduce he was preparing to rescue Alicia.

His next stop was an electronics store. A floor walker in his forties approached from the far side of the store, but Jerome was spoken to first by a member of staff who popped up from behind a row of flat-screen TVs. This one had blue hair, a ring through one nostril and a full sleeve tattoo depicting coiled serpents.

"I'm after a GoPro camera. I want to stream what it records to a fixed location online where I can view it afterwards if that's possible."

"That's pretty standard. Do you want them directly streamed as you record or do you mean you'll upload them at a later time?"

"Directly streamed would be my preference."

"Okay." Blue Hair's hand indicated a variety of GoPro cameras. "These will all do that. You'll need connectivity to make them work. They pair to your phone with Bluetooth and then get uploaded on your cell signal. If you're planning to do this when doing something like skiing, you may have to invest in a satphone or get a special SIM package that allows you to tap into different coverage options."

Jerome followed most of what Blue Hair was saying, but there was one point he had to check. "What about Long Island, will it work there?"

"Sure, they're all waterproof so you'd need a secure bag for your cell if you want to stream footage of you surfing, as the Bluetooth won't reach back to the beach."

"I won't be surfing so that won't be a problem."

Jerome got Blue Hair to set up the GoPro and pair it to his

burner cell. The whole point of this purchase would be to make sure there was a record of his entry into the building. To ensure that whatever happened when he went to rescue Alicia, there would be a trail left behind. He could easily tell Ed what he was doing but he knew his friend would just insist on coming along and he didn't want that.

The final item on his list was the most important and the most extreme. Jerome had never handled a gun before. He didn't like the idea of possessing a deadly weapon, of having the power of life and death over another. Except tonight. Tonight he wanted a gun in his hand. He wanted the power and threat that came with it. As was his way, he'd done the research.

It was as he handled three different guns to see how they fit in his hand that he realized the enormity of what he was planning. His plan was to use stealth. To not harm any of the abductors unless absolutely necessary, but he knew there may come a time when one of the abductors may need to be encouraged to talk. Or subdued. Jerome was no fool, he knew there may come a point where he'd have to pull the trigger. To send a bullet toward another human being. He was a long way from comfortable with the idea, but if that's what it took to save Alicia, then that's what he'd do.

Jerome's hand trembled as he realized how far he was out of his comfort zone. Since Alicia had been taken, he'd planned grand theft and had engaged in petty theft on two occasions. Instead of being a law-abiding citizen, he was now buying a gun. A gun he was prepared to use to shoot a man if doing so helped him rescue his wife. This wasn't who he was, but it was who he'd become. Once again his jaw was tight, clenched in determination as he came to terms with this new version of his self.

A hand was extended and the sales clerk passed Oliver's gun license back to Jerome. Before entering the gun store Jerome had done all he could to obscure the picture without totally defacing the license, and he'd finger brushed his hair into an approximation of Oliver's style.

"Sir. I have to make you aware that to comply with the firearms laws, you must only travel straight home with the gun and once home it has to be in a locked gun safe. Other than that, it's a felony to transport it around the city."

The sales clerk's words just hammered home the scale of his planned transgressions. Five steps in the wrong direction when leaving the gun store would mark him as a felon. It was a fact he was prepared to overlook. Carrying the gun was far less of a crime than defrauding millions, and he was prepared to do whatever it took to get Alicia back.

34

Jerome drove the rental car with care. It wasn't that he was worried about damaging it or picking up a ticket, more that he was following the GPS with one eye and he wanted to make sure he was paying attention to the route. He'd picked up the small hatchback after departing the Long Island Rail Road, at Ronkonkoma. The hatchback wasn't nearly as peppy as he'd have liked, but it had been available and within budget, as he'd already burned through most of the bills he'd withdrawn from the ATM.

Nine times Jerome had checked his cell for a Twitter message from the abductors as he rode the train to Long Island. Nine times he'd found no message. He'd also checked to see if Lucy Sampson had read his message. She hadn't, *damn her*.

The GPS did its job with digital efficiency and led him to the building he was looking for. The closer he got, the more his heart sank. The whole area was depressed. If a human being showed such levels of depression, they'd be medicated or put on a suicide watch. Cars were abandoned, some burnt-out, others not worth the gas needed to ignite them. Graffiti and gang tags littered most flat surfaces, and there were few buildings that didn't have at least several windows boarded over. Every structure appeared to wallow in self-pity at how it had fallen into neglect and disrepair.

Shapes moved in the shadows cast by the moon, the streetlights having long ago flickered their last. It was a feral place, an area where poverty and lawlessness would be rife, and it was as far away from Jerome's world as the moon. He'd grown up in a good neighborhood, attended a decent school and led a professional life after leaving college. He wasn't equipped to travel mean streets, yet here he was walking them.

Ahead of Jerome, the building he believed Alicia was in loomed in the moonlight. Shrouded as it was in shadows, with occasional spotlighting from moonbeams, it looked sinister and foreboding, like a place where evil dwelled and death stalked every corridor. All Jerome could hope was that Alicia hadn't seen its exterior, that she was blissfully unaware of her prison's appearance, as it would surely add to the sense of terror she was bound to be feeling.

Since the Google StreetView images had been taken a wooden barricade had been erected around the building. It stood eight feet high, and beneath a smattering of graffiti a sign proclaimed the premises was protected by a security company. The barricade had a gate, presumably for construction workers should the building ever receive the much-needed repairs and regeneration that would come from when the development wing of Beck Holdings made their move.

The gate had once been hinged on both sides, although the left side was now lying flat on the ground inside the barricade, the right slumped and twisted. A chain was padlocked to the right gate and Jerome could see where it had once been affixed to the left gate.

Security would be nothing more than the barricade and the sign. The street gangs who'd roam the area could be bought off for a few bucks. It was possible they'd be hired as a ring of security by Alicia's abductors, but if Jerome had to guess, he'd say they'd been bribed to stay away with the promise of more money if they did so.

Jerome drove past the building at little more than a crawl, but he was ready to stamp on the gas at any moment. When he'd passed the building he turned the hatchback around and set off back the way he'd come.

As much as he wanted to park beside the gates and sneak into the building, Jerome had enough street smarts to know that if he did so, there was a better-than-even chance of the car being gone or ablaze when he returned to it. He and Alicia walking away from the building was fine provided there was nobody coming after them, but he expected there may be some kind of pursuit and he didn't want to leave more to chance than could be helped, so he carried on a couple of blocks until he was in a somewhat better area before parking the car.

With each step he took back toward the building Jerome felt the threat level increase. There were sounds carrying on the night air that had no place anywhere but nightmares. A dog yelped short angry barks, something howled and there was wild cackling laughter emanating from at least one of the buildings. High to Jerome's right a window flickered with the dancing colors of an open fire. Whether it was someone setting fire to the building or a homeless person seeking nocturnal warmth from a small fire was a moot point for Jerome. It wasn't Alicia's building so it didn't matter.

Onwards he strode; the faster he walked, the more his nerve was bolstered.

35

Jerome was twenty paces from the gate in the barricade around Alicia's building when he stopped walking. His right hand was in his pocket, clasped around the Smith and Wesson pistol he'd bought before leaving New York. Jerome was new to guns and he'd made a point of getting himself a pistol that had a safety catch he could be sure of. One he could see and move only on purpose. The M&P 9 Shield by Smith and Wesson was what the guy in the gun store had recommended. Matte black, squat and square, the Shield looked deadly and that's what Jerome wanted. The pistol was to be used for intimidation, not assault. He had come here on a rescue mission, not one of vengeance or retribution. If he had to pull the Shield's trigger, something had gone wrong, badly wrong.

The flashlight hung from Jerome's left hand. It wasn't switched on, and before he did use it he wanted to scope out the building. Wanted to examine it for signs of life before the flashlight announced his presence.

A service door was boarded over, as was what would have been the former main doorway. The entrance to what Jerome presumed was a subterranean parking garage yawned beneath the building's center.

The parking garage seemed like it may be the best option, but

Jerome didn't want to go down that route if he could avoid it. That was how he suspected Alicia's abductors accessed the building, and he wanted to find another way in to lessen the chances of running into the abductors at the wrong time.

Jerome walked forward until he was beside the gate. In the gloom he could make out more boarded-over doorways, but there was no judging how secure the boarding was. His best guess was the boarding would be half rotted, but that didn't mean he'd be able to discreetly lever it free. The squealing of a pulled nail would be enough to alert anyone guarding Alicia. If not to his direct presence, then enough that they'd pay more attention to strange noises.

No matter how many times Jerome scanned his eyes over the building's exterior, he saw the same thing. Dark shapes colored only by moonlight and passing clouds. There was no movement. No sparks of light emanating from any part of the building. It appeared to be deserted, abandoned to a life of decay until it collapsed on itself.

Behind Jerome there was the scuff of a stone beneath the sole of a shoe. He whirled around, heart racing, to find himself confronted with four youths. One of them was holding a knife whose blade flashed in the moonlight.

The knife holder was slight, but his face was hard and there was a cockiness about him that overrode any lack of threat his diminutive build may suggest. The fact he was backed up by bigger guys didn't bode well.

"Put your wallet, watch, cell and any jewelry you have on the ground and you can walk away. You have three seconds."

This wasn't what Jerome needed, but he didn't flinch. Didn't try his usual pacifist tactics. Tonight he had a higher purpose and he wasn't going to be deflected from it by a knot of street punks.

"I don't need them." Jerome pulled the Shield from his pocket and aimed it straight at Knife Holder's nose.

Knife Holder stared at Jerome. There was no backing down, no retreat from the superior weapon. Just a look of dumb insolence.

"One."

Jerome waggled the gun at Knife Holder's nose. "I'll shoot you."

"Nope. You won't." Knife Holder's eyebrows flicked up. "Two."

Jerome sure as hell didn't want to shoot him, not only did he not want to kill anyone, he didn't want the shot to alert Alicia's abductors of his presence in the area. He needed to end this before the countdown got to three.

This was spiraling out of control. Knife Holder may be a street punk, but that didn't mean he wanted to shoot him. Jerome cursed the fact that now he was locked into this standoff, that there was no way to escape it other than to try and bluff it out. "I have a gun. I *will* pull the trigger."

Something clicked within Jerome's brain and sent minute electrical charges to the synapses of rational thought. Knife Holder had no reason to be so cocky. His knife was a far inferior weapon to the gun Jerome held and yet he wasn't backing down. In fact, he was pressing on with the deadline he'd set. There had to be a reason for this. He wouldn't want to lose face in front of his buddies, that was a given, but as he was outgunned he'd not lose too much face.

The only other reason for Knife Holder's cockiness that Jerome could think of was that he wasn't afraid of the gun. Therefore Knife Holder knew something he didn't. What did he know? What *could* he know that would engender such bravery?

"Pull it then. Three." As he spoke Knife Holder lurched forward, his blade slashing at Jerome's gun hand.

Jerome had anticipated some kind of move and as there was a clear six feet between them, he'd time to withdraw his arm enough that the knife did no more than catch the end of the gun's barrel. As a reflex his finger curled around the trigger and depressed it as his hand spasmed at the sudden movement and the desire to retain control of the weapon lest it be knocked from his grasp.

Nothing happened. There was no boom, no flash of flame as a bullet shot from the barrel and delivered death to Knife Holder, and there was none of the recoil the salesman had warned him to prepare for.

Jerome instantly knew why. He'd left the safety on. Knife Holder had seen this and that's why he'd been so bold. Knife Holder had known the gun couldn't fire and that it was nothing more than a piece of metal until the safety was disengaged.

Knife Holder stepped forward again, his knife making a wild slash left to right. Jerome danced back out of reach and then a fury overcame him. Feelings he'd never experienced before swept over his conscious thought and closed off his mind to everything but base primal instincts. He was no longer a polite accountant. He was a man fighting for his life. His wife's life.

Jerome dropped the flashlight and used his empty hand to catch Knife Holder's elbow and propel the blade to a place where it couldn't be turned against him as he moved toward his opponent. He didn't waste time fumbling for the safety, instead he slipped his finger from the trigger and crashed the weapon into the side of Knife Holder's head.

Knife Holder's eyes went white as he slumped to the ground.

Jerome didn't know whether he'd killed or just stunned him. And he could care less. In that precise moment with his vision narrowed by rage, either was fine with him.

Blows rained in on Jerome from Knife Holder's buddies. He almost welcomed them as he retaliated. His next attempt to slam the pistol against a temple was blocked by a forearm, but he still managed to throw a solid punch with his left hand that was enough to rock his target backwards. A wild elbow swing caught a jaw and then a thunderous punch from nowhere split Jerome's lips and loosened at least one tooth.

He retaliated with a hard groin kick that drew a pained yelp and then the fight fell away from all combatants. The two remaining aggressors backed a pace or two away and Jerome did the same thing. To emphasize his point he made a show of releasing the safety on the Shield. "Beat it."

Jerome had to give the gang credit; they went to pick up Knife Holder intent on taking him with them. He couldn't allow that. He needed to assert his dominance one last time so they didn't try again. "Leave him, and beat it."

Knife Holder's buddies did as they were told, although they stopped fifty yards away and threw insults his way. They could have that. They were out of range and would have to come back for their buddy when he moved on to the building.

37

Alicia eyed the spider crossing the far wall with a mixture of fear and hatred. The multi-legged arachnids were normally her greatest fear, but as much as their very presence threatened to give her palpitations, she'd never once swatted one, nor permitted her father or Jerome to do so when ejecting them from her presence.

To Alicia the two-inch spider represented her current predicament. Terrifying and uncertain. She didn't know what was going to happen to her, or to Jerome. He'd intimated he was coming for her, that he was going to rescue her. She hoped he was going to arrive with a SWAT team. With hostage negotiators and enough cops to pick up this entire building and carry it away.

The idea of many trained men behind serious guns effecting her rescue was a comforting thought. It provided a warm glow of affection strong enough to take the chill off the room.

Except she knew Jerome. Knew exactly how he thought. How he felt. He wasn't the hero type, and nor was he a gambler. But she knew he'd have run the numbers in his head. He'd have weighed up the pros and cons between trying to rescue her himself and going to the cops.

The cops were better at rescuing kidnapped victims, that was a no-brainer. The kidnappers were sure to have made many threats to Jerome about contacting the cops. Another no-brainer.

Jerome would have balanced the risk of the kidnappers having a police source against the dangers of coming himself. Even if he brought Ed or some of his other buddies, they'd still be a bunch of amateurs. Since she'd been kidnapped, she'd never seen Big Guy without a gun in his hands.

Alicia dropped her chin to her chest, clasped her hands together and sent a silent prayer up toward heaven that Jerome had done the sensible thing and gone to the cops. As soon as the prayer was sent, she began to worry that if he did go to the cops, the kidnappers would find out. There were corrupt cops on the payroll of criminals, and she was sure that more than a few cops would be paid retainers in brown envelopes to help out high-rolling business people. The kind of business people behind her kidnapping.

The idea of Jerome going up against Big Guy and his ever-present shotgun petrified her more than a thousand spiders. Jerome wasn't a man of action; at least, not that kind of action. He was her hero, but not that kind of hero. He might fight hard for what he believed in, but never with his fists. Jerome was a kind man, a gentle man.

The more Alicia pictured Jerome going up against her kidnappers, the more she feared for him. He was in good shape, but while his physique was buff and he had plenty of stamina, he had no experience of real fighting. He could wrestle, but she'd never known him to get into a fistfight, nor to mention ever using a gun. If there was any kind of standoff or battle between Jerome and her kidnappers, Alicia knew the smart money would be on the kidnappers.

Alicia's foot began to shake of its own volition. Tremors at first and then full-blooded taps that bounced it off the dusty floor. She lifted herself upright and put the nervous energy to use by pacing back and forth across the room as she offered up prayer after prayer for Jerome's safety.

For all Jerome was a safe and predictable man, he had an

impetuous side to his nature. He'd book a weekend away on a Friday lunchtime and message her, telling her to start thinking about what she'd need to pack when they returned home from work. He'd be scrupulously meticulous about his work, yet his closet was a jumble of work clothes and vivid shirts bought on impulse. She'd always teased him that she thought he was trying to build a collection of the world's most hideous shirts, but as she paced back and forth, she'd give anything to see him in the worst example—a hideous draylon affront to taste with a design that always reminded her of the curtains in her grammy's house.

Jerome wouldn't let her down. Never. Nor would he trust anyone else to get her back safe. If he was coming himself, she knew he'd be calculating every step of any rescue attempt he made, working out each action in advance so it was executed in the best way possible, but he was an amateur going up against armed kidnappers. No sane gambler would bet on his chances of success. No one would back Jerome in a fight with Big Guy. Maybe if Jerome had studied a martial art to a decent level he'd stand a chance, but to the best of Alicia's knowledge he hadn't once stepped into a dojo. Sure, Jerome had wrestled in college, but that was a long time ago and a lot of flexibility ago. Jerome was in shape, there was no question of that, but Big Guy was so huge that his size and power offered him a massive advantage. To even engage Big Guy in a wrestling match, Jerome would first have to get past the shotgun and its murderous threat.

Alicia ended her prayer and her pacing with a glower at the door. Every thought in her head was a nest of worry and, as the door allowed the kidnappers into this rooms and resisted her attempts to escape, it was the focus of her fear and frustration.

Jerome had to have called the cops. Had to have done the sensible thing instead of playing the hero.

The more Alicia thought it, the less she believed it.

38

With the trio of gang members keeping their distance, Jerome could move on with his attempt to search the building looking for Alicia. He didn't move toward the building, instead he pulled the duct tape from his backpack and used it to secure Knife Holder. Left wrist to right leg and vice versa was his chosen method. A series of faint groans emanated from Knife Holder as he did this, so Jerome made sure the gun was tucked into his belt at the small of his back and the knife was away from Knife Holder's hands but always within his own reach.

A few slaps on Knife Holder's cheek brought him back to full waking consciousness. His eyes first groggy and then widening as he realized Jerome was standing over him and he was immobilized.

"The hell?" Puzzlement filled his face and tone. This wasn't how it should have gone down. He screwed his head around, only stopping when he saw the knot his buddies were forming.

"Your gang split when I removed the safety. They're keeping their distance."

"They'll do you, man. Do you good. You ain't gonna last a New York minute 'gainst us."

"I very much doubt you're going to try your luck again. I won't make the same mistake a second time. However, right now is what

I'm interested in." Jerome extended an arm toward the building. "I want to know what you know about that building. Who's been coming and going. How often they've been coming and going. How to get in there."

"What? And you think I'm going to tell you? My head feels like you busted it all the way in. Screw you, jerkweed."

Jerome had anticipated this kind of resistance. Knife Holder must hate him. Not only had a potential mugging victim turned the tables, but he'd inflicted a knockout blow in the process.

"I can think of a couple reasons why you will help me." Jerome pulled out his wallet and showed Knife Holder the last $500 dollars he had in cash. Then with his other hand he dangled Knife Holder's blade in a loose grip. "You tell me what I want to know, and you get some money. You don't tell me, I start removing parts of you. A finger, an ear or maybe I'll just lop off your nose. You have a simple choice, pain or profit."

Jerome stepped back and kept his face as hard as possible. Knife Holder had to believe he'd carry out his threat, otherwise he was wasting his time. No way would he actually use the torture he was suggesting. Not on a random street punk. If his prisoner was one of the abductors, that would be a different matter, but despite being a predator who preyed upon the weak, Knife Holder didn't deserve to lose body parts.

Knife Holder's head rotated until he was sending looks toward his buddies. Whether he was extorting them to help or looking their way for advice was an unknown.

Jerome tapped the top of Knife Holder's skull with the hilt of the knife. "What's it to be?"

Fear pulsed out from Knife Holder to the extent where Jerome almost pitied him. "I can't tell you crap, man. No way."

"You can and you will. Now, do you want your buddies to hear you screaming, or do you want them to be jealous of the money I give you?"

Knife Holder didn't answer and something in Jerome's brain fired the right set of synapses. Knife Holder might want to talk, might well be happy to take his money, but after the failed mugging he'd already lost face in front of his buddies. If they saw him talking and then receiving money from Jerome, his standing would be shattered within their group.

"Much cash you got?"

"Five hundred bucks or thereabouts."

"Okay." Knife Holder's voice was tight. "Here's what to do. Put your knife against my ear. I'll tell you what you want to know, and then you have to cut me a little. Leave the ear on, but make sure you at least cut across the top part. I'll struggle a little, but I won't make no moves 'gainst you."

Jerome did as Knife Holder instructed, his every sense alert to an attempt to overpower him. The three buddies started forward but stopped in their tracks when he put the knife above Knife Holder's ear.

"You gonna talk or not?" Jerome let his voice amplify enough for the buddies to hear it.

"I ain't seen much, man. Just a couple guys going into the parking garage. They come in either a plain blue panel van or a black sedan. They'd go in and after a while they'd come out."

"What did they look like?"

"I didn't see much of them. One was a huge dude and the other looked tiny beside him."

"What about the van? Did it have any markings? Did you get the license plate?" As soon as he asked the last question Jerome realized its stupidity. Knife Holder wasn't a concerned citizen who jotted down the license plates of unfamiliar vehicles. He was a street punk who'd only notice things if they could be stolen and then sold, or set alight for his amusement.

"Have you been in the building?"

"In the past, yeah. Not for months now. Place stinks worse than a hobo's butt crack."

"Are you sure? I thought someone like you would want to check out what Big Guy and his buddy were up to."

"No way, man. The big guy is huge and the first time I saw

them go in, they had guns. Proper kick-ass shotguns. Not going up 'gainst that. No way, man."

"What's the best way for me to get in there?"

Knife Holder's eyes widened further. "You crazy to go in there with the size of that guy, but it's your life you'll be losing. The bottom part of the fire escape round the back fell down last year. The big guy is using the parking garage, so I'd say you either go in that way or through another door. The one at the far end is easy to pull open."

"Thanks." Jerome went to release Knife Holder, who squirmed to make it look as if he was trying to break free.

"Man. You gotta cut me. I need for them to see you cut me." The words came out as a furious whisper.

Jerome felt the knife in his hand tremble. The last thing he wanted to do was cut Knife Holder, but it was what the youth wanted, what he needed to retain his social standing. Jerome drew the blade across the top of Knife Holder's ear. Not far, just a half inch. Far enough to draw blood and leave a nasty scar, but not enough to remove part of his ear.

As he dropped the cash onto the ground by Knife Holder and stalked toward the building, Jerome's brain was trying to process what had just taken place. He'd used torture and Knife Holder had gone along with it. How messed up was Knife Holder's world when he would rather be cut than lose face with his peers?

Another part of his thinking was on the information Knife Holder had spilled. The big guy with the shotgun sounded awfully familiar to him. He sounded just like the guy whose barrel he'd stared down when Alicia was taken. As afraid as Jerome might be, he was also thrilled to have gotten further confirmation Alicia was inside. The comings and goings of Big Guy would be guards changing over.

Jerome padded forward. A part of him wanted to creep like a character in a cartoon, but he knew better. All the same he was watching his step, making sure that he neither kicked anything that would make a noise nor tripped himself. His eyes were constantly moving, scanning the ground and the building ahead of him. Likewise, his ears were alert to any sounds that may emanate from the building. His skin prickled with beads of sweat and he could feel his heart thumping inside his chest.

He'd never been so afraid, not even in the first milliseconds after he'd awoken to stare down the barrel of a shotgun. Jerome's fear wasn't for himself, but for Alicia. He was happy to risk his own life to save her, but he knew that if things ended badly for him, he was sure Alicia's abductors would dispose of her to protect themselves.

He got to the far door. As Knife Holder said, it had been boarded over, but the boarding was loose and the original door stood open.

Upon his arrival at the door, Jerome had a decision to make. Should he press on and enter the building in his search for Alicia, or should he wait for one of the abductors to exit, put his gun to their heads and then extract information from them?

Jerome liked the idea of getting more information. If he had to search the whole building, he would, but the longer he spent searching the greater the chance there was that he'd be spotted by the abductors. It was dark outside the building, so it stood to reason it would be darker inside. To make sure he could see where he was going he'd have to turn the flashlight on. The flashlight had different settings so he didn't have to worry too much about its beam being spotted, but he did worry. In an ideal world he'd know exactly where Alicia was being held and would be able to navigate his way there undetected.

This wasn't an ideal world. If it were, Alicia would never have been taken.

As attractive as the idea of capturing one of Alicia's abductors was, Jerome didn't want to waste hours waiting for one of them to come out. If Knife Holder had been telling the truth, there was also only a slim chance they'd use this door as he'd said they entered and exited via the parking garage.

Jerome had already dismissed the idea of sneaking into the building via the parking garage. That option held far too many dangers. The abductors could be present; he had no way of knowing where the door to access the building would be located, therefore he'd have to either walk right round the perimeter or scan it with his flashlight and risk discovery.

Instead of delaying any longer, Jerome pressed on. His flashlight was on its lowest setting and he kept it aimed at the ground to reduce the chances of its beam being spotted. The building smelled of decay. There was a stillness about the atmosphere inside the building that was unnerving and, even in normal circumstances, the decrepit space would be unwelcoming.

Jerome expected discovery at any moment. He didn't know what would come first, a warning shout, or a bullet slamming into his body. Still he pressed on, his flashlight picking out a set of footprints in the dust and fallen plaster. Ahead of him he heard the squeak of a startled rodent and the pitter patter of tiny feet scurrying. Cobwebs littered every internal corner with their silvery mesh.

The sight of them made Jerome's heart thump that little bit more. Alicia loved all of God's creatures, with the exception of spiders. They terrified her and, as frightened as she would be of her abductors, if where she was being held had anything like the number of webs he could see, it would be a purgatorial hellhole for her.

The footprints led him through the building. At times scuffed and at times clear and distinct, he could make out the pattern of the soles. He'd be the first to admit he was no tracker, but to his eye they were boot prints, made by new boots rather than the kind of worn sneakers Knife Holder and his buddies wore. In his mind he was picturing one of the abductors entering the building the way he had. One person seeking out a space to hide Alicia, a route to and from the parking garage so they could use its depths to hide their nefarious activity.

The footsteps may well lead him on a wild goose chase and they may lead him direct to Alicia. Jerome's expectation was that they'd take him down a meandering path as the lone abductor sought out an area or room that fit his criteria.

The lower parts of the building were damp and there was an overpowering smell of mold that pressed its way up Jerome's nostrils, forcing him to breathe through his mouth.

When the footsteps led him to a stairwell he felt a sense of relief at being able to escape the foul stench.

Jerome followed the footprints upwards. He counted three floors before the footprints exited the stairwell.

A scan round with his torch showed the footsteps returned and carried on upwards. Not knowing whether they'd found a better place to hold Alicia higher in the building, Jerome extinguished his torch and teased the exit door open to take a peek through. The door creaked its way open, the noise enough to bathe Jerome's entire body in sweat even though he knew it wasn't actually that loud.

Off at the far end of the corridor there was a room with an open door. The multicolored flickering of a TV and the muted sounds of canned laughter spilled through the doorway.

Indecision hit Jerome like a heavyweight champion's knockout punch. His eyes had picked out a series of footprints. Back and forth they went from the area where the TV flickered to another stairwell and on to a door that was closed. The closed door had three bolts securing it. All three possessed the pristine shininess of recent additions, and one had a heavy padlock securing it in place.

There was no doubt in Jerome's mind that he'd found where Alicia was being held. The TV was the guards' way of entertaining themselves. Alicia would be unable to break out without creating a massive amount of noise thereby alerting them of her escape.

It was the same for him. He might well be able to shoulder charge the door and break it down, or at the very least damage it enough so Alicia could squeeze out of her prison. But there was no way he could do such a thing without alerting the guard or guards watching the TV. He could do what they did in the movies and shoot the padlock, but that would bring the guards running, and they'd make damned sure they had their guns with them after hearing a gunshot.

Not knowing the number of guards presented a problem he had no way of solving. Knife Holder had said he'd seen two entering, but that didn't mean there weren't others already there. Two made sense, though, as they'd be able to back each other up and keep one another awake during their long night of sentry duty.

If it came to a fight Jerome would stand a chance with one guard provided it wasn't the huge shotgun wielder. Two would mean that he'd have to draw his gun and use it to bring them under control. That was fraught with dangers and having already seen the size of one of the abductors, Jerome didn't relish the idea of getting into any kind of physical battle with him. Not because he was afraid of getting hurt, but because he didn't want to fail Alicia and risk losing her.

The flip side of all his worries was that it was late at night and, to his way of thinking, the guards would be relaxed. No way would they be expecting anyone other than perhaps a hobo or a street punk like Knife Holder coming into the building. Therefore they'd be bored, and as such, relatively easy to surprise.

It sounded simple, but Jerome knew such a thing wouldn't be simple. It couldn't be simple in any way. Every choice he made was beset with alternative options that may work out better. He balanced the wisdom of having two free hands so he could better aim his gun against the idea that his flashlight on its brightest setting could be used to dazzle the guards and therefore hand him another advantage to join the element of surprise.

The roll of duct tape he had in his bag was transferred to a pocket for easy access, although he now wished he'd thought to buy several zip ties. According to the movies, duct tape was the staple go-to thing for binding prisoners, but in those same movies, the hero always found a way to escape the duct tape lashing them to whatever the baddies chose to immobilize them.

Jerome used touch alone to make sure the safety was off on the Shield and slipped through the doorway. Now it was a case of approaching the room where the TV was. Where the guards were.

His aim was simple. Creep up on the guards and jump out with his gun aimed directly at them.

Step by step he crossed the corridor until he was on the same side as the door where Alicia was held and the guards were. He wanted to tap on the door. A series of taps such as one, four, three would let Alicia know he was here, but he daren't do that in case Alicia called out his name or shouted for him to free her.

Jerome knew stealth was his best friend and that everything he did had to be silent. Had to be done soundlessly so that when he burst in on the guards, they would have had no time to prepare for him, no chance to pick up their weapons.

He was ten feet from the guards' room. Four paces or three strides. He inched forward, his grip on the gun in his right hand tightening and loosening in time with the pulsing of his heartbeat.

Every sense he possessed was on high alert. His ears picking up the sounds of the TV, his nose recognizing the wafts of fast food coming from the doorway while his eyes were scanning every possible surface for hazards, threats and anything he could use to his advantage.

Six feet. His mouth began to dry, yet perspiration slicked down his spine.

Four feet. Mouth arid, heart racing, and the slick of perspiration was now a river swollen by heavy rains.

Two feet. To Jerome even his breathing was trumpet loud. The theme tune to a popular show rattled out and he tensed. Maybe if the show was over the guards would patrol the area while the commercials were on. That meant they could be on their feet, guns in hand. The sound of an upholstery spring popping was followed by a man speaking.

"Man, I love that show."

The voice was deep and earthy, sounding as if it was drawn from the bowels of the earth. It could only mean one thing: Big Guy was here.

Jerome had to act right away. There could be no time wasted screwing up his nerve, no time spent trying to ascertain where in the room they might be, or how many of them there were. The time for procrastination had gone. Now was the time for action.

Jerome spun into the doorway, his gun drawn and his torch beaming out a blinding light as he shouted instructions at them.

Alicia sprang to her feet and ran to the door. The shouting she'd just heard was in Jerome's voice.

She banged the heels of her fists on the door. "Jerome. I'm here."

There was no answer. No response to tell her he was coming. Just silence.

When she heard his voice again, it was barking orders so she pressed her ear to the door to listen to what was happening.

As she listened she felt a compelling urge to yell out again. To encourage and inform Jerome of her location. It was an urge she forced herself to stifle. Jerome was up against a minimum of two opponents. He'd need to focus. To deal with the task at hand and not be distracted by her.

Her ears strained to hear what was being said as she prayed she wouldn't hear the boom of gunfire.

———

Jerome kept his gun as level as he could, but in his inexperienced hand the heavy Shield skittered around rather than staying firmly locked on a target. Big Guy was on his feet, a carton of fast food in his hands. As he made such an unmissable target, it was Big Guy he pointed the Shield at.

Another man lay sprawled in a ratty Barcalounger. He was half the size of Big Guy and at Jerome's sudden intrusion into the room his hands had shot skywards.

The yell from Alicia was the sweetest sound he'd ever heard, but he paid it no heed. A primal part of him knew she'd have to wait. That until he'd properly dealt with his two foes, there could be no lapse in focus or concentration.

Jerome aimed the flashlight so it dazzled Big Guy. "Don't move. Don't even think about moving."

Both men stayed where they were. The situation couldn't last, Jerome knew that. Big Guy represented the greatest threat, but that didn't mean the other guy wasn't dangerous.

"Calm down, Jerome. Don't do anything stupid. There's no need for you to worry, we're not going to do anything that will make you pull your trigger."

Jerome took a step to his left so he could see both men. The words from Big Guy could be a distraction while the guy on the Barcalounger drew a gun.

"Do you see this GoPro on my head? It's uploading to YouTube. I've scheduled posts on Facebook and Twitter to share links to the footage. Naturally I've tagged every law enforcement agency I can think of. Those links can only be stopped by the passworded cell phone in my pocket, so if either of you is thinking of pulling a gun and shooting me, you'll be recorded committing a homicidal act."

Jerome flicked the flashlight toward the Barcalounger so he could keep a better watch over the second guy.

The beam of light displayed a face he knew. A face he hadn't expected to see here. As soon as the light hit his face, the man's eyes screwed shut, but not before Jerome registered the man's shame and fear.

The man on the Barcalounger was Lenny Zeller. The CEO of Beck Accounting. His big boss. On some levels it made sense

Zeller was involved. He'd be monitoring the accounts and in all probability would have known about the money being diverted to the Utah account. What didn't make sense was that he'd called Jerome into his office to reprimand him for his searches. Unless it had all been an elaborate double bluff. That was a problem for another time. As was how Zeller must have left the office early for him to have been one of the guys Knife Holder had seen entering this building. Jerome's hands were full with keeping Big Guy and Zeller under his control; the questions ricocheting around his head could be answered at a later time.

Jerome tucked the flashlight under his gun arm and pulled the duct tape from his pocket. As his hand disappeared into his pocket he heard the clatter of the fast food cartons being dropped by Big Guy. He tossed the duct tape forward and snatched the flashlight back into his hand.

Big Guy's left hand was empty, but his right had disappeared behind his back.

"Freeze."

The word might be a cliché, but it had the desired effect. "Nice and slow, let me see your right hand. Be under no illusion, if your hand appears holding a weapon, I will shoot you before you can get the weapon anywhere near me."

"Don't shoot. I don't got a weapon." The wording of Big Guy's reply triggered a thought within Jerome. The use of "don't" instead of "haven't" was very much a Boston thing and he knew a large contingent of the management of Beck Construction were descended from Boston Irish. That would explain how the abductors knew this building was vacant. Jerome would also bet that it must be Big Guy who'd made the typos in the messages he'd been sent earlier, as there was no way the pedantic Zeller could have been here at the time, and he knew Zeller well enough to know the man was the kind of grammar Nazi who never missed the opportunity to correct other people's mistakes.

Jerome bobbed the Shield at Zeller then returned it to Big Guy. "Which of you has the keys to the room where Alicia is?"

The men exchanged a look. Zeller swallowed hard, and Big Guy gave a rapid series of blinks. Sweat beads loitered on both of their faces.

"I do." It was Zeller who spoke. His voice full of resignation and fear.

"Okay." Jerome bobbed the flashlight so it picked out the roll of duct tape and then focused on Big Guy. "Use that to bind him up. You"—Jerome pointed the flashlight so its beam was aimed right into Big Guy's eyes—"Hold your arms in front of you and put your left hand on top of your right elbow and your right hand under your left elbow."

Zeller wound strip after strip of tape over Big Guy's hands, wrists and forearms, then looked at Jerome for his next instruction.

"Wrap some more across both his elbows and then lash his legs together."

Jerome watched as Zeller applied the tape. By Jerome's reckoning there was no way Big Guy would be able to wriggle free of the bindings anytime soon. And all Jerome needed was ten minutes to free Alicia and leave the building.

"Put the keys on the table then put your hands on your head. Fingers laced together and face the wall."

"Please, Jerome, you must believe me, we never had any intention of harming either you or Alicia. This whole scheme is about bringing Beck Holdings to account for the way they've covered up all the sexual abuse cases levelled against members of the Beck family and others who sit on the board."

"That's bull and you know it, *Lenny*. There are other ways of looking after the victims, and you're not going to pass this off as being altruistic, because if that were your only goal, all of the money would be going to the victims. It's not; a sizable percentage of it is going to you guys, therefore you're using the plight of those women as a smokescreen to get me to steal the money. Maybe you're kidding yourself that you're helping them as a way to manage your guilt for what you're doing to me and Alicia, but the simple truth is you're helping yourselves far more."

As Jerome approached Zeller, his boss turned to reply to him.

Jerome jabbed the flashlight upwards and gave a last-minute flick to crash it into Zeller's chin.

Zeller's knees went weak, but he didn't go down so Jerome slammed the butt of the flashlight into Zeller's kidney.

With a gasp Zeller slumped to the floor. Two minutes later, Jerome had Zeller's hands bound and several wide wraps of tape around his ankles.

A quick search revealed a pistol holstered against the small of Big Guy's back and a pair of shotguns lying beside the Barcalounger.

Jerome lifted all the guns and the keys, then backed out of the room. "Don't worry, I'll send the cops to rescue you."

As he padded toward the room where Alicia was imprisoned, Jerome found a cubbyhole he used to stash the guns he'd taken from the abductors. He didn't want to lug them along with him, but neither did he want to leave them anywhere obvious in case Zeller and Big Guy managed to slip free of their bindings.

"Alicia. I'm coming, darling." Jerome's shout echoed along the hallways, but for the first time since entering the building, he was happy to make a noise.

———

Alicia's heart did a double backflip upon hearing Jerome's yell. He'd triumphed against the kidnappers. He was coming to get her.

She resumed her banging on the door and did what she could to quell the tears of intense relief that were flooding down her cheeks.

"In here."

"I'm coming."

Alicia stepped back from the door so it didn't hit her. She could hear the now-familiar sound of a key being fed into a padlock and, while she knew it was only seconds, it felt like hours passed between the sounds of the padlock being unlocked and the door beginning to open.

Jerome barged through the door, his eyes sweeping past Alicia in case she was being held at gunpoint by a third abductor.

She wasn't. She was alone.

A thin white sheet was draped over her shoulders and her hair was everywhere, but she was upright. Alicia's eyes blazed with happiness and grit and determination. She was ready to get out of here, and he could only imagine the mental torment she'd undergone while held captive with only spiders and her thoughts for company.

To Alicia, Jerome appearing was the most wonderful thing ever. He looked so handsome, so dashing when he burst into the room carrying a gun. This was a side of her husband Alicia had never seen before. Nor even imagined he possessed.

Jerome was no Vin Diesel. He loathed guns and yet here he was, saving her with a pistol in one hand and a heavy flashlight in the other.

His embrace was fierce and beneath the determination in his eyes she could see him examining her for damage. She returned his hug with equal ferocity even though she could feel him guiding her toward the door. Her joy at seeing him sent tears cascading down her cheeks.

"Come on. We need to get out of here fast."

"Agreed."

"I'll lead, hold on to my shirt as I want my hands for the flashlight and..." Jerome's voice took on a sheepish tone. "And the gun."

As much as he was issuing direct commands, Alicia knew the real Jerome was also present. That showed in his hesitation at mentioning the gun. "Good plan. Now let's get the hell out of here."

Alicia took a handful of Jerome's shirt and padded after him, her bare feet slapping on the floor. Lord alone knew what she was stepping in, but she didn't care. Anything that put distance between her and that hateful room was a bonus, and her feet could always be washed when she got home.

Jerome was setting a fast pace as he led her down a stairwell. For the most part he stuck to the center so she could hold the rail with her free hand, but there were times he'd slow and guide her around an obstacle. Bless him, he had the sense to shine the flashlight in a way that meant she could also see her footing and avoid tripping as they moved from stairs to landing.

When they neared the bottom Jerome slowed to a near halt. "Easy. I'm not sure what's ahead, this is a different stairwell than the one I came up. Don't worry, though, there's lots of footprints in here so I'm sure it's the one the abductors are using."

How like Jerome to give her that reassurance. As soon as he'd said he wasn't familiar with this route, she'd worried that he was leading her to a dead end. That at any moment the kidnappers would appear and capture them both.

"Where are the kidnappers?" Alicia blanched as she recalled Jerome was carrying a gun. *Had he shot them? Was her husband a murderer? No, he couldn't have shot them. She'd heard no gunfire.*

"They were in a room along from yours. I tied them up and took their guns away."

"So we're safe. I'm going to be free?"

"We're safe as long as no more appear. There were two up there. How many have you seen?"

"Since I got here. Just two."

"You'll never guess who one of them was."

Before she could ask, Alicia heard the clatter of footsteps above them. She could see from the way Jerome had tensed he'd heard them too. He stuffed the gun into the waistband of his pants and grabbed her hand.

"Quick."

Jerome burst through a wide door and they exited the stairwell into a large parking garage. A large sedan was parked beside the door, but it was otherwise empty.

Straight ahead, moonlight dappled the ground of the parking garage's entrance and exit. Instead of trailing after Jerome, she released his hand and lengthened her stride. She'd always outpaced him on their joint runs and now the desire to breathe fresh, clean air was driving her forward.

Alicia was ten paces from the moonlight when she felt something bite into her left foot. Unable to put weight back onto the foot she tried hopping, but her momentum was too great and she sprawled to the ground. Jerome was upon her in an instant, his flashlight tossed aside as he scooped her up.

"Sorry, I stepped on some glass or something." She wound her arms around his neck to try and ease the burden of her weight in his arms.

"No problem."

Jerome's gasps suggested otherwise. He was panting hard, his face set solid in grim determination. Sweat beaded his forehead and face, yet his pace never faltered as he pounded forward.

She glanced over Jerome's shoulder. A figure passed through the beam of the dropped flashlight.

"Faster, darling. One of them is after us."

"Keep me posted. Look for guns. Can you stand?"

"My other foot is good."

The conversation was foreign to Alicia. Doubly so as she was having it with Jerome. They talked about work and future aspirations. They discussed movies and friends and books and TV shows. Not people pursuing them. Not potential gunfights.

"I can see no gun, but he's closing the gap."

"How close?"

"Maybe thirty paces."

Jerome's breath was ragged as he thundered forward. His sentences a rapid jumble of minimalist words. "Car round next corner. Throw you in back. Can't risk gunfight."

Alicia squinted backwards at the pursing man. "He's in shadow but his hands are empty. I'm sure of it. Oh no."

"Gun?"

"No gun, but the sedan from the parking garage is coming our way."

No answer came. Instead Jerome somehow lengthened his stride to put on a final burst of speed. The way the car was parked, he changed tack and instead of throwing her in the back as stated, he dumped her into the front seat.

Alicia had to scramble upright as he dashed round and launched himself behind the wheel. The backpack he wore was shrugged off and tossed into the rear seat. Alicia's injured foot scraped against something unyielding, causing her to yelp as the agony in her sole doubled.

As Jerome gunned the hatchback's engine, the sedan bulleted round the corner and shot past them before realizing its mistake and screeching to a halt that left it slewed across the road. Big Guy's frame hunkered over the wheel while Zeller was in the passenger side.

Both vehicles started moving at the same time.

43

The little hatchback's engine purred rather than roared no matter how savagely Jerome stamped on the gas. Its power no match for the sedan pursuing them, but it was nimbler in the corners, the larger, heavier sedan either fishtailing and bleeding off speed if it took a corner too fast, or having to slow down and then accelerate again on the tighter turns.

"Hit the GPS, see if you can reverse the directions so I can get us back to the train station."

"How did you find me? Who were those guys?"

"I'll explain everything later, but the smaller one is Lenny Zeller."

"Your boss? The CEO of Beck Accounting?"

"Yep."

"Damn. I should have recognized his voice."

"Don't sweat that now. Focus on the GPS."

Getting to a busy area was paramount for Jerome. It would mean their pursuers would be much more reluctant to try anything nefarious. Crowds offered safety, and while it was unlikely there would be crowds at this time of night, there were always people entering or exiting stations.

Jerome got the desperation Zeller and Big Guy would feel.

The GoPro camera had worked wonders in keeping them compliant, but they would have realized its recording would be used against them in a courtroom. For them to retain their freedom, they'd have to make damned sure the video was removed from YouTube and that the posts on his social media feeds were never published.

Beside him Alicia was fumbling with the GPS, but the road wasn't smooth and neither was his driving. Her fingers bumbled against the screen, and he heard her mutter gentle curses beneath her breath.

"Arrgh."

"What's up?" Jerome tore his eyes from the road ahead to look at his wife.

"My foot. I just jarred it, that's all. Don't worry about me, just get us somewhere safe."

As Jerome refocused on the road he could see Alicia reaching a hand down toward the foot she had propped on top of the opposing ankle.

A glance at the rearview mirror made his heart sink. The sedan was behind him and coming on strong. Its headlights were on full beam and he had to twist the rearview mirror askew so he wasn't blinded by them.

"Ow, ow, ow." Alicia reared back in her seat. A bloody piece of glass between her thumb and forefinger.

Jerome hooked a left, the little hatchback missing the curb by inches. "You okay?"

"I will be now I can't keep banging that piece of glass into my foot."

Jerome jerked his eyes away from his wife again. What he saw in front of him plunged his heart into despair. The road ahead was straight. Arrow straight with no obstacles. No curves and no intersections where the hatchback's superior handling was an advantage over the sedan's greater power.

The sedan rounded the corner after them, its driver having learned the optimum balance between speed and safety.

Jerome knew their escape attempt was a double-edged sword for their pursuers. The closer he and Alicia got to safety, the more desperate Zeller and his partner's efforts to stop them would become.

The sedan was gaining and with nowhere to turn, it was a straightforward contest of speed. A contest the hatchback was never going to win.

The rearview mirror started to fill with the hunkering sedan. Its lights ablaze as it edged closer and closer. In another few yards it would get the added benefit of being in the hatchback's slipstream.

Jerome didn't know what the abductors planned to do when they caught up with the hatchback, but he guessed it'd be one of two things. Either shooting at them, or trying to ram them off the road. Perhaps both if the first idea they tried didn't work.

To try and make things harder for the abductors, Jerome had to keep moving. Had to keep one step ahead of them. To do that he needed Alicia's help if his wild idea was to stand even the merest chance of succeeding.

"Alicia. Lower yourself as much as you can without losing sight of the road ahead. I need you to be my eyes. You're looking for a side road, an intersection, anything that lets us turn off this road before they catch up with us. Just tell me left or right. Nothing else."

"On it."

Alicia's voice was strained, but in the way a tightrope only works when tension is applied, Jerome trusted his wife to come through for them. By giving her the task of watching for a turn, he could focus his full attention on the sedan and keeping the hatchback on the road.

Behind them the sedan moved closer still. Its headlights now obscured below the solid part of the car. No arms poked from windows holding guns, which was a positive thing, but for all he knew they could be planning to drive alongside and then either shoot them, or their tires.

If that happened Jerome would return fire, but he didn't fancy his odds of scoring a telling hit. To fire a gun for the first time when driving at high speed in a built-up area couldn't possibly lead to any degree of accuracy. If they came up on the passenger side he'd have to scrap the idea as no way was he going to risk shooting Alicia by accident.

As the sedan neared, Jerome drifted across the road until his wheels were close to the curb. He wanted to see what their tactics were. Whether they'd pull in behind to ram them or whether they'd draw alongside so they could shoot.

Alicia's voice cut through his intense concentration. "Right."

Jerome switched tactics as the sedan pulled into position on their rear fender. The larger heavier car must now be mere inches from making contact, but his swing of the wheel carried the little hatchback across the sedan's bow and onto the wrong side of the road.

Alicia had said there was a road to the right, so he'd pulled across to the left to give himself the best racing line. He'd never driven a real car in a race, but he'd spent many hours on his PlayStation and enjoyed various driving games. *Nascar Heat* being a particular favorite.

Jerome's eyes scoured the road ahead, but instead of Alicia's road being on the right, it was on the left.

In theory he could pull back across the road and still make the turn, but there wasn't enough distance left to do so without having to bleed off a large amount of the hatchback's speed. Rather than pull behind them, the sedan had stayed central to the road and had crept forward far enough to prevent him from taking a proper racing line. Therefore he'd have to slow even further. Jerome pressed the gas pedal so hard he felt his leg tense from the effort. Taking a turn wasn't an option, so the best he could do was try to outsmart Big Guy.

"Dammit, Jerome, did I get them mixed again?" Alicia knew her flaws. She also knew about racing lines as she'd often play *Nascar Heat* against him.

"You sure did." Jerome tried to keep his tone light, but he could hear the tightness in his voice. The unspoken finger of blame he was pointing at Alicia for her mistake. He'd never really let that finger be pointed, never speak a word of criticism to her as he knew she'd give herself a hard enough time about it. The blame was as much, if not more, on him anyway. He *knew* his wife, knew that left and right were foreign concepts to her and despite that knowledge, he'd instructed her to use left and right.

The sedan drew level with them, Zeller's face hard and uncompromising in the passenger seat.

The road ahead had changed. Instead of swathes of grass between road and sidewalk, there were now trees interspersed with areas cut out for parking on one side and a rough stone wall on the other.

"A turn ahead. My side."

"Got it."

That was his wife, that was Alicia. She'd put her mistake behind her and moved on and devised her own system of communication, one neither of them could get wrong.

Jerome stamped on the brakes until the pedal juddered back at his foot. He kept the pressure there—the ABS could protest all it wanted—and spun the wheel hard over. The little hatchback spun a one-eighty as the sedan slid past, its nose dipping as Big Guy tried to match their emergency stop.

The aroma of tortured rubber filled the hatchback as Jerome's foot returned to the gas pedal.

Behind them he could see the sedan had copied their move, but Big Guy hadn't been able to pull as neat a one-eighty as he had. With the tires spinning, Jerome hauled over on the wheel, reversed his compass heading and shot past the narrow gap between the wall and the sedan's rear fender.

The size of the sedan meant it was too large to ape the move Jerome had performed with the hatchback, and the extra seconds it needed to back up gave Jerome the chance to once again put some critical distance between the two vehicles.

He took the turn at speed but was again disheartened to see a long road stretch ahead of him.

"Have you got your cell?"

Alicia's words shook Jerome. It was a simple question. Of course he had his cell. The burner was in his backpack and his regular cell was in the trunk with his other personal possessions.

"There's one in the backpack." He jerked a thumb over his shoulder. "I tossed it in back."

Alicia squirmed round in her seat and tried to reach the backpack. "I can't reach it. It's gone under my seat."

"Can you climb in back and get it?" As soon as he asked the question Jerome knew it wasn't possible. The little rental car was too small for Alicia to slip between the front seats, and therefore the only way she'd get into the back would be to recline the seat she was sitting on, thereby blocking her from getting hold of the backpack.

Alicia began reclining the seat. When it was halfway down she turned to clamber over it.

A shrill scream escaped her lips.

Before he'd even had a chance to question the reason for her scream, Jerome felt the hatchback jolt. The big guy driving the sedan had given up playing nice and just tailing them.

Jerome's knuckles turned white as he corrected the hatchback's errant path and mashed his foot to the floor. In the rearview mirror the sedan was coming again, looming larger with every second.

"I've got the backpack. Where is the cell?"

"In the main part." Jerome wanted to tell Alicia to hurry, but he didn't want her loose in the back seat for the next impact. If they were forced off the road she'd pinball around the rear seats taking punishment from every surface she collided with. "Quick, get back in front and put your safety belt on."

Alicia's feet led her scramble into position. But before she could return the seat to its original position or put the safety belt on, there was another crashing thud as Big Guy rammed the sedan into their rear a second time.

This time he'd changed his tactics. Instead of a square hit, he'd positioned the sedan so half of its front fender collided with half of the hatchback's rear one.

The resulting effect was a lot harder to counteract. The first impact had driven them forward with only a slight lateral force. This second blow carried far more lateral press and as such the hatchback veered across the road.

Jerome managed to correct the new direction enough to not have a devastating crash, but he still left a portion of the hatchback's paintwork smeared along the side of a parked SUV.

A glance in the rearview mirror showed the sedan in a similar slide that Big Guy managed to straighten.

"My side, maybe a hundred yards."

Alicia's update was as welcome as hearing the click of her safety belt. It would be fifty-fifty as to whether they made it to the turn before another impact, but with luck the turn would lead them to an area where there would be enough turns to allow them to either evade the sedan or for Alicia to call the cops.

"What's the code for this cell?"

"The date we met." Jerome's gaze jumped to the rearview mirror. The sedan was maybe ten feet behind them. "Brace yourself. There's going to be another hit."

Jerome held the hatchback at maximum speed as they approached the turn. At the last second he slammed on the brakes. He was trying to cause as much damage as possible to the sedan. The rear of the hatchback held no vital parts that would suffer from the collision, but a powerful enough impact would perhaps puncture the sedan's radiator, or trigger the sensors that controlled the airbags.

Alicia was typing the numbers into the cell when the sedan thumped into them. Despite his warning, Jerome saw the cell fly from her grasp at the thudding impact. The hatchback squirmed but not uncontrollably. He got it back under control in time to whip the wheel over and make the turn.

The hatchback hadn't escaped the collision unscathed. Something at the rear wasn't right and Jerome suspected that part of the car's bodywork was rubbing against a wheel as the hatchback wanted to veer to the left all the time. Ahead of them the road ran to a sandy slipway leading down to the beach between a raised bank on either side. A crossroad ran each way, so Jerome prepared to make a left turn as the hatchback was pulling that way.

He'd begun easing into the turn when a fourth shunt from the sedan succeeded where the previous three had failed. The hatchback rocketed sideways and Jerome's efforts to control the car saw him forced to steer it at the raised bank.

No matter what he tried, Jerome couldn't halt the hatchback before it crested the bank and rolled down the other side.

44

When the hatchback came to rest, it was lying on its roof. Through the missing windshield Jerome could see a weird world where the moon appeared to be glittering below the ocean. Both he and Alicia hung upside down, held in place by their safety belts. The air was thick with talcum powder from the airbags and the briny smell of the ocean. Worst of all there was the sharp tang of gasoline.

Jerome knew he had to act, had to get them out of the car and away from the abductors, but his mind was foggy and there was a crushing pain on the side of his head where he'd smacked it against the door frame. Beside him Alicia was emitting low moans and cradling her left arm against her body.

Jerome fumbled for the keys and turned the engine off. His next move was to reach for the catch that released his safety belt. The drop to the hatchback's roof was only a few inches, but it was enough to increase the grogginess of his thoughts. As best he could, he ignored the wooliness and wriggled into a position where he could help Alicia.

"Owwww. My arm, Jerome. I think it's broken."

"It's okay, darling. We'll get it seen to real soon. But for now, you're going to have to release your belt. I'll hold you as best as I can to break your fall. When I say so, release your safety belt."

Jerome rotated and maneuvered himself until he was confident he was able to give Alicia the softest drop possible.

"Now."

Alicia's jaw clenched tight as her hand reached for the catch. She dropped, but Jerome was able to break her fall and lower her as gently as possible. It was a struggle to get her broken arm free of the safety belt, but Alicia was stoic and never let out so much as a whimper.

With them both kneeling on the roof of the car, their bodies were bent forward. A look around him showed Jerome the doors were dented. He tried to push his open but it was immovable. He recalled the missing windshield and looked to the front of the car.

There was a two-foot high space between the sand and the hood of the car. It was tight but there was enough room to allow them passage.

Jerome began to crawl out; he had to roll onto his back and slide between the steering wheel and the hatchback's roof, as Alicia was on her side of the car and with her broken arm, she'd need his help to get out.

As desperate as the situation was, Jerome gave no thought to the abductors and where they may be. He'd worry about them once he and Alicia were free of the car.

The gasoline tang grew stronger with each passing second, and the idea of he and Alicia dying in a fireball spurred his every movement. He could picture the explosion in his mind. The gasoline spill forming a river that carried fumes to a heat source or a part of the engine that had shorting electrical circuits from the crash. There would be a huge *whoomp* as a fireball engulfed the entire car. He and Alicia would be scorched by the flames, their agonized screams drawing the fire deep into their throats and lungs. Their throats would blister and their limbs contort as the fire ate at them. When discovered, it would only be their dental records that made them identifiable.

As Jerome wriggled his way out of the windshield, he felt something catch at his waistband. He squirmed and writhed until the obstruction freed itself. Once free, he immediately spun around and reached back in for Alicia.

"Come out on your back. Lead with your good arm and I'll help you."

"Okay." Alicia's voice was tight with pain, but Jerome heard her innate strength underpinning her tone as he encircled her wrist with his fingers.

Inch by torturous inch Jerome helped Alicia drag herself through the opening where the windshield had once been. With only one working arm she was unable to offer much help, but once they got to a position where she could put her good foot on the passenger seat she was able to add some very welcome thrust.

Jerome's back was tight against the hood as he drew Alicia back, and as soon as he could, he crawled out from under the upside-down hood and reached back in for Alicia's good arm.

As he looked down at Alicia's face, Jerome could see her eyes were pressed tight and the skin around her jaw seemed as if it was painted onto her facial bones. No sound came from her lips. No moans. No complaints.

Jerome drew Alicia free and bent to pick her up. As he lowered himself he saw movement to his left. He turned his head for a better look. Zeller and Big Guy were coming his way.

His first thought was that they should be running at him. That they ought to barrel into him and capture him.

They weren't. They were holding back. To Jerome's way of thinking that could only mean one thing. They weren't armed. They had no weapons to speak of, although he guessed one of them might have a small knife that they'd used to free themselves of their bindings.

Their hanging back surprised him until he realized that as far as they knew, he had a pistol. The mighty Shield he'd used to intimidate them back at the building.

Jerome's hand flew behind his back to reach for the Shield. It wasn't there. It was at this point Jerome realized two things. First, it had been the Shield that had snagged and come loose as he'd been escaping the hatchback. Second, there was no way he could get back into the hatchback, find the gun and retrieve it before the two men were upon him.

Even if he did achieve that impossible task, he wouldn't achieve anything. The threat of Big Guy breaking Alicia's neck was one he couldn't fight against, and with her broken arm, Alicia was already vulnerable.

Not being able to get the weapon, Jerome had only one option left. To fight. Two on one wasn't good odds. They were doubly bad when one of the two was as huge as Big Guy.

Jerome never faltered, never hesitated as he charged forward. Alicia was at risk and he was prepared to die protecting her.

Jerome knew he wasn't likely to win this fight, but that didn't mean he wasn't going to give it everything he had. Other than the skirmish with Knife Holder and the grade school scuffle, Jerome had no experience of fistfights, but that wasn't going to hold him back. What he lacked in experience, he'd more than make up for in his desperation to survive.

Big Guy offered the greatest threat. That was logical and basic common sense. On some levels it may be wise to tackle Zeller first, but that wasn't Jerome's thinking. Even if he disposed of Zeller with a single punch, taking Big Guy on without weighting the fight to his advantage would be a Herculean task.

Jerome directed his charge at Zeller. Curses flying from his mouth, each one aimed at his boss. Big Guy stepped aside, leaving a clear space between himself and Zeller. Jerome carried on at Zeller, until the last second when he sidestepped and drove his shoulder into Big Guy's midriff.

Back in college Jerome had abandoned football in favor of wrestling. One-on-one was his preference; there were no team mates to either let down or be let down by. Wrestling was a pure test of individual skill. Jerome hadn't forgotten what he'd learned on the football fields though; he'd been tackled and had made tackles. It was there he'd learned no matter how large and powerful your opponent, if you fully committed to hitting them with everything you had, the opponent would always come off second best.

Big Guy couldn't withstand the sudden impact. He was rocked backwards and because Jerome kept his legs pumping, Big Guy couldn't backpedal fast enough, his feet catching on the loose sand until he went tumbling backwards. Jerome stayed with him. Making sure his shoulder drove even further into Big Guy's gut when he flumped onto the sand.

———

Upon seeing her husband's reckless charge at the two kidnappers, something snapped inside Alicia. Gone was her placid, pacifist nature. Jerome didn't stand a chance against two opponents, especially when one was as huge as Big Guy. She had to do whatever she could to help him.

The pain from the sand grinding into the gash in her foot was ignored, as was the agony of her broken arm. All thoughts of self-preservation were eclipsed by a desire to help Jerome, to balance the uneven scales of the battle he was charging into.

Jerome had taken on Big Guy so Alicia focused her attack on the other one. She'd met Lenny Zeller at a function or two but didn't know him beyond his professional reputation. Right now, that counted for nothing. He was winding up a punch at Jerome and that couldn't be allowed to go unpunished.

Alicia hurled herself at Zeller, her one good arm swinging hard for his head. Zeller didn't see her coming so she managed to land a solid blow, although it only rocked him rather than felling him as she intended.

A scream of rage flew from Alicia's mouth as she went to repeat the punch. Zeller reacted by raising a boot and planting it in her stomach. Alicia was already off balance from her wild punch, and the way she was subconsciously favoring her uninjured arm and foot, she had no way to resist as Zeller straightened his leg and thrust her backwards.

Alicia's bare feet caught on the sand and she went down in an untidy heap, her broken arm flying above her head and sending waves of nausea-inducing pain throughout her entire arm.

Even as she emitted agonized howls, she was on the move, preparing to stand and rejoin the fray. No way could she let Jerome down. No way could she leave him to fight both men at once.

———

Anger, the release of terror and a desperation to survive and protect Alicia were the fuel Jerome used to power his attack. He scrambled up so he was sitting on Big Guy's chest and pummeled blow after blow at his head. Big Guy wound his arms over his face, so Jerome changed tactics and aimed a punch at Big Guy's windpipe. Rather than get a full hit, his fist was deflected by a monstrous forearm.

Something hard slammed into the side of Jerome's head. Zeller had joined in and was winding up for another blow. As much as Zeller's first punch had rocked him and returned the grogginess Jerome felt after the crash, he ignored Zeller and concentrated on Big Guy. He had to put him out of commission before worrying about Zeller. One-on-one, fighting Zeller held no fears for him, but if Big Guy was allowed back onto his feet, Jerome knew he stood little chance against him.

Another blow rocked Jerome's head sideways as a scream erupted to his right. From nowhere Alicia had joined the fray. Her one good arm reaching out nails first for Zeller's face and then a bare foot rising and arrowing toward Zeller's crotch.

Jerome drew his arm back, intent on delivering a mighty blow that would crush Big Guy's windpipe, or at the very least leave him gasping for breath long enough that he could deal with Zeller and then escape with Alicia.

As Jerome thrust his fist downwards Big Guy started to fight back. Instead of using his mighty forearms to protect his head, he thrust them forward. Jerome's punch was caught and deflected on to Big Guy's sternum as the powerful thrust continued.

"Run, Alicia. Get away from here." If Alicia could flee, Zeller and Big Guy would have no leverage over him. They wouldn't be able to control him and as soon as they realized Alicia was gone, they'd have no reason to continue with him as she'd surely raise the alarm.

Big Guy's arms flicked straight and both of his massive fists crashed into Jerome's face.

———

Alicia heard Jerome's words but she had no intention of heeding them. No way could she abandon him to face the two kidnappers alone. Instead of fleeing, Alicia delivered another kick toward Zeller's groin. He deflected the kick onto his hip and reached for her foot.

Zeller's fingers grasped Alicia's toes, but she was able to twist her foot free before he could begin to control her movements. Her good arm lanced forward, the knuckles of her fist white as they arrowed toward Zeller's chin.

He leaned back, evading the blow and leaving Alicia's momentum to carry her arm past him. Alicia now had her back to him, so she thrust the elbow of her broken arm back at Zeller.

It thudded into his ribcage, the impact juddering back through her arm and turning the dial of her agony up to eleven. She bit down on the pain and prepared to repeat the move when a strong arm wound itself around her throat and pulled her backwards.

Alicia had no room to wind up a blow, so she reached back with her good arm and tried to claw at Zeller's eyes. Behind her she felt Zeller twisting so his hip was against the base of her spine. Alicia's back arched to the point where her feet were only brushing

the sand. Every backward elbow she threw either missed altogether or did no more than scuff off Zeller's torso.

At the side of her head, Alicia felt movement. A glance that
way sent icy shivers throughout her entire being. Zeller was
fumbling to open a clasp knife. Desperation flooded her body as
she tried to knock the knife from Zeller's grip and simultaneously
writhe herself free.

———

Jerome's world went sideways. He could feel the damage that had
been done to his face. The loose teeth, the burst lips and nose. His
eyes were streaming tears but worst of all his thinking had slowed.
He tried to throw a series of punches at Big Guy, but his arms felt
leaden and uncooperative.

Even as he struggled to order his thoughts, he was praying
Alicia had followed his instruction to flee and had gotten herself
away.

Another hammer blow crashed into his face and he reeled back
and levered himself into a standing position. Big Guy rolled onto
his front and rose to hands and knees. With the last of his comprehension, Jerome buried his right foot into his opponent's groin.

Big Guy yowled in pain, a deep sonorous sound akin to the
howling of an injured bear. To Jerome's ears it was the world's
sweetest sound. He repeated the blow twice more, and then added
a third for good measure. Each kick he delivered exploded a ball of
agony in his toes as they collided with the steel toecap, but he knew
Big Guy would have it far worse.

Big Guy was rolling around, his hands clasping his injured
crotch so Jerome turned his attention to Zeller. When he sought
out Zeller in the moonlight, his shoulders drooped in defeat.

Zeller's left hand held Alicia's forehead. Her back was arched
over his hip and her neck was stretched, exposing her throat.
Zeller's right hand held a small Swiss Army knife, its blade pressed
against Alicia's throat with enough force to dimple the skin.

A hammer blow thudded into Jerome's right kidney and he felt his knees giving way.

Alicia watched as Big Guy wound up another blow. Her heart was breaking for Jerome who was balanced on his knees and fighting to stay conscious.

"Stop!"

The yell from Zeller was deafening to Alicia as his mouth was by her ear, but the only thing that mattered to Alicia was that Big Guy obeyed the instruction and didn't strike Jerome a second time.

"Why?"

"The GoPro. We need to get that and his cell and stop it getting posted online."

"That was a bluff. We don't got nothing to worry about."

Zeller's voice dripped scorn the way hot toast drips butter. "You want to take the chance? I sure as hell don't. Check his pockets for the cell."

Big Guy cuffed Jerome's head, knocking him to the sand and as Jerome flopped and flailed listlessly, Big Guy began patting Jerome's pockets. When he didn't find what he was looking for he drew back a monstrous fist. "Goddammed lying—'

"Wait. His cell is in the car. I got it from his backpack."

Alicia's words weren't enough to stop Big Guy from throwing the punch he had cocked. His fist scudded into Jerome's unprotected face with a thud that sickened Alicia.

As Jerome lay in a heap, Big Guy rose to his feet and wandered off toward the car.

There was nothing Alicia could do but watch as Big Guy peered into the car and then knocked out a side window with a powerful elbow jab. His arm snaked through the shattered glass and came back holding the cell.

Zeller's grip on Alicia tightened as Big Guy returned.

"Damn thing is locked with a passcode." He pointed at Alicia then took up position beside the still-prone Jerome. A boot was lifted from the sand and planted onto Jerome's throat. "What's the code, buddy boy?"

Jerome's hand patted at Big Guy's foot with no effect.

Alicia willed Jerome to give up the passcode rather than suffer any more, but he was tight-lipped.

When Big Guy tensed then leaned more weight onto the foot covering Jerome's throat, it became too much for Alicia to take and she blurted out the phone's code: the date they'd met.

Big Guy dropped a viperous smile her way when the code allowed him access to the cell. A minute later he tossed the cell away. "That's it all dismantled. He wasn't bluffing, but he also wasn't smart enough to run a live feed rather than a delayed one." He took his foot off Jerome's neck, drew his foot back and delivered a powerful kick that rolled Jerome onto his front. Rather than let the kick be enough, Big Guy fell to his knees and began pummeling Jerome's inert body, heedless to Alicia's pleas to stop.

46

Jerome's face was pulp. No matter how tenderly Alicia tried to dab away the blood, she felt she was going to hurt him.

What they were talking about regarding the GoPro and social media was a mystery to Alicia, but she knew Jerome would explain everything when he came to. For perhaps the twentieth time since they'd been put back into the room she checked for his pulse.

It was there, right where it should be. Strong and regular. He was out cold, though. Watching Big Guy beating up on him had been the worst experience of her life. She'd thought at one point that he was going to beat Jerome to death, but that fear had abated when Big Guy had stopped punching Jerome's head and had pounded his torso, thighs and biceps with great scudding punches.

When he came round, Jerome would be adrift in a sea of pain, and a large part of Alicia was hoping that he'd stay unconscious for a few hours while his body began the healing process. She wanted him to wake, though. She needed to know he was okay, that the beating hadn't left him with any kind of brain damage.

A while after depositing her and Jerome back in this infernal room, the kidnappers had tossed in some medical supplies. She'd taken some of the Advil, put her broken arm into a rudimentary sling, then had concentrated on treating Jerome's wounds as best she could with one working arm. Once she'd done what she could for him, she washed out the gash in her foot, applied Band-Aids and wound a bandage around it.

Jerome stirred then fell still and silent again. His eyes half closed, half swollen shut. Alicia squeezed his hand but got no response. Time and again she repeated the move, interspersing each attempt with a head on his chest so she could listen to his heart beating.

He'd been so brave on the beach. So immensely courageous to take on Big Guy in the way he had. Jerome wasn't a fighter yet he'd taken down a guy twice his size and beaten him. It was her fault they'd been recaptured. If she'd only heeded Jerome when he'd told her to run, then she'd have been able to raise the alarm and summon help. Instead she'd failed to best Zeller and that had led to them both being imprisoned.

Thoughts of getting help hadn't entered her head in the moment. No way was she going to abandon her husband when he'd been so brave. How he'd found her, how he'd managed to get her free was all a mystery, but he'd come up trumps for her, and there was no way she could have left him to fight two guys on his own.

Alicia leaned over Jerome and using as tender a touch as possible, teased one of his eyelids open. She wasn't sure what she was looking for, she just had to see his eyes, had to see for herself if there was any spark of him that would give her hope he'd make a full and proper recovery from the beating.

Jerome's eye was bloodshot and she knew that wasn't good, but without a doctor to diagnose whether the blood in his eyes was due to the swelling or there was some neurological issue she was no further forward.

For only the second time in this room, Alicia surrendered to her emotions and let fat tears roll down her cheeks. The sobs that wracked her body weren't for herself, but for her ingenious, brave and loyal husband who lay battered and unconscious beside her. Somehow against all the odds he'd managed to find where she was being held. If that wasn't enough, he'd personally come to rescue her. To free her from the kidnappers. She trusted he'd have a good reason for not leading the cops here. A solid reason, borne out of the logic he so loved. She'd ask him when he was conscious again. He *had* to regain consciousness. Him not doing so was unthinkable.

After locating her he'd risked his life to get her free. They had been close, so so very close. If she had been able to tell left from right, they might have been safe by now. Slowly, on an individual basis, Alicia's tears morphed from being inspired by Jerome's suffering to being fueled by bitter self-recrimination as she thought of all the ways she was responsible for the pasting he'd taken.

Even as she sobbed she kept squeezing Jerome's fingers.

The tears stopped as if a dam had appeared in her eyelids. Jerome's fingers had curled. Not just curled, but they'd attempted to return her squeeze. Jerome tried again and this time she didn't just feel his fingers move, but felt the pressure of their grasp.

"Awwiciya." Jerome's voice was slurred as if drunk, and from the state of his ruined mouth it was no wonder.

"Yes, darling. It's me."

"Are you owkay? Are you hurt?"

The dam disappeared and Alicia's tears flowed again, this time cascading into the dimples on her cheeks as she beamed down at her husband. This was typical of Jerome. His every thought put her first and foremost. Richer and more handsome guys than Jerome had spent years hitting on her and they could all go hang. Nobody could ever make her feel as precious, as loved as her husband. Who else would have gone to such lengths for her?

"I'm fine, darling. Just fine. How are you?"

"You're owkay, so I am." Jerome's reply threatened to fill her heart to bursting. He levered an eye open, wincing as he did so. "Where are we?"

47

Jerome levered himself to a sitting position at the sound of the door opening. It was only a short while since he came round after his beating, and this was the most movement he'd dared to attempt. As much as he played things down to Alicia, there wasn't a part of his body that didn't feel like it had been run over by a convoy of road rollers.

Lenny Zeller entered trailed by Big Guy. It pleased Jerome to see the damage he'd wrought on Big Guy's face. The man's nose was crooked and stuffed with tissue, both eyes were swollen and already purpling. His lips were split, and the way he now walked like a cowboy gave Jerome no small amount of pleasure.

Less pleasing were the shotguns both men held. They were the ones Jerome had stolen from them and stashed in the cubby hole. Short, stubby shotguns that spoke of menace and destruction. Zeller's was in the crook of his arm, but Big Guy's was held ready to shoot from the hip, and if the grimness seeping out from his battered face was any indicator, he'd be only too happy to pull the trigger.

Zeller took up a lecturer's stance and wagged a finger at Jerome. "You really are a foolish man. All you've achieved in trying to rescue your wife is a broken arm for her, and a damned good beating for yourself."

Jerome kept his mouth shut. He wanted to say it was worth the beating, but to say that would imply it was also worth the break to Alicia's arm, and for him that could never be the case.

Since coming to, his brain had kept returning to the same point. Now that he'd seen Zeller's face, there seemed to be little chance of them surviving their captivity. Whether Zeller was the main man in their group or only halfway up the chain of command was a moot point. He'd recognized the man and as such blown any chance of them being allowed to live.

Alicia wasn't so silent. She extended a finger at Big Guy. "Now I know for sure Beck Holdings is involved: I know who you are. You're George Hunt and you work for Beck Construction. You are the CEO of the Opportunities Assessment team who scout out new construction projects and assess their profitability. As I remember it, you beat up one of your colleagues in a bar after work. The only reason he didn't file a suit against you was because Beck Holdings paid all his medical bills and gave him a generous severance package, even though the altercation took place outside of the workplace."

Hunt gave a derisive snort. "You think what you like, lady. Truth is he was paid a visit and advised of a dramatic shortening of his life expectancy should he try going down the legal route."

It was all Jerome could do to not clamp a hand over Alicia's mouth. He loved her feisty, sassy nature but this was one of those times when she needed to keep it bottled up. It was bad enough he and his wife knew the identity of one of the gang, but she'd just doubled that total and increased their jeopardy tenfold.

To make matters even worse, Hunt was gloating about threatening a life. Should they be killed, it was Jerome's guess that Hunt would be their executioner, and that he'd fulfil the role with a smile on his face.

Jerome hadn't voiced his fears to Alicia, but he knew she must have come to the same conclusions he had. No way could Zeller and Hunt allow them to live.

It was time for Jerome to speak. As his mouth opened he looked directly at Zeller. "What now?"

"Very little has changed for you. You're still going to get us what we want. Still going to steal the money from Beck Holdings so each of the victims of sexual assault can be given fair recompense for their individual ordeal."

"I'm guessing you're not going to release me, so how am I meant to do that from here?"

"I said at the start of this conversation that you were a foolish man. Now you're proving I am correct in my assessment. We've got Alicia's laptop—you yourself had it in your car. I'll tell Carthew I've given you permission to work from home so you can care for Alicia." Zeller's finger wagged twice. "I know all about the lies you told that foppish twit Jessop. That plays right into my hands, because tomorrow morning I will send a link to your personal email that will give you access to the computer in your office. Then when you steal the money, any traces of your actions you leave will lead to your door, not mine. If you're identified as the criminal, I'll do a whole big act of being shocked at your crime and insist I had no idea what you were planning."

"And if I refuse to do as you say?"

"Then I repeat the threats made against your wife. Except this time you'll be able to watch as George here carries them out."

Jerome recognized defeat when it appeared, but there were still opportunities that may be presented to him and Alicia. He didn't for one second think Zeller would be dumb enough to leave him alone with access to a laptop, but to steal the money he'd need Ed's help, and to get that he'd have to contact Ed. There might be a way he could insert a distress flare into the wording of his communication with Ed that would see Ed send the cavalry.

"You're an asshole, Zeller. How you can threaten an innocent woman like Alicia is beyond me. She's a good person, a saint, someone who knows the difference between right and wrong. If you'd had the balls to do the right thing and made her aware of these cover-ups then she'd have done everything in her power to get proper justice and recompense for those women. But that's not why you're really doing this, is it?" All caution flew from Jerome's mind. His and Alicia's futures were so bleak as to be desolate, and therefore he had nothing to lose by speaking his mind. "The real reason you're doing this is because you're greedy and you haven't got the know-how to steal the money yourself. There's thirty million that's not going anywhere near those women. There's you and the lumbering ape at your side, plus whoever was with you when you abducted Alicia. I don't need to be an accountant to work out that you each stand to get ten million dollars out of this."

"Oh, Jerome. Jerome, Jerome, Jerome." Each time Zeller said his name it was accompanied by a wagging finger and enough disdain to pave Central Park twice over. "You really don't get it, do you? Thanks to the Beck family holding half the seats and them not being the trusting kind, I've been passed over for a place on the board of Beck Holdings twice now. George here has also missed out twice despite making tens of millions for Beck Construction, and our colleague, who of course shall remain nameless, has also failed to reach that elevated status on three occasions. The ten million you mention, that's a minimum annual salary for a board member. I know for a fact some board members get thrice that amount plus bonuses, so I think that whatever money we receive for this endeavor will be fair reward for fair labor." The finger wagged three times in rapid succession. "Now do be quiet with all your moralizing. You've stolen, you've lied, you've cheated and you have pointed a gun at us. You may think you're superior, but the truth is when you're backed into a corner, you behave like a feral animal, intent only on your own aims."

Jerome wanted to tear Zeller's wagging finger from his hand and jam it up his ass. The rage he felt at the man was foreign to him, and yet, it was also natural, its source a primal part of his nature buried deep and only tapped now he was in this nightmarish situation. Where he'd always seen himself as a pacifist, he now entertained thoughts of extreme violence against Zeller and Hunt.

As much as he hated to kowtow to Zeller's demands, Jerome knew complying was his only hope of success. "To get the money undetected, I'm going to need outside help. It's pretty much all set up, but I need to be able to contact my buddy. First to make sure he's got his ducks in a row, and second to let him know when I'm ready to make the transfers. To do that I'll need my iPad and access to the notes that were in my backpack."

Zeller's mouth widened in satisfaction. "So you were going to get us the money all along? If you hadn't found this place, you'd have stolen the fifty million and handed it over?"

"Of course, I would have. You had my wife as a hostage. I'd do anything, anything at all to save her." Jerome allowed his mouth to form a sneer. "But you knew that, didn't you? That's why you chose me as the person to steal the money for you. I'm sure you probably wanted to steal it yourself and save the trouble of abducting Alicia, but you're not smart enough to find a way to steal that much without getting caught. That's why you involved me. Tell me, *Lenny*, what happens to Alicia and me once the money is transferred? A bullet? Or will you just leave us here to die of starvation?"

Zeller's face paled. "You'll be released. Your silence on us looking after Alicia for a couple days will be guaranteed because we'll keep Alicia's laptop. It will be loaded with evidence of your wrongdoing, and it'll be your word against ours when it comes to us holding Alicia hostage. The theft of the $50 million, on the other hand will, quite literally, have your fingerprints all over it."

Jerome would have believed Zeller had Hunt's face not shown so much disagreement. Hunt made no secret of the fact he thought Jerome and Alicia were loose ends that required snipping off.

Jerome watched as the door closed behind Zeller and Hunt. They had bested him, both physically and mentally. In a more normal situation losing on either count wouldn't affect him, but the injustice of it all was stoking the fires of a burning rage within. He clenched and unclenched his fists rather than use his hands to start throwing things around the room. He'd never before experienced the urge to throw a major tantrum, but he was living that moment now and he knew he couldn't give in to the desire to let fly regardless of how strong it may be.

The worst thing of all for Jerome was that his mind was every bit as focused on the catalogue of mistakes he'd made as on the consequences he and Alicia would likely face for making them.

A look around the room revealed rough walls that sounded of solid brick when he rapped them with his bruised knuckles. The door was stout and while he might fancy his chances of shoulder barging his way into the room, the way the door opened inwards meant that as well as having to break the lock free of its housing, the door stops attached to the door frame would hold the door in place.

Alicia stood in front of him as he hauled himself to his feet. Every attempt to move sent corkscrews of pain through his battered muscles, but he gritted his teeth against the agony and levered himself upright.

As he'd wanted to do so badly since she was taken, he gripped Alicia's shoulders and delivered a tender kiss to her forehead.

As much as she melted at his kiss, Alicia's voice was full of sorrow. "I'm sorry, Jerome. So so very sorry."

"What? You have nothing to be sorry for, darling. It's me who's failed you."

"Fail me? You found me. You got me outta this hellhole. If I'd only got my directions right we might have gotten away from them. If I'd run when you told me to I could have gotten help from one of the houses by the beach. It's my fault we got captured."

To hear Alicia's dejection as she blamed herself for their capture twisted the knife of guilt that was embedded in Jerome's gut.

"You're talking bull, Alicia. If I'd searched them properly, I would have found that knife Zeller had. If I'd done a better job of tying them up they wouldn't have gotten free, or at least not so quick. If I'd shot out one of the sedan's tires. Made sure to get a rental car with a decent engine. If I'd thought to leave a cell phone in the front of the car. If I'd had the sense to make sure I took the gun with me when getting out of the car. If I'd called the cops and had them come for you instead of trying to do it myself, we'd be safe right now. I've made so many stupid mistakes, Alicia. It's my fault that we didn't get away, not yours."

Alicia's fingertips cradled his cheek. "Don't be so hard on yourself. You achieved a miracle just by finding me. Then you managed to get me away from here. Sure, we didn't manage to escape the kidnappers, but you did your best and your best has always been more than good enough for me. Wasn't those guys beating up on you bad enough without doing it to yourself?"

"I'll stop blaming myself if you do the same." Jerome knew he'd never be able to stop blaming himself, but he'd realized Alicia didn't need to hear him do it any more than he needed to listen to her self-recriminations.

Alicia twisted so her broken arm wasn't between them and pulled Jerome into an embrace. "You got yourself a deal. One. Four. Three."

Jerome repeated the three precious numbers to Alicia and held her as tight as their injuries allowed.

Somehow, by whatever means he could find or devise, or opportunities he could take advantage of, he had to find a way to save Alicia. And if possible, himself, but he was prepared to forfeit his life if it could in some way give his wife a chance at survival.

"Are you going to be able to steal that money for them?"

"Yeah. Ed and I have worked out how to do it."

Jerome didn't say what he thought would happen once the money had been transferred. He was sure Alicia had worked it out for herself, but the last thing he wanted was for her to spend what might be her last hours on earth worrying about her execution.

"And when they've got their money, they're going to kill us. To hell with what Zeller said about releasing us, there's no way they can trust we won't go to the cops. The big guy, Hunt. He'll shoot us, won't he?"

Jerome kept his mouth shut. He was in total agreement with Alicia, but he didn't have the heart to confirm her fears. Nor could he try and put a positive spin on their survival chances. Alicia deserved better than that, and if they were to die soon, he didn't want her last thoughts to be that he'd lied to her.

Alicia released her hug and moved back enough so she could look into his eyes. "You aren't answering me because you agree with me. You always do that when there's bad news."

"I'm sorry. I don't want to scare you, but nor can I lie to you."

"It's okay. Well, it's not okay at all, but since I got kidnapped, I've never for one minute expected to survive. I got to see you one last time, and while I'd rather I hadn't, that I'd much prefer to die knowing you were safe, I've come to terms with what's going to happen."

"No." Jerome squeezed Alicia's shoulders tight. "Don't say that. Don't you even think like that. We're not done by a long way.

There's got to be a way I can raise the alarm with Ed. A way that I can draw things out long enough that Ed goes to the cops. Don't give up hope just yet. I'm not going to lie to you, I don't have a plan, or anything resembling one, but there's no way I'm going to let anything happen to you while there's breath still in my body."

As he cradled his wife, Jerome was sending a silent prayer that he'd find a way to back up his words with actions, while also bending his brain to every possible opportunity that may come their way, and how he could create one himself.

49

Jerome prized his eyes open and took in the room. A bleary glance at his watch showed him the time was a couple of minutes before 6:00 a.m. He and Alicia had fallen asleep on the mattress with him spooning her to protect her broken arm.

He slowly rolled free of her and dragged himself upright. His body an ocean of agony, and he knew that if he was to examine any area of skin he'd find it bruised or bloody. All the same, he eased himself into a series of slow stretches.

Jerome leaned forward to try and touch his toes. He got his fingertips as far as his knees before the pain grew too great. Still bent over, he rotated his arms as if swimming. His shoulders protested the movement, but not so fiercely he was forced to stop.

"What you doing?"

Alicia's voice was laden with sleep but it still carried puzzlement.

"Limbering up. I don't know if we'll get a chance to escape, but if we do I want to make damned sure I'm ready." Jerome looked at his wife until their eyes locked. Hers, brown pools of beauty, his, serious as the grave. "I want you to promise me something, Alicia, something huge."

"What is it?" Jerome heard the fear in her voice. She knew him well enough to know he wasn't one for dramatic statements and would therefore have divined what he was about to ask of her would be something she wouldn't want to do.

Jerome hesitated before speaking, but only for a fraction because what he was about to ask of Alicia shouldn't be delayed.

"If we do get another chance to escape, I want you to promise me that if I'm lagging behind you don't wait for me. If I stop to delay Zeller and Hunt, you won't turn back to help me. I know it's a lot to ask of you, Alicia, but I need you to know that whatever happens in the next few hours, I'm going to do everything I can to get you out of this mess alive." Jerome took a deep breath and used the pause to steady his voice. Even as his words had fallen on Alicia's ears, he'd seen the change in her eyes. "I love you with all my heart, but there may come a time when I have to sacrifice myself so you survive. I'm happy to do that, but I *need* you to promise me that you'll do as I ask and make sure you get away."

Alicia's eyes closed. The action squeezing out a pair of large tears that rolled down her cheeks and dripped from her chin.

"There has to be another way, Jerome. I don't want to lose you. You're my world."

"And you mine. That's why it's so important to me that you make this promise."

Another pair of tears tumbled from Alicia's eyes when she opened them. "How can I make a promise like that? I couldn't leave you to be recaptured. They'll kill you. I couldn't do it."

"You must. You're faster than I am even when I'm in my best shape. Like I am now, you're probably twice as fast. Believe me, Alicia, I want to survive, but if it's a straight choice between us both being recaptured, and me delaying them so you can get away, then so far as I'm concerned it's a complete no-brainer." Jerome squeezed Alicia's hand. "Please, promise me you'll do it."

"On one condition." The squeeze was returned. "You make the same promise. If you're ahead of me, you'll not come back for me."

The idea of leaving Alicia behind wasn't something Jerome could envision himself doing. It went against his every instinct.

Alicia returning his request made him realize just how much he was asking of her, what such a promise would cost her to make.

The easy thing to do would be to lie, but Jerome couldn't do that. Sure, he could tell Alicia a white lie about something that didn't matter, but he couldn't tell one about something of this magnitude.

Inspiration struck Jerome, handing him a knockout response to Alicia's request. "Me leaving you behind wouldn't work. They'd still have you as leverage over me, and before you try and suggest I not do what they tell me, no matter what they threaten you with, we both know that as long as there's a chance to save you I'll do anything that's ever asked of me."

Alicia tilted her head as she assessed his logic. "I get what you're saying, but jeez, Jerome, there's got to be another way."

"I hope there is." Jerome gave a wan smile and winced as the movement pulled at the cuts in his lips. "I want to be around a good while longer. After all, you'll never manage one boy, one girl, two dogs and three cats by yourself."

A nod from Alicia as she fought back a sob at hearing their desired future. "I promise, but only if you swear that sacrificing yourself is the absolute last resort."

"I swear. Thank you, Alicia. One. Four. Three."

"Stand clear of the door."

Jerome and Alicia looked at each other and, upon seeing Alicia's face, he tried to show strength and defiance to combat the naked terror in her eyes.

50

Two men entered the room. Hunt carried a shotgun that his bulk dwarfed enough to make it seem like a child's toy. The other wasn't Zeller, which is what Jerome had expected. Instead it was a third man, and the fact he wore a ski mask told Jerome the person would be recognizable to either him or Alicia. The top of the third man's head was no higher than Hunt's shoulder. That he was trying to hide his identity gave Jerome a faint glimmer of hope he and Alicia may survive the ordeal, but he was shrewd enough to figure it may be a bluff to keep them compliant, so he didn't dare put too much energy into his hoping.

The man stood with his fingers interlaced across his gut. "You've not helped yourself, Jerome. It's most unfortunate what happened yesterday, and while my colleagues suffered at your hands, I think it would be fair to say that you and your wife have suffered more. And all that suffering on all sides has not progressed things for you one iota. In fact it's only made things worse."

To Jerome's ears the man's voice was odd, as if he was feigning an accent. Like the ski mask, it suggesting the man was known to Jerome and was trying to hide his identity.

Jerome stood in front of the man. Not close enough to strike, but as close as he dared get while Hunt brandished the shotgun. If he got the slightest opportunity he'd pounce with everything he had. "What did you think I'd do? Lie down like a good boy? You had my wife, I wanted her back safe and sound. Your goons kicked my ass. So what? I'd do anything to save her and you must be stupid not to realize that."

"By your own admission you'll do anything to save your wife. My colleague is setting things in motion for you to get the money we've asked you to."

"You mean Lenny Zeller? There's no point hiding it. I'm sure he's told you we saw his face. The big lump at your side is George Hunt. You're trying to disguise your voice, which tells me it's familiar to me, although I honestly can't place it. You've got a ski mask on so that tells me you're afraid either Alicia or I will recognize you. That would give me some hope we'll survive this, but I can't see how you're going to let us live once you've gotten me to steal the money. We know too much and despite what Zeller said, your buddy with the shotgun doesn't seem the trusting type. So if you think that I'm going to steal the money for you then you're very much mistaken."

"Those are brave words, Jerome. Perhaps you even mean them. You expect us to kill you and you'd sooner die without first stealing for us. I understand that. It's both very noble and principled of you." The man reached into his jacket and pulled out a pistol. It wasn't a hurried move; his hand just got the weapon and then aimed it at Alicia. "If your theory about us not letting you live is correct, and we believe your stance on acquiring the requested funds, then we're now at the end of the line. You and your wife have now outlived your usefulness, so to protect ourselves we ought to kill you both."

"No." Jerome took a step sideways so he was standing in front of Alicia. "Don't shoot. Damn you, I'll do it."

"I know you will. I've always known you'd do whatever I wanted. Your wife's arm is in a sling. My guess is that it's broken." The man nodded toward Hunt. "If you show further resistance to what we ask of you, I'll instruct him to start twisting it. As you can see for yourself, he's more than strong enough to break her arm with his bare hands. Can you imagine the pain your wife will be in if he does that?"

Jerome felt a shove at his back as Alicia barged past him. "That pig isn't going to lay one hand on me. Jerome told me all about your supposed altruism for the people who are alleged victims of sexual assault in the workplace. That might sound good to you, it might be a salve on your conscience, but it's as hypocritical as hell. Hunt has been leering at my boobs every chance he can get. He even grabbed them when bringing us back here. He had a right good feel, so don't give me any crap about him hurting me. He's a goddamned pervert and I'd sooner take a bullet than have him touch me again."

Jerome saw nothing except Hunt's face. The guns aimed his way, the room, even Alicia all faded from his vision. That filthy great lump had laid his grubby paws on Alicia, had molested her.

His injuries were forgotten as he aimed a wild swing at Hunt's nose.

Pain exploded in Jerome's gut and he went down gasping.

Alicia ignored Jerome's plight as she directed her venom at the clear leader of the kidnappers. He'd had the butt of the shotgun thumped into his ribs. It'd hurt, but he'd survive and she could look after him once the kidnappers had gone. For the moment, she was intent on pressing her point home until it skewered something vital inside the kidnapper's group.

"Your man there groped me. He didn't just grab my boobs, he grabbed my ass as well. Every good thing you may think you're doing by giving each of the assaulted women a million bucks, it's all been undone by him." Alicia jabbed a finger Hunt's way without taking her eyes off the leader. "He's every bit as bad, if not worse than the people whose actions you're trying to achieve redress for. Well, what have you got to say about that?"

The leader's head twisted to look at Hunt.

Hunt raised a hand as his head sawed side to side. "No way. She's lying. She's making it all up."

"Typical." Alicia put as much snort into the word as she could muster. "That's the way of all predators. I've heard it all before, they accuse the victim to shift the blame from their own shoulders. The victims are always portrayed as overreacting to a friendly gesture, misinterpreting a well-intentioned comment, or finding offense where none was intended. He makes me sick to my stomach."

"Shut it, bitch. You're talking nonsense." Hunt pawed at the leader's arm to spin him round. "She's lying. I never once grabbed her ass, or her boobs."

"You did too, you pig."

Alicia hadn't been groped by Hunt, but she was desperate to convince the leader she had been. If she could cause dissension in the kidnappers' ranks, there was a chance Hunt would be kept away from her. Without his huge frame and immense power to contend with, she and Jerome would stand a chance of overpowering the kidnappers and being able to escape. The leader was clearly the brains of the outfit and Hunt brought in to provide muscle. If her allegations could see Hunt sidelined, then the blow to the gut Jerome had taken was a small price to pay. She loved that he'd flung caution to the wind upon hearing her lie about Hunt's action. It was a shame Jerome had gotten hurt, but she knew he'd understand why she'd told the lie.

"Enough. Both of you." The leader turned back to face Alicia. "I don't find your account of events to be entirely credible. I have known Mr. Hunt for some years, and I've never known him to do anything like the things you're accusing him of."

Alicia allowed the leader's words to bounce off her. She wasn't done trying to drive a wedge between them. "You forget what I do for Beck Holdings. To remind you, I'm an HR lawyer. As such I've spoken to countless female employees who have requested transfers across Beck Holdings' subdivisions. I've also spoken to women who have left so I could assess their reasons for leaving. This might be anecdotal, but by my count around sixty percent of those women leaving Beck Construction said they wanted to move or leave due to Hunt's constant leering at them, and the way he made them feel that he was constantly undressing them in his mind."

"This is a load of bull. Surely you can't believe this bitch. Sure, I pay attention when I see a pretty woman, who doesn't?"

"Paying a moment's passing attention is one thing." Alicia

glared at Hunt, her eyes daring him to contradict her. "Creeping women out with lechery is another thing altogether. You're a pervert and the way those women shuddered when they told me about you spoke volumes. I've endured it myself from you. Every time you came in here, either with Zeller or this guy, the way you've run your eyes over me has totally creeped me out. In my opinion you're nothing less than a sexual predator, and the idea that you're involved in paying compensation to victims of sexual assault is nothing less than laughable."

The leader craned his head round to look at Hunt. "She has something of a point. I myself caught the way you were looking at her the night we brought her here."

Hunt squared up to the leader, his shoulders hunched and his chin jutting forward. "Get real. That was part of the act. Sex has always been used as a weapon. Victors raped losers; prisoners were routinely stripped. All I was doing by looking at her was making sure she was creeped out. I wanted her to fear me in every way possible so she'd do as we said. That's all I was doing."

"You pig. You utter, utter pig. You had no need to do that to me. Wasn't the gun in your hand enough? I was terrified of being shot. Being left to rot in this room. There was nothing but your own lechery to be gained from what you did to me."

Jerome clambered back to his feet, his breaths coming in strained gasps as he once again positioned himself in front of Alicia.

"Shut up, bitch. I've heard more than enough of your lies." Hunt clutched the shotgun tight enough that Alicia thought he was about to pull its trigger.

"I think we've all heard enough." The leader pointed at Hunt, then the door before turning back to look at Jerome and Alicia. "When we return you will be given access to a laptop so you can acquire the money for us."

With his point made, the leader marched out leaving a furious Hunt to stomp after him.

Jerome pulled Alicia into a fierce hug. "Oh Alicia. Poor, poor you, getting molested by that pig."

Alicia leaned until her lips were at Jerome's ear. "He didn't molest me; I was just trying to cause trouble for him in the hope he'll be kept away from us in future. It might give you a better chance to overpower the others."

52

Jerome tensed when he heard the key being turned in the lock at the door. Since their early morning altercation with Hunt and the leader, they'd been left alone. He and Alicia had breakfasted on the last contents of the fridge and had formulated the best plan they could muster between them.

Above all else, they had to delay things as long as possible. The longer he and Alicia were still needed to steal the money, the longer they held value to their abductors.

Together they'd discussed every possible way they could draw things out. Alicia's lies about Hunt molesting her were a stroke of genius so far as Jerome was concerned, and he accepted her reasoning that if he'd known her plan before she said it, his reaction would have been false, or if he got his timing wrong, one of the abductors would have realized he reacted ahead of her admission.

Jerome's biggest hope was that Ed's buddy had yet to fulfil his part of their plan. That would cause the greatest delay. As much as they hoped they'd be left alone with a cell or computer, neither of them thought it likely. Their abductors might be amateurs, but they weren't idiots. Both he and Alicia expected them to watch over his every move. Every action he committed would be monitored to prevent him from summoning help.

That he hadn't told Ed he was coming out here galled Jerome. He should have told his buddy about his rescue attempt. If he hadn't made contact by a certain time, Ed could have called the cops and have them descend on this building with SWAT teams and everything else at their disposal. At the very least he should have told Ed he was doing something, and if Ed heard from him without a certain codeword inserted into his communication then things had gone bad.

Jerome pushed the negative thoughts from his mind. There were enough worries to contend with without beating himself up for past mistakes. If he got the chance to break free, he'd make damned sure he didn't repeat his errors. No mercy would be shown to any of the abductors. He'd do whatever it took to stop them from coming after them a second time.

The door opened and the leader strode in. Instead of Hunt following him in, it was Zeller who carried the shotgun.

"Follow me. Both of you."

The leader exited the door and left Zeller to cover them, so Jerome laced Alicia's fingers with his own and started following. If the chance to run came, he'd set off at pace and drag Alicia with him. She was primed to follow his lead, to take her cues from him. This was her idea. Normally they'd share all decisions, but they'd agreed that when the moment came, they wouldn't have the luxury of time to discuss things, so she'd told him she'd trust his judgement.

It was a mighty burden and, as they padded after the leader, he was tempted to barge Alicia into the stairwell and take his chances that Zeller wouldn't shoot him as he barricaded the door. It was only a fleeting idea and it turned out to be a moot point as the leader paused beside the stairwell door to point them in the direction of the room where he'd found Zeller and Hunt the previous evening.

Jerome entered the room and saw Hunt dwarfing a plain desk. On the desk Alicia's work laptop, his tablet and his burner cell were laid. A lead from the laptop was connected to a separate cell Jerome presumed was there to give him access to the internet.

Hunt took up position behind the easy chair that faced the desk, a shotgun in his hands and fury on his face.

"Alicia, you sit in the easy chair. Jerome, you're at the desk." The leader's voice was taut and brooked no argument.

Jerome walked to the ancient dining chair by the desk and hoped it would hold his weight. Both Zeller and the leader stationed themselves behind him. Their proximity close enough to make him feel crowded.

Hunt moved his shotgun so it was aimed at Alicia's head.

Jerome felt a tap on his shoulder as the leader's voice cut through the air once more. "I feel I need hardly say this, but I shall say it anyway. If you try and make any contact with anyone outside these four walls, my colleague will shoot your wife in the face. The same thing will happen if you try to attack us. Now, get to work."

"Before I start, I want to inform you of something I told Zeller last night. I've a buddy whose help I need to steal the money. Without him, I can't get the money for you."

"I was informed. That's why your cell and tablet are there. Any communications you make with him must be shown to me before sending. Now, if you'd be so kind..."

Jerome picked up the cell and using deliberate slow movements held the cell where Zeller and the leader could see its screen.

ARE YOU SET? WANT TO PROCEED ASAP. FAKE INVOICES COMING TO YOU VERY SOON. x

The "x" at the end of the message wasn't supposed to be a kiss. It was there to represent "X marks the spot." The idea Ed would pick up on it was tenuous at best, but Jerome had never signed a kiss when messaging Ed, and he knew his friend was very astute when it came to reading between the lines.

Jerome lifted the cell a little higher. "Is that okay to send?"

A hand slapped against the side of his head with enough force to jolt it sideways. "No. Remove that kiss at the end. Guys don't sign off with kisses. Once that's removed you may send it. The next time you try anything cute like that, your wife will be punished. Do you understand?"

"I understand. Please don't hurt her."

With the message sent, Jerome logged into Alicia's laptop and, following the instructions given him by Zeller and the leader, activated the link that allowed him remote control of his work PC. His first task was to email the fake invoices he'd created. To do this he used his tablet and sent them via a new email account he'd set up for the purpose.

"I've gone as far as I can without my buddy's help. We need to wait on him answering."

In an ideal world, Ed would be in a day-long meeting and wouldn't answer for hours. Better still if he and Alicia were moved back to the room where they'd been held until Ed replied.

Jerome leaned back in the chair, his eyes rising above the screen to look at Alicia. Part of their plan for delaying was that she'd claim to need the bathroom. When he wanted to activate this ruse, he was to scratch his nose.

Alicia looked petrified. No wonder. After her accusations yesterday she'd know Hunt would hate her. He'd positioned himself so that she'd be able to see the shotgun he held two inches from her cheek.

At that range, the shotgun would blow half of her head away. It was unnecessarily intimidating and, as much as it was a tactic used to force compliance, there was no doubt in his mind that Hunt would be only too happy to pull the trigger.

As he worked, he was analyzing the body language he'd observed from the leader and logging it in his memory banks along with the snippets of the man's real voice that bled into his commands, and the leader's general body shape. All of these details were then cross-referenced against people he knew worked for Beck Holdings. The list of candidates wasn't long, since if he was leading a CEO in Zeller and an executive-level engineer in Hunt, then he had to be of at least an equal or higher position within the company.

With females discounted, there were six people on Jerome's suspect list. Four he only knew by reputation and the other two were guys he'd only met a few times at company social events or in passing at the Beck Building.

His deliberations were interrupted by a double beep from the cell phone.

Ed's message was brief and to the point.

ALL SET. WHEN YOU ARE READY SAY THE WORD AND WE'LL SEND THE EMAIL.

A tap on the shoulder from the leader. "Explain what he means by him sending the email."

"To make sure that the theft of this money doesn't come back to me, I've created false invoices. These invoices are being presented to the Chief Finance Officer of Beck Holdings for approval, but to make sure they're going to get the necessary approval, a friend of my buddy has hacked into TriMail and the emails will purport to have originated from Thomas Beck Junior. The emails state that the collection of invoices is to be paid at once." Jerome ignored the intakes of breath from the men at his shoulder. He hadn't expected they'd be on board with his methods. "Once the money goes into the account listed on the invoices, I'll use it to buy cryptocurrency, which I'll then deposit into the various accounts as you instructed. Essentially it all hinges on the CFO paying the invoices. If he responds to the email, my buddy will answer as Thomas Beck Junior. If he picks up the phone and calls Thomas Beck Junior, we're sunk."

There was only silence in the room, but Jerome could see Hunt's face and that told a story. A big story complete with prologues and epilogues.

Hunt's eyes were wide and full of questions. His mouth hung

open enough that his plaque-laden teeth could be counted. There was disbelief, worry and no small amount of consternation in his eyes.

Something clicked inside Jerome's head. Hunt's expression had changed because he'd heard the details of his plan for the first time. Therefore he knew something that affected the plan, and that could only be one thing. The leader—the man in the ski mask— actually was the Chief Finance Officer for Beck Holdings, Christopher Adamson. Adamson was a man who saw vast sums of money each day and now it seemed he wanted some of it for himself. Another indicator of Adamson's guilt was his height. He wasn't a tall man and despite his likable nature there were many hushed office jokes about the fact he wore discreet heels.

Jerome knew Adamson would have had the opportunity to steal the money himself, his levels of access would be far greater than Jerome or Zeller's, but the CFO obviously lacked the ingenuity to pull off the heist without implicating himself. That's why Alicia had been taken and he'd been press-ganged into stealing the money.

The abductors now had a problem. The leader was being careful not to reveal his identity—the one crumb that made Jerome think he and Alicia might not be murdered out of hand—and if he was the CFO, then he could hardly announce it and change their plan. For all they'd called Jerome dumb from time to time, they'd have to know that he wasn't.

"Tell your friend to send it." The tautness was still there in the leader's voice, but it was now stretched as if being tested to breaking point.

Jerome typed out the command to Ed, showed it to the leader and upon receiving permission sent the message.

Now it was time for Jerome to turn the screw, to disrupt the abductors' plans with a little side detail he'd so far omitted from his briefing. How they reacted to what he was about to say would confirm whether the leader was the CFO or not.

"There is one other tiny thing. The email is copied in to me with the instruction that he can 'check with Zeller' if he has any queries. Why would you involve me in your schemes?"

"Believe it or not, Lenny, you have a reputation for complete honesty. Your word is taken at face value. But those of us who work under you know you're also a corporate climber. An ass kisser of the highest order. I figured that if you'd gotten that email for real, you wouldn't dare question its origin and would vouch for it because it came from Thomas Beck Junior. It might be best that he returns to the office so he's at his desk should the CFO contact him. Unless of course he has remote access."

"You're not making any friends here, Jerome." The leader's voice was now harsher and vibrating with suppressed anger.

Jerome pulled a face. "Yeah, and after you guys have treated us so well."

"You are leaving me pissed, Jerome. I'd advise that you stop pulling stunts and withholding things from me. There's an awful lot of things that can happen to your wife that won't kill her."

"Maybe this will help you." Jerome rotated round to face the leader. "My friend has inserted a code into the email that he can activate once the money has been transferred. The code will remove all traces of the email from the CFO's computer. It'll be like the instruction to pay the invoices never happened, and there will be no trail back to the CFO as he's also going to trash the CFO's computer history. He's assured me that there will be absolutely no way anyone can pinpoint who transferred the money from the Beck Holdings' account."

"For you and your wife's sake, I do hope that you're telling me the truth."

As he felt silent, Jerome was left wondering if he'd overplayed his hand and scuppered any chance he and Alicia had of being allowed to live.

53

Hunt and Zeller escorted them back to the room that was their prison. Both were alert and Jerome didn't even consider making a move against them. The shotguns they held would decimate him and Alicia, and it wasn't like he was in any fit state for a fistfight should he manage to disarm them.

Jerome knew that now the email was sent, a countdown clock had started ticking. If the leader was the CFO, Adamson, then he'd have to return to the office and act upon the email. If he wasn't, Zeller would so he was around to be questioned by the CFO.

Jerome's entire plan hinged upon the CFO making the payment, but if Adamson was the leader, he'd be cautious about making the payment himself. He wouldn't want to do anything that would incriminate himself. He and Ed had made sure the email would appear genuine, but Adamson's knowledge of its false-ness would stay his hand. For Adamson to authorize the payment, he'd have to be convinced that his position was, and always would be, one that was supported by utter deniability, and that would only come if he could argue the email was entirely plausible. That's why Jerome had lied about Ed removing any trace of the CFO issuing the transfer. He wanted the CFO to believe he'd be safe from prosecution, to believe Jerome hadn't set him up for a fall. The safer Adamson felt, the greater the chances were of him and Alicia not being executed.

By Jerome's reckoning it would take Zeller or Adamson at least two hours to get back to the office. If they made a pretense of normality and checked in on their juniors, which common sense dictated they'd surely do, it could be another full hour before they managed to make the payment. Then there would be a short spell while the money was transferred and a call put into Hunt or whichever one of them hadn't returned to the office. After that Hunt would get him to buy the cryptocurrency and deposit the requisite amounts in the various sub accounts.

In total, Jerome counted that in a minimum of three and a half hours, the abductors would have no further need of him and Alicia. Even if Adamson instructed Hunt to release them, he didn't trust the man not to go rogue and execute him and Alicia.

The knowledge that there was a specific expiration time on his and Alicia's lives spurred an even greater urgency within Jerome as the door slammed shut and he heard the snap of the padlock being fastened.

The room's walls and floor were sound, and the door unbreach- able, so the only possible way left to escape the room was via the ceiling. He'd looked at it previously: it was plastered over and was feet above their heads. All the same, it was the only potential route out, so they'd have to find a way to not just reach the ceiling, but to get through the plaster and the drywall.

Jerome licked one of his fingers and made a smear on a wall at shoulder height. With that done he stepped back and ran a couple of geometric calculations. There was perhaps four and a half to five feet between the smear and the ceiling. Too much for his plan to work. He had to lessen that gap somehow.

A scan of the room revealed its scant contents. The mattress, the mini-fridge and the porta-potty were the things that caught his eye. In its ancient state, the mattress was too spongy to be trusted as a platform, but the porta-potty and the mini-fridge were candidates.

The porta-potty was the larger of the two square items, so Jerome stood upon it where it sat in the corner and added another shoulder-height smear. It was a lot closer, but he wasn't sure it'd be enough.

Alicia's hand was warm on his arm. "What are you doing?"

"Trying something. Bear with me while I see if it'll work."

The mini-fridge was unplugged and placed on the porta-potty. The books that had been on the fridge were considered as being good for an extra inch or two, but Jerome tossed them aside not wanting to risk too precarious a platform. With the fridge as secure as he could make it, Jerome clambered atop the two and raised his right arm.

It was still over a foot short of the ceiling, but he'd expected that.

"Damn, you can't reach."

"No. But if you sat on my shoulders, you could."

Alicia's eyes sparkled. "But how do we get through the ceiling? Surely there'll be drywall or sheetrock up there."

"There will, but I've had an idea about that."

The room was devoid of anything they could use as a tool, but Jerome still wore a belt around his waist. It had a nice square buckle that could be used to gouge a track or hole in the drywall.

"Here." Jerome handed Alicia the belt and showed her how to hold it so the prong could be used as a spike. "First off, stab a series of holes in the ceiling in a line parallel to the wall. At some point you'll find the studs the drywall is fixed to. Once you've found them use the corner of the belt buckle to score a line in the drywall. Behind the plaster on the ceiling the drywall is just plaster sandwiched between two pieces of paper." Jerome had worked a summer through college for a builder and had spent many hours fixing drywall to ceilings and walls. "What you are aiming to do is cut a hole large enough between two joists for us to climb through."

Jerome's plan hinged on there being a crawl space above the ceiling that they'd be able to use to get away from the room and effect their escape via another part of the building.

Alicia's jaw tightened as she listened. "That sounds like a good plan, but are you going to be strong enough to hold me? No offense, darling, but you look like crap after that beating and I've seen how you're moving."

"Sure I am."

Jerome understood Alicia's worry. He shared it, but as painful and strenuous as supporting Alicia might be, it was a lot better to endure a lot of short-term pain than to die at the hands of Hunt's shotgun.

Before he got Alicia on to his shoulders, Jerome ran through the necessary movements in his mind, then did a practical rehearsal. To get Alicia on his shoulders, it made sense for her to stand on the mini-fridge so all he had to do was duck his head between her legs then clamber up the makeshift platform. To practice his moves he climbed on to the parts of the porta-potty that weren't covered by the mini-fridge. The step up onto the mini-fridge was a balancing act as the mini-fridge's feet were slick on the porta-potty's lid. To counter this he reached down and flipped the mini-fridge upside down. It lowered the platform by an inch, but he figured they'd have enough height for the missing inch to not be a problem.

"Which way will the beams run?" Alicia pointed at the ceiling, her good arm swiping left and right then back and forth.

"I don't know. You'll be near the corner, so I'd suggest you use the belt's prong to stab a line of holes parallel to each wall. When you find a stud you'll have your answer and will know which way to go. Try not to look up if you are working above your head or you'll get lots of dust in your eyes."

"Pass me the sheet, will you?"

Alicia handed it over. Puzzlement in her eyes.

Rather than explain why he wanted the sheet, Jerome tore off a strip three inches wide and two feet long. With the strip of cloth in his hands he gathered up handfuls of Alicia's hair and used the cloth to pull it into a ponytail.

"What are you doing that for?"

"If we have to crawl our way out up there, I'm guessing there will be spiders. This means there'll be much less chance of them getting in your hair."

Alicia's lips twisted and her eyes clouded, but her jaw was firm as she jerked a nod of thanks. Jerome wasn't just thinking of Alicia's welfare, he was doing everything he could to minimize the chances of her shrieking and giving away their attempt to escape.

"Okay." Alicia clambered on top of the mini-fridge. The belt tucked into her sling and her good hand braced against the wall to give her balance. "Let's do this."

Jerome dragged the mattress across so that if they fell for any reason, Alicia would have a softer landing.

Alicia shifted her feet until they were right at the edges of the mini-fridge and squatted until there was a space between her thighs for Jerome's head to pass through.

As Jerome positioned himself, he kept his back as straight as possible. His legs had the far superior muscles and while working construction he'd been shown how to properly lift a heavy load.

Alicia's weight on his shoulders wasn't too bad initially, but when Jerome raised a leg in preparation for stepping onto the porta-potty, he felt a shift in balance that almost toppled him. He corrected the lateral movement in time, but when he went to make the step up, he felt every ounce of Alicia's weight pressing down on him, pinning his standing foot to the floor.

"Brace yourself against the wall."

"I am anyway."

Jerome eased his standing foot onto tippy-toes and then as he lowered it, he bounced it back up to full extension. Twice more he did this with Alicia bouncing on his shoulders. For a split second her weight eased as his bouncing movements crested then fell, and it was in one of these moments when he thrust upwards and jumped his standing foot up so he had both feet planted on the porta-potty.

Sweat enveloped Jerome's head, and he couldn't work out if it was from the exertion or from the body heat emanating from

Alicia's thighs. He was grateful she was wearing silk pajama bottoms rather than coarse denims that would scrub the exposed wounds on his head.

Jerome tested his balance and then lifted a foot onto the mini-fridge. He had to press down with the top foot, as with all their weight on the edge of the porta-potty, he was afraid any lateral pressure he applied might topple the whole precarious structure.

"And again." Three bounces of his foot later, Jerome thrust down with his standing leg and hoisted himself up until he had both feet on the mini-fridge.

The move worked, but not fully. Jerome's heel was caught on the upturned foot of the mini-fridge. He had to screw and twist his foot until he had both soles firmly planted.

Above him Alicia had wasted no time and was already rhythmically stabbing the prong from his belt into the ceiling. Every movement she made reverberated through him, and he was constantly correcting his balance, but no way was he going to ask her to slow down. The quicker she cut the hole, the sooner he'd be able to thrust her upwards and relieve himself of her weight.

Sweat bathed Jerome's body as Alicia stabbed away at the ceiling, and although he could feel his legs trembling he gritted his teeth, ignored all the discomforts and strains on his body and concentrated on making sure he kept Alicia balanced above him.

54

Alicia's ninth thrust upwards hit an obstacle. Unlike the previous eight the belt's prong didn't spear through the plaster. It hit something solid and stuck fast. Three twists later she had it freed and knew where one of the studs was.

From the stud's position she worked out which way the studs were running and began scoring with the belt's buckle.

Jerome had been right about the dust. She could feel it sprinkling her hand and tumbling into her hair. That she might look snowed upon was neither here nor there. She'd face a lot worse than drywall dust to be free of this infernal room.

Below her she could feel Jerome's head and shoulder were sodden with sweat as he fought to support her. From time to time a juddering tremble would carry upwards through her butt, yet Jerome always managed to bring his muscles back under control, even though his breathing rasped more with each passing minute.

Rather than waste time asking Jerome if he was okay, she soldiered on with her scoring, trusting him to bear her weight as long as was necessary.

After five minutes of dragging the belt buckle across the plaster she felt it break through the other side. Three more strokes saw the gash extended to its full two-foot length.

"One side done." Even as Alicia spoke she was starting work on the next score. Her hand aflame from the effort of holding the buckle and applying as much pressure as she could against the plaster and drywall.

"Good work."

Jerome's words were uttered through clenched teeth, and the knowledge of his suffering spurred Alicia to work even faster.

The extra pressure and speed she applied caused them to totter, and she had to stop working to brace the heel of her hand against the ceiling to help Jerome regain their balance.

As soon as she was certain they wouldn't fall, Alicia resumed work, but she'd learned a valuable lesson about the perils of rushing.

Time after time she scored away until the second and third sides of an access rectangle were cut into the ceiling.

Alicia bent her head down and adopted a strong whisper. "That's three sides done. It's hanging down a little and I think I can pull it down."

"No, don't do that, drywall can often break with a crack and I don't want to risk making too much noise."

"Okay."

Alicia's heart broke a little at hearing the strain in Jerome's voice, but she followed his instruction and reached up to score at the fourth side.

Try as she might, she couldn't twist her body enough to get the required purchase for the belt buckle to gouge the plaster and drywall.

"Jerome. Can we turn around?" Alicia tucked the belt back into her sling and placed her free hand flat against the ceiling to help with balance. She knew that Jerome wouldn't refuse her request.

Slowly, with shuffling movements, Jerome started to wheel counterclockwise. Their balance was good, but there was a faint cracking sound that grew louder as they tensed awaiting disaster.

The cracking ceased only to resume again when Jerome tried to complete the turn.

"It's the porta-potty. I think it's had enough of supporting all our weight. Can you manage from where you are?"

"Sure, but keep a hold of my legs as I'm going to have to lean back a little."

Alicia felt the shift in balance and Jerome's correction as she began scoring. As soon as she broke through the plaster and the first layer of paper, the piece of drywall sagged further, closing on the gash she'd made.

It felt like a betrayal to Jerome as she wasn't following his instructions to the letter, but she again tucked the belt into her sling and grasped the drooping drywall. Slowly she pushed it back up into the hole until it snapped with a gentle pop. Alicia gripped it tight and tore it sideways, ripping the last shreds of paper free.

Alicia took aim and dropped the piece of drywall onto the mattress where it landed with a dusty flump.

The sparse light from their room illuminated enough of the hole for Alicia to see there was a crawl space. That was the good news. The bad news was the proliferation of spiderwebs that criss-crossed the area she could see. Once up in the crawl space where there was no light, they'd have to pass through God knows what with only their sense of touch to give them information.

Even as she shuddered at the idea, Alicia was snaking her good arm toward the hole. No matter what arachnid terrors the crawl space held, it was still preferable to staying in the room and waiting for Hunt to murder them.

55

Jerome gave Alicia's leg a tiny squeeze followed by a half dozen applauding taps to congratulate her on getting a section of the drywall cut out. "What can you see? Is there enough space for us to get up there?"

"There's space. I can feel the timber beams the drywall is fixed to."

"Okay. I'm going to put both my hands under your right foot." Jerome didn't worry about Alicia getting her left and rights mixed up. She'd feel where his hands were. "If you straighten your leg, you should be able to put your other leg on my shoulders. Then you should be able to wriggle into the space. When you get up there, stay on the timber beams as the drywall itself won't support you. And keep back so I can get up there too."

"Well, durrh." Alicia blew a soft raspberry at him after speaking. Jerome loved that even in this awful situation she had retained her innate sense of fun. He had to save her. Had to get her away from Hunt and that damned shotgun he always carried.

Jerome interlaced his fingers and placed both hands beneath Alicia's foot. He had to adjust his standing as the movement created a shift in balance. The porta-potty creaked and splintered some more.

Alicia's leg straightened, and Jerome ground his teeth against the strain and did all he could to give Alicia a boost upwards. Her calf biffed his already broken nose, and he could feel a fresh trickle of blood descend toward his top lip as tears leapt to his eyes.

The heel of her unsupported leg bumped his shoulder next and traced its way to where it could be planted. Once the foot was sited, Alicia straightened that leg and eased the pressure on Jerome's hands as her right foot sought Jerome's other shoulder.

"How far through the hole are you?"

"To my belly button."

"Okay. Can you lie forward enough to support your own weight for a minute?"

"I think so."

"Okay, on three, do it. I'm going to squat down and put my hands beneath your feet so I can use my leg muscles to give you enough of a boost to get up there. Ready?"

"Yes."

"On three. One. Four. Three."

As Jerome squatted down, he slipped his palms beneath the soles of Alicia's feet and maintained as much pressure as he could while also allowing his arms to straighten and lock together.

The second he could sink no further, he started back upwards. The screaming agonies from his muscles were ignored as he boosted Alicia up enough that she removed a foot from his grasp and clambered through the opening she'd made.

Jerome started when he heard a thud immediately followed by a muffled yelp. His instinctive look up achieved nothing beyond an eyeful of dust.

"You okay?"

"Fine. I just landed on my bad arm." Alicia's face poked through the hole after a moment's scuffling, a pained grin etched into her features. "Trust you to count like that. Now get your ass up here." Alicia patted the side of the opening beneath her chin. "There's a beam here that will support you."

As Alicia's head ducked away, Jerome assessed the gap

between the tips of his fingers and the top of the beam Alicia had indicated. He knew from his construction days the correct name for the beam was "joist," but such semantics were right at the bottom of his list of priorities.

There was more than a foot between his fingertips and the top of the joist. Yet the distance wasn't so great as to be approaching two feet.

Jerome squatted until his thighs brushed against his calves. As he sprung upwards he felt the porta-potty giving way beneath the powerful thrust. This would be his only chance of using the platform. Jerome's hands shot up into the opening, his fingers scrabbling for purchase on the joist.

Jerome's right hand caught, but his left wasn't able to get a meaningful grip of anything substantial before his thrust was thwarted by gravity. He hung one-handed, unable to haul himself up with just the one arm. No matter how he stretched upwards with his left hand, it never got close to the ceiling, let alone high enough to get a grip on the joist above it.

To counter this, Jerome abandoned his efforts to grab the joist and fastened the fingers of his left hand around his right wrist. Now he had two hands planted. Two arms whose strength he could employ in his efforts to get into the crawl space. He wanted to rest. To catch his breath and give his tortured muscles a moment to heal.

There wasn't time. Any seconds spent recuperating would be offset by the extended effort required to support his entire weight from the one hand that was gripping the joist. Inch by inch he hauled himself upwards, all the while fearing he'd lose his grip or that the agony in his wrist was a precursor to the joint separating.

When Jerome raised himself to a point where his biceps were at right angles to his forearms, he released his left hand and shot it up toward the joist.

This time he got a grip of the wooden beam. Not a great one, but enough that he could improve it and hang from two hands instead of one. It took reserves of strength Jerome didn't know he had, but he managed to lift himself high enough to hook an elbow over the joist.

From there it was a simple enough task to drag the rest of his body upwards and enter the crawl space.

The first task Jerome gave himself was orientation. It was critical he and Alicia didn't pass above where Hunt and the other abductors were stationed. They needed to go in the opposite direction and then search for a hatch or a place where they could cut a fresh hole and descend from the crawl space.

To complicate matters the only light they had to see by was what came up from the room they'd just exited.

Jerome looked at the hole, worked out how it lay with regards to what he knew of the building's layout and got his bearings. By groping around he found a set of water pipes that were suspended from the floor above. He eased his weight onto them and when they didn't give way he smiled in the darkness. The pipes ran left to right. Left was where the abductors had taken over a room, therefore freedom lay to the right.

"Alicia, there are pipes we can use as a pathway. I'll go first, okay."

"Yep."

The sole word of Alicia's clipped answer gave Jerome a good indication of how his wife was coping. She was on board, but struggling. Since entering the crawl space, he'd felt the clinging grasp of spiderwebs on his head and arms. How she'd coped up here so far was a miracle, but he'd have to do everything he could to ease her fears, as if she was to feel one on her bare skin there would be no way she'd be able stifle the scream he knew would rise in her throat.

As he crawled along the pipework, Jerome swept a hand ahead of him in a circular motion to catch as many spiderwebs as he could. The fewer that were left to make contact with Alicia the better. His back would periodically brush against the underside of the floor above, but a few scratches were small beer compared to his many other injuries.

Jerome gave Alicia whispered warnings of hazards such as valves, and after they'd progressed maybe twenty yards into the darkness, he felt two of the outside pipes take a right and go off in a new direction. This left them with just four pipes as their pathway. It was narrow but not impossible.

Where it became more of a problem was where the supporting rods dropped down. Before there had been plenty of room to squeeze between them, but now it was a case of wriggling through a narrow gap, the slender threaded bars tight against their bodies.

Behind him he could hear Alicia laboring. With only one hand fit to use, she was sliding that hand along the pipes rather than a proper crawl. Her breaths were ragged, and he knew she'd be totally strung out being encased in a dark space that held countless spiders. It would have been bad enough to see the spiders, but to have no sight meant her imagination would fuel her fears. There would be nothing but terror for her with every second she was up here.

Still Jerome pressed on. As horrible as this ordeal was for Alicia, he knew he had to put every possible foot between Hunt and the place where they dropped from the crawl space.

A whimper escaped from Alicia, but somehow she managed to keep it low and it was shut off after a brief second.

"Nearly there, darling. Hang in there."

Even as he spoke the words, Jerome cursed them for their futility. They were a long way from *there*, wherever *there* turned out to be. They still had to get out of the crawl space and exit the building without discovery for them to be anywhere close to *there*.

Jerome's hand did its usual sweep to remove the spiderwebs from their path and lowered back to the pipes he was crawling along. As he slid his hands forward he found the left two pipes making a ninety degree turn away from the remaining two.

This was the end of the line for them. As far as they could easily go without clambering over joists, and in the stygian, spider-infested darkness, Jerome figured that wouldn't end well. By his calculations they were at least thirty yards from the room where they'd been held. Not as far as he'd like, but still far enough that he rated their chances of success around seventy-thirty.

"We're as far as we need to go." Jerome saw no point in burdening Alicia with any further worries. "Rest up while I cut a hole through the drywall."

Jerome set to work with the belt. Because he had two hands and could apply his weight to the buckle, he cut a hole far quicker than Alicia had scoured one into the ceiling of their prison.

Faint light crept up from the hole and when Jerome ducked his head through he saw beams of moonlight splintering their way into the room via a broken window. The room had dilapidated shelving, a sole window and one door that was closed. Whether the door was locked or not was unknown, so Jerome shimmied his way along the joists until he was convinced he'd passed the point where the sole door was.

So far as Jerome could figure, the room had once been a storage space for the building's super. That meant that on the other side of the door there would be a corridor or passageway.

He cut another hole and when he scored the fourth side and the drywall hinged downwards, he again dipped his head to see what lay below.

It was the promised passageway, so he made his way back to Alicia.

"I've got us a place to drop down. There's a passageway below the second hole."

"Thank God." Alicia's tone carried relief the way a packhorse bore saddlebags.

"You'll have to crawl along the joists. Put your hand on one and your knees on another. Try to lift your hand and knees rather than slide them as they're rough and will have lots of splinters."

"Okay." Jerome couldn't see his wife's face, but he could hear the determination in her voice as she steeled herself for what lay ahead.

"When we get there, sit on one joist with your legs through the hole. I'll lower you down via your good hand and then drop after you."

"Got it."

It took three minutes for Alicia to make her way along the joists, not that Jerome was aware of this. He just knew she was struggling to make the trip with only one good arm and the constant fear of a spider dropping onto her.

When she was in position, Jerome lowered himself onto the joists until he was lying flat across four of them. He braced his left hand on the one upon which Alicia sat, and clasped her wrist with his right. "Hold my wrist not my hand. When you go to drop, try and do so as slowly as possible as I don't know if I'll be able to hold you if there's a sudden jerk."

"You will." Conviction filled Alicia's tone. "I know you'll never let me down. On three I'll start easing my way down."

Jerome gripped Alicia's wrist and felt her fingers wrap around his. "Ready when you are."

"One four three, darling. One four three."

Alicia's body began to slither forward. When it got to the point where she fell forward, Jerome increased his grip on her wrist and braced himself for the sudden jarring that was bound to happen when he suddenly had all of Alicia's weight to bear.

There was the rent of tearing fabric as Alicia's pajamas snagged on something. By the faint light Jerome could see her face scrunched in pain.

Alicia wriggled and there was another ripping sound as she

dropped down. Even though he was braced for the jolt, Jerome felt as though his shoulder had just been pulled from its socket. From the gasp that escaped Alicia's lips he guessed she'd felt the same agonized jerk.

Below him, Alicia swung back and forth in lazy arcs, her feet thrashing for a source of purchase that wasn't there.

"Keep still."

Alicia stopped fighting the swing and it bled its energy until Jerome felt it was safe to release her.

As soon as Jerome saw Alicia land upright, step aside and start roughing her hair clear of cobwebs he was on the move. He swung his legs into the hole, placed two hands on the joist, and followed his wife.

Jerome bent his knees as he dropped and allowed himself to roll to the left when he landed. As he rose to his feet, his eyes picked out Alicia. She was peering into the darkness, her eyes focused and locked in the general direction of the room they'd just vacated.

Alicia's body language gave no sign that she'd detected a threat, so he eased out a relieved sigh. His biggest fear when dropping down from the crawl space wasn't turning an ankle, but making so much noise he drew Hunt's attention.

Now it was a case of slinking out of the building, and getting well away before their escape was discovered.

Jerome knew where he was. The corridor he'd dropped into was the one he'd exited the stairwell into when he'd come to rescue Alicia. It should be a simple task to return the way he'd first entered. He took Alicia's hand and led her along the corridor. It was a tougher task than his arrival as he didn't have the flashlight, but his eyes had adjusted to the darkness enough that he could see the worst hazards as he navigated his way along the passageway.

From the far end of the building there was the faint glow of a television set, and when he listened hard Jerome could hear the sounds of canned laughter.

Upon reaching the door Jerome grasped the handle and gave a

gentle push. The door didn't swing open. It didn't budge. It just stood there, all firm and immovable. He tried again and got the same result.

Jerome ran his hands over the door thinking there may be some lock mechanism that had been activated. He didn't find a lock, but his fingertip snagged on a raised piece of timber that buried a splinter into his flesh. Jerome stifled down the yelp that sprang to his lips. Compared to his myriad injuries, the splinter was nothing, but the unexpectedness of the pain almost caused him to betray their escape.

The splinter ran deep into his finger and no matter how he tried to remove it, there wasn't enough protruding from his skin for his fingers to get a meaningful grip, so he dug a nail under the free end, gritted his teeth and snapped the tip of the splinter off. It hurt, and it would be harder to remove when the time came, but at least it wouldn't snag on anything and inflict fresh agonies at inopportune moments.

Jerome reached out for the door again and using slow gentle movements located the area where he'd picked up the splinter. In the darkness he couldn't give the door a proper inspection, but from what he could see, the area was paler in color, which suggested the area had recently been exposed.

As Jerome probed the area he felt a dimple in the door's frame, so he fed a fingertip into the dimple to confirm his fears. Jerome's fingertip located the head of a screw. Not just a screw head, but a screw head that was angled, its position suggesting the shank of the screw was securing the door to the frame and effectively locking it.

To Jerome it made sense that Hunt or one of the others had made sure there was only one route of access to their floor, but internally he cursed them for their efficiency and forethought.

Whether there were more screws affixing the door or not was a moot point. Even if there were only this one screw, it was impossible to break through the door with any degree of stealth.

Rather than waste any more time on the door, Jerome returned the way he'd come, Alicia trailing after him. He had to find another way to get down. Whether there was a stairwell he hadn't yet found, or a fire escape outside the building was unknown, but he intended to learn these things.

Jerome tried every door handle he passed. Every door was either locked or led to an empty apartment.

At the far end of the building he found a fire door, its crash bar suggesting that it led to a metal staircase that provided an external means of escape for the building's occupants. Knife Holder had said the bottom part had fallen away, but Jerome hoped they'd be able to drop or jump the last portion. Whomever had secured the building when it had been abandoned had affixed a block of wood in the space between the door and the crash bar, thereby preventing the crash bar from being activated.

Jerome tried to lever the block out, but it was stuck fast and when his fingers explored it they found a screw hole at both ends. Like the door to the stairwell, this was a bust.

An idea sparked for Jerome and he wasted no time in checking out if it was feasible. He quit trying to get through the door and tried the rooms on either side. The one on the left was locked but the one on the right opened at his touch.

With Alicia at his back, Jerome padded softly into the apartment, his eyes searching for a window close to where he reckoned the fire escape would snake down the building.

A window was right where he wanted it to be and through it he could see the framework of a fire escape.

So far, so good. The only issue was the window was intact, save a small hole where someone had managed to pierce the glass with a projectile. They were at least three floors up so the windows had largely escaped the bored youths who'd taken potshots at them.

The bottom sash of the window was divided into six panes, each of them twelve inches high by eight wide.

With the door closed, Jerome reckoned he could knock out enough of the glass to afford their escape without drawing the attention of Hunt. Once the glass was removed, the thin lattice of woodwork could easily be riven free. The timber was sure to be rotten, everything about this building stank of mold and decay. There was just one thing to check before putting his plan into action.

Jerome bumped his wedding ring against the lattice bisecting the window. But it didn't thud or provide a dull knock. Instead it gave the dull clank of metal upon metal. It wasn't the rotten wood he'd been counting on.

There was no way he could remove the metal lattice, so Jerome abandoned the idea at once. Hunt or one of the others could decide to check on them at any moment, and as soon as they discovered he and Alicia weren't where they should be, a search would begin.

Jerome was under no illusions about what would happen if they were caught. The fact they'd made the escape attempt would prove to the abductors they couldn't be trusted, and that would leave the leader with only one surefire way to ensure their silence.

He remembered there was an elevator shaft central to the building, but the doors were closed and any attempt to open them would either create noise or require electrical power. And that was on the assumption the elevator mechanism would still work.

The more Jerome thought about it, the more he realized the only way to get off this floor of the building was to use the stairwell the abductors were watching over.

To that end he had to create a plan, devise a way to ambush them and make sure he could best them before they could turn their shotguns on him or Alicia.

A glimmer of a plan began to form in his mind. It was risky and would mean he had to utilize Alicia, but the more he prodded at the idea, the more he came to believe it could be successful.

Jerome's plan was simple. He had to lure the guards to him, in order that he might disarm them and claim their weapons for himself. To do that he would need the element of surprise. And a weapon of some sort, so he tracked to the room he reckoned had been the super's. Slowly, carefully, he tried the door handle. It turned without sound so he gave the door a gentle push and breathed a sigh of relief when it swished open. The room was given a quick examination, and Jerome found a pair of ancient brooms.

Jerome planted a foot on the back of one broom and leaned the handle from side to side until it popped free. He passed the handle to Alicia and repeated the move with the second broom. Now they both had a weapon of sorts.

The broom handle would be useless against a shotgun, but in an ambush situation it would be far more effective than a clenched fist.

"Here, hold it like this." Jerome demonstrated the way he was holding his. He'd placed one hand at the end and the other perhaps two feet further along. The technique wasn't something he knew, but he had watched enough movies where either Jackie Chan or Bruce Lee had used a broom handle in this way, and while he knew that neither he nor Alicia could begin to match their skills, he was working on the theory those movie stars would know what they were doing.

"I've only got one working arm."

"Oh crap. Sorry, that shouldn't have slipped my mind." Jerome altered his grip and held the broom handle by its center. He tried a few moves and found that it was most effective when used with jabbing movements, although he reckoned that it could also be used to deflect incoming blows.

Alicia copied his grip and made a few practice swipes and jabs with the broom handle.

"Okay. Now what?"

"I go down to the corner where they are watching over us. I want you to go back to the room right at the far end. The one where I was looking at the window."

"Got it. What then?"

Jerome laid a hand on Alicia's shoulder and gave it what he hoped was a reassuring squeeze. "You are to let out a loud, pained scream followed by a shout for help. As soon as you've done that, hide yourself in the apartment."

Even in the darkness Jerome could see his wife's eyes widen.

"But that will have them come running, won't it?"

"I hope so. They'll do one of two things. They'll either check out the room where they think we are. Or they'll charge along the corridor. If they go to the room, I'll be on their heels and will make sure I get at least one of them locked in. If they come along the corridor, I'll use my broom handle to trip them and then grab their weapons."

"What happens if you can't trip them? If they don't let go of their weapons?"

"Then I'll have to improvise." Jerome gave his wife's shoulder another squeeze. "We have to do this, Alicia. It's our only chance."

"I know." Jerome felt her lips brush his. "Stay safe, darling. One. Four. Three."

Jerome returned the message and set off along the corridor.

When he was in position, he waved to Alicia as she watched from the doorway of the room with the metal window.

Even as Jerome was taking a deep breath to steel himself for what was about to come, Alicia's scream rippled down the corridor, a pained shout hot on its heels.

"Owwwww. Jerome, quick. Help me. I'm stuck."

The thud of running footsteps was audible before Alicia had finished her part in his plan. Jerome gripped the broom handle until his knuckles ached. Their lives depended on what happened in the next few seconds, and he was determined not to fail her again.

59

Jerome had enough time to recognize there were two lots of footsteps thumping along the passages. One heavier than the other. To him it suggested Hunt was accompanied by either Zeller or Adamson. His money was on Zeller, as he suspected Adamson had returned to the office to fulfil his role as CFO and authorize the payment.

Jerome expected to have two opponents. His calculations were based on that assumption. If it was only one, then this takedown would be easier than expected. Unless there were more members of the gang he didn't know about, either Zeller or the leader had to return to the Beck Building.

As the leaner man, Zeller would be first to get to where he was hidden. Which meant he'd have to deal with him first. He'd much rather it would be Hunt that arrived first. The bigger man carried a greater threat and he wanted the element of surprise on his side, so Hunt was ambushed before he had time to react. This would be lost if he had to spend even two seconds dealing with Zeller first. Then he'd have to deal with an alert Hunt who held an advantage that wasn't just from his physical size but from the coldness that exuded from his eyes. He'd be far more likely to pull a trigger. There would be little, if any, hesitation from him when it came to using violence.

The thuds of running feet grew closer, and Jerome ratcheted up the tension in his already poised muscles. At this moment in time, his ears were his greatest weapon. Sound was his information stream, and he had to strike at the perfect moment to maximize his chances of success. There was the weaving beam of a flashlight that bobbed in a runner's hand, but there was no way to tell from its beam how close it was.

Too soon and he wouldn't trip the first abductor, that in turn would leave him two standing opponents to deal with. Both of whom would hold far superior weaponry.

Too late and he might miss the first runner altogether. Again, this would lead to him having to deal with two standing foes.

As well as getting the timing right, he had other worries. The broom handle he was holding was old and coated in grime. As tight as he might grasp and grip it, he couldn't be certain it wouldn't slip from his hands if violently jerked. Worse, it might snap at the first telling contact and leave him shorn of its greatest asset: its length.

With the broom handle intact, he could strike at the abductors from a distance once he'd disarmed them, away from the powerful blows Hunt would send his way. Without the safety its length provided, he'd find it harder to keep the abductors away from him and the weapons he intended to knock from their hands.

When he judged the time was right, Jerome exhaled a harsh breath as he stabbed the broom handle downwards past the corner. He was gambling the abductors would come round the corner both at pace and tight to the wall. If they walked round with care and preparation for potential ambushes he was sunk.

"Jerome. Please hurry. It hurts, and there's so much blood."

Alicia's extra words weren't part of his plan, but as soon as Jerome heard them he saw the value in them. She was drawing the abductors to her. Luring them in with protestations of agony and the suggestion of grievous injury. Alicia was their leverage over him and they wouldn't want her to escape while they needed him to transfer the money. They also wouldn't want her to die from her injuries as they'd then lose their lever.

The tip of the broom handle was six inches above the floor with Jerome's end held at waist height. Jerome was a fraction too late to catch the front leg of the first abductor, but the man's trailing leg caught its foot on the timber shaft. Rather than trip him direct, the man's momentum pressed the handle forward until its tip jammed against the heel of his standing foot.

He didn't stand a chance of maintaining his balance and went crashing forward in a sprawling heap. Attuned to every sound as they were, Jerome's ears heard the clatter and skittering sounds of the shotgun and flashlight being thrown forward to slide along the floor.

Jerome didn't waste time celebrating his success or striking down at the man to make sure he was immobilized. The man was too slight to be Hunt; that meant that only a small portion of the threat had been dealt with. Even as he drew his broom handle from between the man's legs, Jerome was arcing it upwards. By his reckoning, the abductors would be carrying their weapons with their barrels aimed either up or downwards. As soon as Hunt realized what had happened to his buddy, Jerome expected him to level his shotgun ready for use. He wouldn't need to pull the trigger: the shotgun's threat would be enough.

As Jerome swept the broom handle toward where he expected the shotgun to be, he was moving his hands in different directions. The one at the end of the broom he pulled downwards toward his body as the other drove the makeshift weapon upwards. The opposing forces created a fulcrum that increased the velocity of the end of the broom handle Jerome was employing as a weapon.

There was a pained yelp as the broom handle made contact. Jerome hadn't dared hope to score a hit on Hunt's fingers, but it was an added bonus he wasn't going to refuse. The power and centrifugal forces at work in his move drove the shotgun up until it was aimed at the ceiling.

Perhaps in reflex, or agony, or just outright fury, Hunt pulled the shotgun's trigger as he withdrew his injured hand from the weapon's barrel.

At such close proximity the blast from the shotgun was deafening. The air filled with the scent of gunsmoke as fragments of ceiling rained down upon Jerome's head.

Jerome wasted no time in pressing home his advantage. Until Hunt could pump another round into the shotgun, the weapon wasn't a direct threat. The end of the broom handle continued upwards until it thumped into Hunt's chin.

The blow rocked the big man, but although rocked he didn't go down. Twice more, Jerome slashed the end of the broom at Hunt's face. The man's nose pulped and the shotgun clattered to the ground, but somehow he stayed upright, his arms moving up to offer an instinctive defense of his head.

Rather than allow Hunt to protect himself, Jerome drew back the broom handle and then jerked it forward in a stabbing motion. The end of the broom handle landed square on Hunt's temple with enough force to see the big man crumple to the floor.

Jerome didn't bother waiting to see if Hunt would move. He stepped forward, the end of the broom handle crashing against the back of Hunt's skull as Jerome leaned down and scooped up the shotgun.

With Hunt out of action, Jerome's greatest concern was the other guy. He put the shotgun against his shoulder and pumped a new shell into it in one slick movement as he turned to face the guy on the ground.

Now Jerome was looking, he saw from the beam of the flashlight the guy on the ground was Zeller, and that Zeller had used the brief seconds he was fighting with Hunt to retrieve his lost shotgun. A shotgun that was being brought to bear on him.

There was no doubt in Jerome's mind that Zeller would have him in his sights before he had Zeller in his.

60

Alicia padded her way along the passageway. Jerome might have told her to hide out, but that was never an option for her. No way was she prepared to let Jerome face all the danger alone. They were a couple, bound together for life by the vows they'd exchanged in the chapel where she'd worshipped since childhood.

Jerome had needed her on the beach and if he needed her here, by God she was going to be there for him.

She'd witnessed the fight. The way he took down both opponents made her heart swell with pride. His plan was working perfectly, except Big Guy was super tough and took a lot more blows to fell than he should have.

This handed the advantage of time to the guy on the ground, who in the dim light Alicia recognized as Zeller. The shotgun in his hands was going for Jerome, and she was the only one who could stop it.

The man's head was pointing her way, so Alicia tucked one end of the broom handle into her armpit and swept the makeshift weapon sideways through a low arc.

As intended the end of the broom handle knocked the shotgun's barrel sideways. Unlike Hunt, Zeller didn't pull his trigger. Instead he tried to train the shotgun Jerome's way again.

Alicia unclamped her arm from her side, allowing the part of the broom handle that had been in her armpit to drop down. This tip of the broom handle was driven downwards into the man's face.

Blood exploded outwards, but the shotgun never stopped moving. The passageway lit up for a brief instant as the shotgun was fired. Alicia had thought the first blast was loud but now she was this close, it sounded as if the second blast had been amplified by a rock band's sound system.

The ratcheting sound of another shell being fed into the shotgun sounded as she heard Jerome issue a harsh command.

"Freeze! Don't you dare move a muscle. If you get so much as a twitch, Zeller, I'll blow a hole in you a semi-truck could drive through."

Zeller froze. No wonder. The strength and certainty in Jerome's voice was mesmerizing. He wasn't his usual self; he was commanding, forcefully assertive and his tone suggested he'd do exactly as he threatened. It was a Jerome Alicia didn't recognize, yet she was as drawn to this new side of him as she'd ever been to the Jerome she'd always known. This was Jerome stepping up to the plate and making damned sure he hit the home run required to save them.

Alicia used the tip of her broom handle to press the shotgun to one side so it wasn't aimed anywhere near Jerome.

Jerome shook his shotgun as he stepped toward Zeller. "Nice and slow, take your hand off the trigger and push the shotgun away from you."

"Please, Jerome, don't shoot me."

"I can't think of one good reason why I shouldn't." Jerome shook the shotgun again, and even in the faint light Alicia could see the rage on his face. "You abducted my wife, threatened to hurt her if I didn't steal money for you and then you beat the crap out of me when I tried to rescue her! You imprisoned us and we know you would have killed us once we'd gotten you the money."

Before Jerome could do anything stupid like pulling his trigger,

Alicia crashed her broom handle into Zeller's forehead. His eyes rolled back in an instant.

"Come on, Jerome. Let's get out of here."

"No, not yet." Jerome thudded the butt of the shotgun into the heads of both Zeller and Hunt, then handed the weapon to Alicia. "I'm going to drag them into the room where they kept us. I'll take Hunt first. If Zeller wakes up, hit him again."

Jerome grasped one of Hunt's feet and started to haul him toward the room. Alicia could tell he was struggling and her instinct was to go to his aid. With only one good hand she knew she wouldn't be much help, and Jerome was right, she *had* to watch over Zeller in case he awoke.

Alicia liked how Jerome stopped short of the room with Hunt and came back for Zeller. It meant Big Guy would never be out of their sight until he was dumped into the room. Now she didn't need to watch Zeller, Alicia swapped her attentions to the task of covering Hunt. The broom handle tossed aside in favor of the shotgun Jerome had given her. As she stood over Hunt, she noticed their room's padlock remained locked. Therefore they'd have to find the keys.

She was tempted to lean down and check Hunt's pockets, but she didn't trust the man not to play possum and launch a surprise attack on her.

When Jerome had positioned Zeller beside Hunt, he trotted back to retrieve the other shotgun.

"I'll watch this pair." Jerome's arm pointed toward a room with flickering colored light spilling from its doorway. "You see if the key for the padlock is in that room."

Alicia entered the room and found a pair of ratty chairs facing a table. There were pizza boxes on the table along with a tablet that was being used as a TV. By the light of the tablet she could see a pair of keys on a ring. They looked to be as new as the padlock, so she scooped them up and made her way back to Jerome.

The keys opened the padlock, so Alicia covered the kidnappers with a shotgun as Jerome dragged them each into the room.

Jerome snapped the padlock shut and pocketed the keys. Alicia understood his actions. When the two men woke up, Hunt would easily boost Zeller up through their escape hatch. Zeller wouldn't have to follow their route. As soon as he was clear of the room he'd be able to kick his way through the ceiling and drop down. Then he'd either run to save his own skin or try to break his fellow kidnapper out. Either way, she got why Jerome was making things harder for them.

"Did you see the laptop in there?"

"No, I didn't. But I didn't look for it. Only the keys."

"Don't sweat it. I've only just thought of it. It's not the laptop I'm after. It's the phone that connected it to the internet that I really want so we can call the cops."

"I'll get the flashlight and take another look."

"No. I want to get out of here. There's no telling when Adamson will come back."

61

Jerome led their escape with a shotgun tucked under each arm. Behind him Alicia held the flashlight in a position that illuminated their way down the stairwell. He'd considered tossing one of the shotguns but wanted to make damned sure he stayed armed in case they met the leader or any other accomplices on the stairs.

As much as Jerome wanted to get out in a hurry, he was wise enough to exercise a certain amount of caution. Every time he reached a landing, he leaned over the safety railings and took a peek down the central shaft of the stairwell.

On the third landing he saw what he most feared: the bobbing beam of a flashlight as someone ascended the stairs.

Jerome shot a hand up to halt Alicia, and gestured she cut the flashlight and crouch down. She did so at once, the act pitching them into utter blackness.

The sound of trotting footsteps on the stairs assaulted Jerome's ears. To him it was a welcome noise. He laid the shotgun in his left hand on the ground and shouldered the other.

As best he could, Jerome trained the barrel of the shotgun at the landing below them. His chief desire making sure his ambush was absolute.

Jerome listened carefully to the footsteps as they clattered on the stairs. As best as he could judge there was only one person coming up. One he could deal with. At least he could unless it was some elite soldier, but the way he was feeling he'd still give it a go if Rambo himself came up the stairs.

The flashlight bobbed its way onto the landing below him. Behind the beam a silhouette showed a figure whose body shape was the same as the leader's.

"Don't move, Adamson. I have one of your buddies' shotguns aimed right at you." Jerome pumped a fresh shell into the barrel to give proof of his claim. A shotgun shell was ejected and even as it dropped to the ground, Jerome sent a prayer the fall wasn't enough to detonate it. He'd deliberately used the name of the CFO in the hope the shock of identification would add a layer of confusion to the man's thinking.

"Don't shoot. I'm unarmed." The origins of the beam from the flashlight rose, and Jerome figured that instinct had raised the leader's hands. "How did you know it was me?"

"Alicia. Put your flashlight on, please, and let's have a proper look at him. If I see a gun in your hand, Adamson, I swear I'll shoot you where you stand. We haven't come this far to fail."

"Please, Jerome, don't do anything foolish. My hands are above my head." Alicia's beam picked out the leader, and Jerome got a look at his face. Fear decorated every pore, even with his eyes scrunched against the glare of the flashlight. His mouth opened again. "Look, I'll admit we made a mistake involving you. That was wrong of us. We should have stolen the money ourselves. You've still got control of the money. You're going to get away and you'll have a bank account with fifty million dollars in it. There's no need to kill me."

Adamson's words bounced off Jerome. He didn't care about the money. All he wanted to do was get Alicia out of there. Get her someplace safe. Someplace she could be treated by a doctor. Someplace where she wouldn't spend every waking moment in fear for her life. Someplace he could relax knowing she was safe.

All the same, he had to get past Adamson. Jerome was at a loss as to what to do until he remembered what cops did in all those shows he and Alicia had watched while entwined on their couch.

"Put your hands against the nearest wall and spread your legs."

Jerome's idea was simple. He was going to approach Adamson and then fell him with the butt of the shotgun. As furious as he was with the man who'd put him and Alicia through such a traumatic experience, he wasn't prepared to kill him. Homicide was a whole step up from the violent acts of self-defense he'd committed so far, but Jerome knew he'd have nothing to offer by way of a legal defense if he shot Adamson dead.

Adamson turned as if to put his hands on the far wall of the stairwell. Just as the fingers of his right hand made contact, he pushed left and took off down the stairs.

Jerome's finger twitched on the trigger, but he didn't fully depress it until Adamson had gone. Instead of aiming down the stairs he blasted the shotgun at where Adamson had been. The move had two purposes. The first was to show that he was prepared to shoot Adamson, with the second being that he wanted Adamson to keep running. If he was armed the last thing he wanted was for Adamson to lie in wait for him.

The recoil from the shotgun was far greater than Jerome expected it would be. He knew about the noise and the smell, but his shoulder felt as if it had caught a wild kick from a bucking bronco.

There was no time to spare massaging it. He took a rapid look over the railings and saw the beam from Adamson's flashlight descending the stairwell.

"I'll go first, Alicia. Come after me, but always stay two landings above me in case he sets up his own ambush. Put the flashlight in your sling and bring the shotgun with you. I'll shout you when I know it's safe. If I don't come back up and he does, shoot the scumbag."

Jerome set off down the stairwell. Now the ringing from the shotgun was dissipating, he could hear Adamson's footsteps on the stairs. There was a clattering noise as Adamson bumped into something, then a muffled curse. This gave Jerome confidence he'd sufficiently scared Adamson into fleeing, but he still didn't take any chances.

When he was on the first floor, Jerome heard what sounded like the slam of an automobile door, followed by the coughing bark of an engine being kicked into life. Best of all was the screech of tires that suggested Adamson was burning rubber in his attempts to get away.

Step by step Jerome descended. He made sure his feet made no sound, and he kept every sense he possessed on high alert in case the moving vehicle was a ruse designed to fool him into making a fatal mistake. As desperate as Adamson might be to get away, he'd be equally determined to stop Jerome and Alicia exposing his crimes to the cops and the best way of doing that would be to kill them.

When he got to the bottom of the stairs, he examined as much of the parking garage as he could without showing himself. There was light spilling into the parking garage from the access route and he was able to see there was one van parked to the left, its rear doors backed up tight to the wall. He scanned round to the right and found the parking garage devoid of any human life.

That only left the van as a hiding place. Its sides were fully paneled with the only doors being the ones for the passenger and driver.

Jerome lowered himself down until he could look underneath the van. There were no shapes beneath the van's body. No legs supporting a gun-toting Adamson.

If Adamson was in the van, he would be lying across the front seats. His gun ready to steal Jerome's life away.

Without stepping into the main parking garage, Jerome hefted the shotgun up against his shoulder, pulled it tight against the bruise it had inflicted with his first shot, and set his aim on the front wheel.

He was ready for the recoil this time, and while it still hurt its impact was lessened by the tighter grip he now employed. What he wasn't ready for was the way the front tire exploded with a boom that was louder than the shotgun's. The tire was instantly shredded and the bodywork of the van around the wheel was beset with a myriad of jagged holes.

No return fire came. Nothing came hurtling through the van's bodywork to slam into Jerome.

Jerome stepped forward and skirted the van. His muscles ready to react at a micro-second's notice, and his eyes seeking out a human shape in the front seat.

When Jerome saw the front of the van was empty he ducked back to the stairwell to shout Alicia's name, even as his shoulders slumped in blessed relief.

Jerome led Alicia out of the parking garage without any drama, although he was alert to even the merest hint of danger. The shot he'd fired at the van had shredded the tire, so he need not worry about anything other than a foot pursuit from Hunt and Zeller, should they manage to break free.

The streets of the downtrodden area still managed to look ominous in daylight, but after everything he'd been through, and with the shotgun in his hand, there was little for Jerome to have serious worries about.

In daylight they could see along the streets far enough they could plot a course toward a better area. A place where the locals would help the strangers who'd gotten into trouble.

After a half mile, Jerome saw a woman hanging laundry in her back yard. He nudged Alicia forward and made sure the shotgun he carried was hidden below the low wall.

The woman had been happy to let them call the police from her cell. She'd given the cops her address and upon hearing their tale, the cops made sure they attended within minutes.

Jerome had laid the shotgun on the ground and made sure he and Alicia were several feet away from it with their hands raised by the time the cops came.

A squad car pulled up, lights flashing but without sirens blasting out deafening whoops.

Name badges identified the cops, but Jerome didn't bother remembering them. He expected that as soon as the two cops heard what he and Alicia had to tell them, they'd refer him to detectives, or the FBI, as he was sure kidnapping would class as a federal crime, and if that wasn't enough to involve the feds, the amount of money he'd stolen was surely large enough for the FBI to take an interest.

————

Jerome now sat in a police interview suite across from an FBI agent called Gonzalez, who had the body of a runner and bright intelligent eyes. Alicia had been taken to hospital to have her arm set, but so far he'd only been treated by the paramedics called by the officers who'd been dispatched.

The interview suite was like every one he'd seen in the movies. A bare room with a utilitarian table, chairs that were fixed to a floor and a huge mirror on one wall that was sure to be two-way so observers could monitor his every reaction.

Now the exertions were over, Jerome's body was letting him know of every assault, every slight it had suffered. He ached in places he didn't know he had, and the idea of doing something simple like tying his shoelace carried the same prospective pain levels as swimming in lava.

"This isn't yet a formal interview, Jerome. I'm just going over everything you've told us. You are admitting that you've conspired with your friend Ed Dunsfold to defraud Beck Holdings of $52 million dollars. You've told us that your wife was abducted to force you to do this. I'll not waste your time asking why you didn't contact us. I'm sure there were enough threats made to prevent you daring to do that." Gonzalez reached up and rubbed the small gold crucifix that hung around her neck between her forefinger and thumb. "You've told my colleagues that the people who abducted your wife and extorted you to steal the money were Christopher Adamson, Lenny Zeller and George Hunt. Christopher Adamson is the CFO of Beck Holdings; he's shown my colleagues the company accounts. The very accounts you claim to have stolen the money from. But there has been no theft."

"We didn't get the money?" This news sideswiped Jerome like a semi-truck barreling across a busy intersection and clearing all in its path. His breath shortened and his chest tightened. His and Ed's plan had failed. They'd been unable to steal the money. The consequences of that could have been immense, and it was only because he'd managed to effect an escape that he and Alicia hadn't been punished for the failure of their plan.

"I can see you need a moment to compose yourself after hearing that news. Take a drink of water, and let me know when you're ready to hear more." There was a compassionate edge to Gonzalez's voice, and she sat with patience while he tried to wrap his mind around her revelation.

Jerome took a slug then three sips from the paper cup. "Please continue. I've held nothing back from you, and I know that I'm due to face some consequences for my actions. I accept that, and quite frankly whatever they are they're a small price to pay for the knowledge Alicia is safe. I'd like to hear what else you have to say. Did you find Zeller and Hunt? Please tell me I didn't kill them when I knocked them out."

"They weren't in that building, but we did find everything else you said was there. As for Zeller and Hunt, we picked them up an hour ago in Montauk. Your wife told one of my colleagues the same story you've told me. Either the two of you are telling the truth, or you've rehearsed one hell of a tale."

"Thank God you caught them. As for Alicia and me, we've told the truth. We agreed that we had to. It's the right thing to do."

"That may well be the case, but you are still admitting that you attempted to steal a huge amount of money."

"Yes, but it was for the right reasons. You have to see that."

"I do see it, but"—Gonzalez pulled a face—"very few of my

colleagues see it that way. We have, of course, pulled Adamson in. As you'd expect, he's surrounded himself with enough Wall Street lawyers to have us chasing our tails for years."

"Surely you'll get him on something. I can't see you getting Hunt to cut a deal, but I'll bet Zeller will."

"Oh, we will get them all for this eventually, but we'd like something quicker. Long trials waste resources and taxpayers' dollars. That's why I looked at another angle. I had questions I couldn't answer so I took a different, sideways look at things. I spoke to my boss and he agreed with my assessment and the plan I put to him. In short, you say you stole the money, but the Beck Holdings account isn't missing the money. I needed to speak to a digital specialist. Someone who knows more about these things, and how that anomaly can be explained. I'd like you to meet him so he can explain to you what happened. He's quite simply the smartest man I have ever met. I'm not allowed to know which agency he works for, but suffice it to say he's at the forefront of our efforts to keep America safe from any form of digital attack." Gonzalez rose from her seat and knocked on the door of the interview suite.

The man who walked in was tall, around two-fifty pounds and had a squashed nose. If Jerome had thought the news about the money not leaving the Beck Holdings account was a sideswipe, the presence of this man in the room was a gut punch that left him winded and gasping for air.

Jerome leapt to his feet, his aching muscles forgotten about. "Ed? What the hell?"

Ed's hand rose in a gesture that was half placating, half halting. "All will be explained, buddy. Don't worry."

"Don't worry?" Jerome slumped back into the chair. "How the hell can you say that?"

"Calm down, buddy. It's all going to be okay."

Jerome wanted to believe Ed, but Gonzalez's revelation about him being a government employee was a game changer. He had no secrets from Ed, and thought that was something his buddy had reciprocated.

"How? How is it going to be okay?"

Ed took a seat opposite Jerome, his long frame dwarfing Gonzalez. "I have some stuff to tell you that I couldn't before. I apologize for deceiving you, for not telling you the truth right from the start. Believe me, buddy, when I say that I wanted to, but I couldn't until I got clearance. Basically I have been working for the government for the last ten years. My employers are an agency that you haven't heard of. Other agencies get the credit for what we do and that's how we want it to stay. We're not law enforcement. We have no pull with the cops, the CIA or the FBI. We're not investigators, we're anti-hackers and hackers and malware designers. You remember that storm two years ago when the Russians were annexing Crimea again?" Jerome nodded, not trusting himself to speak. "That eventually got halted and nobody knew the reason. The reason they didn't invade was that we dropped a virus into their Astra Linux operating system, which scrambled all of their weapons. They couldn't fly jets, control warships or fire guided rockets. In short, we took away all their fancy toys and stopped them from rolling all the way through the Ukraine."

"What's this got to do with what happened to Alicia and me?"

"What you asked of me—the truth is I could do that in a half hour. There was no friend helping me help you. It was all me, but I had to make it look real as you were not allowed to know what I do. I have to be, and remain to be, anonymous. There are a lot of people around the world who'd put a huge price on my head, and the heads of the guys I work with, if they ever learned my identity. I've told you this so you'll realize I'm way more than you've ever thought I was. Once you gave me the details, I set things up so the money would appear in the account, but it would never actually be stolen. I also had it set that for a four-hour period, the money would appear to have left the account so that the CFO would see it gone. I didn't know he was part of the gang that took Alicia. I was just covering bases. I couldn't tell you, but I had to get authorization from my boss before I could even agree to help you."

Jerome didn't speak. Couldn't speak. His friend. No, scratch that, his *best* friend had spent years lying to him. All those conversations about Ed's work had been a tissue of lies. Yet when he'd needed Ed's help, Ed had come through for him. A thought struck Jerome and it centered on the consequences of Ed's trick with the money that both was and wasn't stolen.

"And what do you think would have happened to Alicia when Adamson and co couldn't get their money? They'd have killed her."

"Easy, Jerome. The money was there. If you'd tried to buy Bitcoin with it, you'd have gotten $52 million bucks' worth. I might have lied to you about my job, but you were still my buddy. Alicia's your wife and there was no way I could take any chances."

"So why didn't you call the cops? The FBI? With your connections and skills you could have easily found the abductors. Alicia's in hospital with a broken arm. She'll likely be in therapy for years after what she's been through. You could have stopped that, Ed. All these years we've been friends and you hung her out to dry like that. That's cold, dude. Real cold." Jerome could hear the scorn and anger in his voice, and see its effect on Ed's face. He didn't care. It was all he could do not to rise to his feet and start throwing punches at Ed for the way his cover-ups had extended Alicia's captivity. "You could have saved me the worry about her. You could have saved her long before I went to Long Island to get her back. Why, Ed? Why didn't you step in and save her?"

"I spoke to my boss. I tried suggesting all those things. Her assessment was that the abductors were amateurs, and that it would be safer for Alicia to aid you giving them the money and then pick them up afterwards by tracing where the money went. None of us expected you to go rogue, and I would have been watching your back except there was a situation I got sucked into."

"A situation? What the hell was more important than Alicia?"

"Remember that plane that went missing a few years back— MH370? A plane disappeared the same way last night. It had a couple senators and congressmen on it. A supposed fact-finding trip in the Philippines and their plane goes AWOL. The president tasked us with finding it."

"I'm guessing from your tone you did find it. And that you somehow saved the day."

"We did, and, we did."

Gonzalez leaned forward and planted her elbows on the table. "Mr. Dunsfold is helping us build our case against Adamson and the other two. The fact Zeller and Hunt were apprehended trying to steal a boat in Montauk speaks volumes about their guilt. Adamson is trying to tough it out, but we'll get him."

"And me and Alicia? What happens to us?"

"There is quite a list of charges I could bring against you." Agent Gonzalez's eyes hardened. "I won't name them all, but trust me when I say that if I wanted to, I could build a case that would see you jailed for a minimum of ten years."

Jerome picked up on the clues in Gonzalez's choice of words. "If you wanted to. That tells me you don't want to. Or someone above you doesn't want you to."

Gonzalez let her gaze wander to Ed. Her face a mixture of admiration and consternation. "In exchange for Mr. Dunsfold's expertise, whenever I need it, for the next twelve months, it has been agreed that I am to release both you and your wife without charge. The money was never stolen, so we can't prosecute you for that. Neither Hunt nor Zeller have yet made complaints of assault against you. I'm told they have refused to speak without a lawyer present. All we have at this time is your confession. You're lucky this is New York; deals get done here every day and Mr. Dunsfold has done one to keep you out of prison."

Jerome looked at Ed who held his gaze for a moment then gave him a cheeky wink.

Ed had come through for them in the end, the way a good buddy should.

Jerome squeezed Alicia's hand, her cast brushing against the back of his hand. Today was his first day back at work. It had felt weird to be back in that office. Beck Holdings had wasted no time in drawing their forces together. Carthew had been promoted to replace the still-absent Zeller, and Jerome had twice been spoken to by Thomas Beck Junior.

Beck Accounting had a continued place for him, and as concocted with Ed, Jerome stuck to the lie that the money he purportedly stole would never actually be real. It was all a digital sleight of hand to fool those who'd extorted him.

Thomas Beck Junior had bought the lie, but Jerome had already started looking elsewhere. For him the Beck Building was tainted. His office stained with the memories of the worry he'd carried while trying to find a way to save Alicia.

Jerome and Alicia were sitting in a booth at Melvilles. There were bottles of beer in front of them, and although Alicia wasn't her normal self, she was close enough that Jerome had no fears for her long-term mental health.

A woman walked into the bar. Her head turning as she looked for the people she'd agreed to meet.

Jerome raised a hand to attract the woman's attention. The

woman walked over, her movements fluid and lithe. The dress she wore caressed her figure as she walked with the sultry stride of a panther stalking its prey.

As the woman neared, Jerome rose to his feet. "Lucy, thanks for coming to meet us. This is my wife, Alicia."

The women exchanged greetings, and Jerome flagged a server to get Lucy a drink.

For Jerome, this was the final piece of the jigsaw. So much about the last week had confounded him or sent his mind into endless questioning, and he needed to check this last detail to give his overactive brain a chance of closure.

Lucy Sampson was the former colleague of his from Beck Accounting he'd been trying to get hold of since seeing the list of names from the kidnappers, and she held the details he needed.

"I'm going to get right to the point, Lucy. Alicia is an HR lawyer for Beck Holdings. She specializes in conflict resolution. This isn't common knowledge, but we're trusting you with this. Last week Alicia was kidnapped. I had to steal $50 million to secure her release; $30 million went to the kidnappers and the rest was supposed to be shared equally among a list of former Beck Holdings' employees who had apparently been victims of sexual assault in the workplace."

"I see. Thank goodness you're okay and Alicia is home safe, but what has this got to do with me?"

Alicia leaned forward, her voice soft and gentle and sincere. "Your name was on the list of sexual assault victims. Can you confirm—"

It was Lucy's laughter that cut off the end of Alicia's sentence. Not a giggle, but a full-throated belly laugh that ricocheted around the room turning heads.

Jerome couldn't see where the humor belonged in the situation, but he knew better than to interrupt Lucy's mirth with questions. For all he knew, laughter could be Lucy's way of keeping the bad memories at bay.

Lucy hauled herself under a semblance of control and tried to speak as her head sawed from side to side. "Didn't happen. Not to me. Never in all my days have I heard such bull."

"Are you saying you were never sexually assaulted while an employee of Beck Accounting?"

"You're damn right I am." Lucy wiped tears from her eyes, the action smudging her mascara. "I've sure as hell never been bothered by anyone beyond the usual requests for a date. If anyone tried that crap with me, I'd knee their balls up into their chest."

Both Alicia and Jerome tried rephrasing the question in several ways, but Lucy was adamant she'd never experienced such a thing. After a while Lucy left, and when she'd exited Melvilles, Ed joined them from the next booth.

"The cunning jerkweeds. That whole line about the money being for victims of sexual assault in the workplace was nothing more than a salve to my conscience. A way to make the crime of theft seem less of a guilt trip."

"I don't get why they felt they needed to do it." Ed's head shook as he spoke. "Anyone who knows you guys would know saving Alicia was more than enough motivation for you. I think that was them trying to kid themselves more than you."

Jerome raised his beer in a toast. "Here's to the FBI making damned sure all three of them get a long prison sentence."

Alicia and Ed joined in with the toast but Ed's face was serious rather than celebratory. "This isn't over yet. There's still the question of what happens to the money."

"What money?" Jerome and Alicia asked the question at the same time.

"The $52 million. It's still in that bank account. The world believes it isn't real, but I can tell you it's real. It's there in that account waiting for us to do something with it. Don't ask me how I did it, because I'll never tell you. But know that it's there."

Jerome's first reaction was to do the math. "Fifty-two split three ways is seventeen and a third each. Or twenty-six million each if you want to go halves with us." Jerome looked at Alicia and saw his own thoughts about taking the money reflected in her eyes. "I don't want a single cent of that money and neither does Alicia. Either take it yourself or share it out among some charities."

Ed's shoulders drooped as a wide smile underlined his nose. "I would have bet my 401K on you saying that, but it was still a relief to hear you say it."

"It was never going to be any other answer." Alicia caressed Jerome's cheek and turned his head until he was looking into her eyes. "One. Four. Three."

Jerome smiled his brightest smile. All was well in his world. He'd just heard the woman he loved more than life itself say his three favorite words.

A LETTER FROM JOHN

I want to say a huge thank you for choosing to read *The Hostage*. If you did enjoy it, and want to keep up to date with all my latest releases, just sign up at the following link. Your email address will never be shared and you can unsubscribe at any time.

www.bookouture.com/john-ryder

The Hostage was a very different novel for me to write as I wanted to mix things up a little and create a hero who wasn't a hero in the traditional sense. Instead of a gun-toting ex-marine like Grant Fletcher or a detective/fixer like Kyle Roche, I wanted Jerome to have no training in his background that would help him in his efforts to rescue Alicia. He had to be an everyday person who faces the same trials, tribulations and worries as the rest of us. Sure, I gave him some skills as a former high school wrestler, but they didn't really help him too much.

Another element I wanted to add into *The Hostage* was that the greatest driver of the story would be Jerome's love for Alicia. To this end I had him determined to save her himself and made him willing to cross lines he'd never previously have considered crossing. Of course, the crossing of these lines gave me some opportunities to have Jerome beat himself up for his sins against Beau, the Good Samaritan, and the drunk guy whose briefcase he stole.

For those of you who have read my previous novels, you may have noticed the body count was a lot lower than usual. This too was intentional as I wanted to write a thriller that didn't litter the page with dead bodies. The death toll of *The Hostage* is a big fat zero, although I'd like to think there are enough moments of dread to have readers expecting the worst to happen, especially so when Jerome and Alicia are making their attempts to escape.

What comes next for me is still up in the air as I have several ideas of what to write next, and while none of them are fully formed in my brain, I can say for certain that whichever idea I choose to be my next project it will be crafted to hopefully keep you, dear reader, turning the pages as fast as possible with that familiar feeling that anything can happen next.

I love hearing from my readers—you can get in touch on my Facebook page, through Twitter, Goodreads or my website.

Thanks,

John

www.johnryderauthor.com

facebook.com/JohnRyderAuthor
twitter.com/JohnRyder101

ACKNOWLEDGMENTS

As always I'm going to start off the acknowledgments by thanking my family for their support of my writing career. They put up with lots of vacant looks as I work on a plot point and many instances of me having my focus firmly on the laptop with only the most minor complaints.

I'm hugely lucky to have a wonderful editor, Isobel Akenhead, who gets my silly sense of humor and plays along with the jokes I leave in the comments. Not only is she eagle-eyed in the professional sense, she and her team are a delight to work with as she plays pedant to my grump. Over in publicity, Noelle Holten and Sarah Hardy continue to prove on a daily basis why they are among the best in the business. Over in marketing, Alex Crow and his team perform miracles as easily as I make a cuppa and their efforts to get my books in your hands are truly appreciated.

I'm incredibly fortunate to have a wide circle of friends in all areas of the writing community and all of them have been very supportive mines of vital information and damned good mates. A special shout-out as always goes to my Crime and Publishment gang, and special thanks to Jeff Sexton who keeps me right on all things firearms. Any mistakes in this department are down to me employing artistic license rather than an error in the advice he gives me.

Finally, I've done my usual thing of leaving the most critical people to last. You, dear reader, are the most important part of this relationship. For all I may love writing, without readers and their enthusiasm for my stories, I'm just a lonely typist who's not very good at typing.

Thank you all from the bottom of my heart.

Printed in Great Britain
by Amazon